Consumed

by

T.S. Charles

W&B Publishers
USA

Chapter One

New Kid

It was my first day of school, and I knew exactly what was in store for me. You see, I have this whole "new guy" thing down. Five schools in three years—I've been bounced around so much that nothing surprises me anymore. As much as it pains me to admit this, I wanted this one to stick. It was more than hope, to be honest. It wasn't that I was particularly fond of Stone Creek High—heck, I knew virtually nothing about the damn school—I was just sick of the routine of starting anew. Now, don't get me wrong. I wasn't a perfect angel at any of my other schools. Not even close. But I really wasn't all that bad either. I just never seemed to fit in, and was too damn stubborn to turn the other cheek.

First, it's important to make something perfectly clear so that you don't get the wrong idea: just because anxiety wasn't coursing through my veins doesn't mean I was thrilled about the prospects of returning to school. In fact, while standing outside of Stone Creek High, its faded red bricks and grimy windows an eyesore for all to see, I dreaded entering the small school gearing up for its 136th birthday. Like any kid whose favorite time of the year is summer break, I had grown fond of my extended vacation.

My previous school, Brunswick High School, located in the *bowels* of New Jersey—smelled like it, too—gave me the boot when my fist accidentally smashed into Dante Jacob's nose. I meant to hit him. That was undeniable. But sending a bloodied version of him to the emergency room had not been my desired end result. Adrenaline is to blame for that. You see, he was getting on my nerves, harassing me about a highly sensitive topic—we'll get into that later—so I clocked him. I wanted to send a clear message to him and all the other students at Brunswick High that I was not the type of kid you wanted to mess around with unless, of course, you didn't mind a consultation with a plastic surgeon. Even if no one believed me, in particular the faculty, there had been no intent on my part to change the landscape of Dante's face. The moment the blood came spurting out of his now crooked and swollen nose, I knew my time was up. That twerp Principal McAdams wasted no time in calling my foster parents to inform them that I was no longer part of the Brunswick High family.

Jesse and Dana Gilchrist, my foster parents at the time, seemed to take it well. They didn't yell, didn't badger me about the stupidity of my actions, and most of all, didn't give up on me. They simply hit the phones searching for any school that would take me. They weren't the problem. As it turns out, I was. My reputation must have preceded me because no schools (excluding private schools the Gilchrists couldn't afford) within a reasonable driving distance would take me. That left the Gilchrists in a precarious situation. They couldn't homeschool me—they both worked—and I was too young to legally drop out. In the end, there was only one viable option: pack my bags and send me on my way. Naturally, it was more intricate than that.

To make a long, drawn out story short, they somehow finagled the system to move me from my home state of New Jersey, all the way to Stone Creek, West Virginia, to live with Bill and Susan Baniak, old college buddies of theirs. How the Gilchrists accomplished the feat of shipping me all the way to the mountainous region of Stone Creek, West Virginia, who knows? What I do know is that the move enabled me to miss a substantial portion of my sophomore year of high school. Lucky me.

Before making the six-and-a-half hour hike to Stone Creek, the Gilchrists gave me one piece of advice: STAY OUT OF TROUBLE. They also forewarned me that the Baniaks, although good-natured people, are a bit rough around the edges and quirky as they come.

When I first met Bill and Susan, it immediately became apparent what the Gilchrists had meant. Bill was a tall and lanky character who was either shopping at the wrong stores or didn't know how to dress properly. His prehistoric, faded jeans fit snuggly around his thighs and upper calves just like capris, although my gut tells me his pants were not designed to be worn in that particular style. His shirt was just as bad. He wore one that resembled a brown potato sack, cut in just the right places so his hairy arms and gigantic, bearded head could fit through. In terms of classification, Bill was your typical late forties to early fifties longhaired hippy. Susan, who also bore the flower-child look, was dressed from head to toe in what appeared to be pure hemp. Her incredibly long and dreadlocked hair, filled with an array of flowers and peace symbols, careened all the way down her back, stopping right above her shapely posterior. Like Bill, she was also in her late forties to early fifties. Standing a foot shorter than her husband, she had one of those plump yet firm builds. Hours spent chasing after Frisbees must have done her body good. As far as first impressions go, even without uttering a solitary word, the Baniaks left a memorable one.

Shortly after settling in, Bill and Susan arranged for me to start school. I had wanted to wait until the following week, you know start fresh on a Monday, but they thought it would be a good idea for me to begin my career at Stone Creek High on a *Friday*, of all days. I thought it made absolutely no sense, but it was their house, their rules.

Sick of reminiscing, I drew a deep breath and threw open the splintered oak door and stepped inside Stone Creek High. Watching the door slam shut behind me, I knew there was no turning back. My first day had officially begun. Locating the main office, which just happened to be the first room off to the left, I approached the receptionist.

"Excuse me," I said, clearing my throat. "Do you know where I can pick up a copy of my schedule?"

"Name?" she asked curtly, her bulging blue eyes staring through me.

"Zack...Zack Treadwell."

"Okay, have a seat and I'll be with you in a minute," she said, pointing a slender, well-manicured finger towards a row of chairs.

Sitting there bored out of my mind waiting for my stupid schedule, I noticed that it was getting closer and closer to the start of homeroom. Yeah, as hard as it is to believe, after being out of school for nearly two months, I was able to *will* myself out of bed in order to get to school early. Bill and Susan were noticeably impressed. They believed their newly acquired responsibility was doing the conscientious thing. You know, arrive early to scope out the joint and familiarize myself with my new surroundings. Truth is I had an ulterior motive. Being the new kid and all, I simply wanted to dodge the crowds as much as possible. An early bird that day, excited to send off her recently adopted hatchling for his first day of school, Susan offered to drop me off. I gladly accepted in lieu of making the three-and-a-half mile trek, which had been my initial plan to beat out the busses.

What could possibly be the holdup? I thought to myself, standing up to peak over the counter.

I shook my head in disgust, discovering the root cause of the delay. The receptionist, whose thick, curly brown hair looked as if someone had taken a hedge trimmer to it, was piling layer upon layer of makeup onto her pasty, white face. I'm guessing she wasn't a fan of the whole "less is more" fashion trend. No, if I had to guess her fashion preference, I would say she was of the *Elizabethan-era* variety. In addition to thick globs of concealer, blush, and eyeliner, the receptionist's lips looked as if a toddler, one who visibly struggled with the concept of staying in-between the lines, went to town on them with a deep red lipstick tube. Obviously, the receptionist did that to herself, presumably in an effort to make her thin, almost non-existent, lips appear much fuller than they really were. It didn't work.

Hallelujah! I screamed to myself when she finally announced that my schedule, including all of my locker information (combination and number), was ready. I opted not to thank her after grabbing my schedule—not that she would have noticed anyway as she had already turned her attention to her nails, sanding away any uneven surfaces. Schedule in hand, I located my locker, tested out the combination just to make sure it worked, and then headed straight for my homeroom class. To my relief, the room was empty. My bottom wasted no time in parking itself in one of the seats in the far corner of the room, the back row to be exact. In my opinion, it was the best seat in the classroom. Not only could you see if anyone was glancing over in your general direction (important when you're new), but you're also as far away as possible from the worst possible seat in the classroom—the one adjacent to the teacher's desk.

"Are you Zachary Treadwell?" a middle-aged woman asked, entering the room. "I'm Ms. Maddows, your homeroom teacher."

"Uh huh!" I nodded.

Ms. Maddows smirked dryly, and made her way over to the seat in front of her desk. While shuffling the chair, making sure it was perfectly aligned, she turned to me, and said, "Zachary, there appears to be a mix up. You are sitting in the wrong seat. Yours is right here. We do everything in alphabetical order in my homeroom class. So come...take *your* seat."

I reluctantly got up from the coveted back row seat and sat down in the chair she had designated for me. Her desk was full of an array of plants and garden gnomes. Staring at her desk left an impression that she had some real deep-rooted issues. Ones, I had no interest in exploring.

At least I only have to endure this torturous seat for homeroom, I thought, my eyes darting from one plump, red-cheeked gnome to another. As it drew closer and closer to the start of homeroom, in a pathetic attempt to look busy, I began doodling in my notebook. A poorly drawn gnome, slightly resembling Ms. Maddows, somehow found itself decapitated in one of my better drawings.

Brrrrinngg! The sound of the bell shot through my ears, screaming at me that my first day at Stone Creek was officially underway.

With my retinas glued to my notebook—eye contact invites small talk—students slowly began to trickle into the classroom. Ears keenly tuned to my surroundings, I overheard a student complaining to Ms. Maddows that "someone" was sitting in his seat. In a stern tone, Ms. Maddows instructed him that he would have to take the seat behind me, and that everyone knows "the rules." I was perplexed. Why in the world would anyone be upset with losing the worst imaginable seat in the classroom? Unless he shared her apparent gnome fetish or had dreams of becoming a botanist, he should have been thrilled at the prospect of changing seats. I certainly would have been.

After everyone settled into his or her respective seats, and the bell rang for a second time, Ms. Maddows gestured for me to stand. Pressing my lips together, I reluctantly stood up. "We have a new student entering our homeroom today. His name is Zack Treadwell, and he's come ALL the way here from New Jers—"

"Pennsylvania," I interrupted.

"Oh!" Ms. Maddows said, her bright, pink lips turning downward. "I could have sworn your file said you were from New Jersey."

"Well, I'm not. Maybe there was a mix up or something."

My intentions had been to keep a low profile—I have my reasons—but Ms. Loudmouth seemed determined to tell the entire class just about everything there was to know about me. Aside from my name, which would have been impossible to keep confidential, no one, especially not my peers, needed to know anything else about me. The less they knew, the better.

Ms. Maddows apparently did not approve of my insolence. The reddish hue spreading across her grave face, and the bulging veins in her forehead and neck, made that abundantly clear. She gestured for me to turn around and face the class. "Zachary, would you mind introducing yourself to the class?" she snarled, her brown coffee-stained teeth clenched tightly. "Let's start with your origins. If my file is wrong, as you say, I'm curious as to what part of Pennsylvania you are from."

Well that certainly backfired, didn't it? I thought.

I wasn't much of a geography buff so my choices were limited to the only two cities I could think of on the spot—Pittsburgh or Philadelphia. As a lifelong Giants fan, fictitious or not, living in a rival's territory left a bitter taste in my mouth.

"Pittsburgh," I announced glancing around the room ready to stare down any doubters.

"Ohhhh…really?" she said with a doubtful expression, the streaks of white in her mostly dark hair shining brightly in the fluorescent lighting. "What part? I'm very familiar with the area, you know. I did go to school at *Pitt*, after all."

Just perfect. Now she's quizzing me on my fictitious home state. Think, Zack, think.

Then it struck me. It didn't matter what I said since she wasn't going to buy it anyway. "Downtown area," I replied, confidence waning.

"How did I know you were going to say that?" Ms. Maddows mumbled, a strong scent of stale coffee beans wafting in my direction. "Please continue!"

"Hi, I'm Zack Treadwell. And, as you know, I'm from Pittsburgh. Go Steelers!"

After my wonderful introduction, I glanced over at Ms. Maddows as if to ask without asking if that was sufficient for her needs. She just rolled her eyes. "You can be seated now, Zachary."

Plopping back into my seat, it felt as if all eyes were on me. Nerves of steel or not, your first day of school is always the worst. Especially when you don't know anyone and you have people like Ms. Maddows forcing you to do something as stupid as an "ice-breaker." Checking out my surroundings, I noticed that some of the other students, most of the ones in the back, were whispering back and forth to each other. I unsuccessfully attempted to listen in on their conversations. The voices just seemed to fuse together as one muffled and faint voice pulsating from the rear of the room. Paranoid that they were conversing about me, I leaned back, swiveled my head to the right, and tried to listen for any clues that may have suggested the "new kid" was the topic of conversation.

Again, I was unable to hear anything significant. Turning my head back to face the front of the room, my eyes locked with Ms. Maddows' piercing dark gaze. I swear the veins in her bloodshot eyes formed the word "HATE" in fibrous, red letters. Great, within the span of five minutes, I had already made an enemy. I was, however, able to comfort myself with the knowledge that I'd only have to deal with her for the first fifteen minutes of each day. That was a relief at least.

Then, as luck would have it, my eyes caught a glimpse of my schedule. *No!* I thought in pure dread. *Dear God in Heaven! Somebody up there must really hate me.* Next to first period English and eighth period gym was the name **MADDOWS** in big, bold letters. *What kind of school is this? A gym/English teacher!* I just prayed that, come eighth period, Ms. Maddows wouldn't be clad in a tight, pink leotard, accentuating her roundish proportions.

As challenging as it was to shed some positivity on the situation, there was one benefit of having Maddows for homeroom and first period. It delayed the inevitable walk through the halls. The drill is always the same, sacrificial lambs burdened with the task of introducing themselves to you in a friendly manner, all designed to yank out as much information from you as possible. In all the schools I had attended, there was always at least one of them, if not more. I often wondered why teenagers couldn't be more standoffish and content with keeping to themselves. You know, more like New Yorkers.

When the bell finally rang, not soon enough in my opinion, I waited for everyone, including Ms. Maddows, to leave the room before making my move. The plan was simple. Get as far away from Maddows' desk as possible. It was a good plan. As inconspicuous as possible, I grabbed my belongings and stood up. Glancing around the room, eying several seats in the back row, I noticed that there were three other unfortunate souls in the same predicament as me. They, too, had to endure Ms. Maddows for homeroom and first period.

Two steps were all it took. Ms. Maddows, with her seemingly super-human hearing, popped her head in the classroom and pointed with a pudgy finger at my old seat.

"If you haven't noticed already, Zachary, anyone who has me for homeroom and first period are expected to use the same seat as they did for homeroom. It just makes things less complicated. Don't you think?"

"I guess," I muttered, trudging back to the dreaded seat.

Now, not only would she easily see my complete and utter boredom for her class, but she would also be able to smell what I consumed for breakfast. And, trust me that was not a good thing. You see, the Baniaks didn't exactly have the best breakfast menu at their humble abode. If you think it's normal to eat french toast pizza for breakfast then, by all means, trade places with me. PLEASE! Without going into too many details, french toast pizza is a concoction of french toast, pizza dough, tomato sauce, cheese, and maple syrup, all blended together to destroy your stomach and make artwork of the inside of your toilet.

First period fired off the same as homeroom with another awkward "introduction" followed by growing paranoia that everybody was talking about me. The laughter was the worst. Without any real basis for believing the laughter had anything to do with me, I was convinced it did. Fortunately, Ms. Maddows didn't approve of that type of behavior and was highly effective at snuffing it out.

"Class, take out Shakespeare's *Macbeth* and turn to page 57. Nicholas, please start with the first paragraph," Ms. Maddows announced, holding up her worn copy of *Macbeth*.

"Start what?" Nicholas replied, scratching his short brown hair.

"Don't be a smart aleck, Nicholas, you know what I meant. Now will you please start reading from the first paragraph on page 57?"

"Sorry, no can do, Ms. Maddows."

Ms. Maddows bit her lower lip, the bright pink visible on her stained brown teeth. "EXCUSE ME!"

"I don't read, Ms. Maddows. I write." Then, holding up his own copy of *Macbeth*, he added, "Think Shakespeare."

"Would you mind elaborating on that, Nicholas? I am very interested to see where you are going with all of this. And it better be good."

"Okay, Ms. Maddows," he said, sounding confident. "Do you think Shakespeare wasted his valuable time reading the works of other writers? Heck no! He wrote…and wrote…and wrote…and in the process became a literary genius. In fact, avoiding reading at all costs is one of my personal hobbies. Therefore, I would like to pass as it goes against one of my chief principles."

One of the veins from earlier began pulsating again in Ms. Maddows' neck. She looked like she wanted to tear Nicholas' head off. Then as quickly as the rage swept in, it vanished. Smiling, Ms. Maddows casually walked over to Nicholas' seat and stood before him. "All right, Nicholas, if you don't want to read, I will respect your wishes. I'll have someone else read. But it won't be Shakespeare. Nicholas, will you please take out your writings now. You did say you were a writer, didn't you?"

"Okay," he responded without hesitation.

Nicholas then removed a white notebook from his backpack and handed it over to Ms. Maddows. Her mouth turning upward, Ms. Maddows waltzed back to the front of the class and dropped it with a thud on my desk. "Would our Pennsylvania native mind reading a passage from Nicholas' notebook?"

First the introductions and now *this*! Could things get any worse? Probably.

Sensing there was no choice in the matter, I flipped open the notebook and began reading from the first passage. "'The Girl with the Pierced Clitoris,' by—"

"That's enough, Zachary," Ms. Maddows cut in as the class erupted in laughter.

Flustered, Ms. Maddows snatched the notebook out of my hands, walked back to Nicholas' seat, and slammed the notebook on his desk. All laughter ceased. "Nicholas, you are going to read what I asked you to read or you are going straight to the principal's office. I mean it. NO MORE JOKING AROUND. And I never want to see this notebook in my class again," she added, tapping on the notebook with her pointer finger. "UNDERSTOOD?"

"All right," Nicholas replied, sounding somewhat reluctant. "Even if it goes against everything I believe in, I'll comply and do as you wish."

Similar to me, Nicholas also had the misfortune of having Ms. Maddows for both homeroom and English class. In terms of first impressions, Nicholas seemed an intriguing fellow. He was funny, defiant, stood up for his beliefs, and Ms. Maddows clearly didn't like him. All positive attributes in my book. That said, I did not foresee the author of "The Girl with the Pierced Clitoris" and myself becoming friends, but at least I had company on her hit list. I briefly wondered where my ranking was on the list in comparison to his. With his brashness and cockiness, he was surely in the top three, if not number one.

When the class neared its end, anxiety began to rear its ugly head. There was no more avoiding the inevitable. I would have no choice but to roam the halls with everyone else. Those nerves of steel I had talked up seemed more like nerves of aluminum foil, easily manipulated and torn to shreds.

Brrrinngg! The bell rang.

Slowly rising from my seat, I gathered my few belongings (a red notebook, a pen, and a pathetic excuse for a lunch) and headed straight for the door. Before exiting the room, I glanced back and noticed that Ms. Maddows was glaring intently at me with a subtle smirk on her face. The look sent a cold chill down my spine. What was running through that mind of hers? Who knows? And honestly, who really wanted to know? I didn't.

One benefit of attending so many schools is that you begin to get a feel for the general layout. Some are more run down than others, but in regards to floor plans, they aren't all that much different. If your class is in the 100s—first floor all the way. 200s—second floor. 300s—you get the point. Finding room 134, my American History II class with Mrs. Vera, was a breeze. Entering her class, I just hoped, no, prayed, Mrs. Vera was more pleasant to be around than Ms. Maddows.

She was and, better yet, I made it through her class without incident. In fact, in addition to her class, I successfully made it through third period biology, fourth period art, and fifth period algebra, all without any significant social interactions before heading off to lunch. Since pickings were slim at the Baniaks' residence, at least in terms of things deemed edible, all I brought with me were a couple of bruised apples and a homemade brownie, which I hoped was of the *special* variety. With my less than desirable lunch in hand, I made my way to the cafeteria and found an empty table all the way in the back. Even for such a small school, the cafeteria seemed desolate. In total, in addition to myself, there were roughly 16 students scattered about the cafeteria that reeked of foul body order and ammonia. I'm guessing most of the students took full advantage of Stone Creek High's open-campus lunch policy. I chose not to. I wanted no part of venturing outside the confines of Stone Creek High. It was safer that way. Students tend to be a little more abrasive when teachers are not around.

When lunch ended, I headed straight for my seventh period Spanish class where avoiding conversations were easy, especially since our teacher, Mr. Diaz, insisted we attempt to converse exclusively in *Español*. Aside from a friendly "hola" and "no," I was useless when it came to speaking Spanish. Minutes before the end of seventh period, I glared at my schedule with utter disdain. I still couldn't come to grips with having Ms. Maddows for English and gym class. My days would start and end in the same fashion: miserably.

To wear a pink leotard or not to wear a pink leotard, I thought entering the gym. *That is the question, Ms. Maddows.*

The moment she came into my line of vision, I nearly burst into laughter. She wasn't wearing a pink leotard. Her outfit *was* pink, I had that part right, but it was actually much more ridiculous. Clad in a pink and black referee shirt, pink parachute pants, and an ensemble of pink accessories, including a headband, wristbands, kneepads, sports goggles, fanny pack, and a whistle around her neck, the mere sight of her nearly induced tears. It was almost too good to be true.

With a smile curving a path upwards on my face—a path less traveled—I approached Ms. Maddows and tried my hardest to maintain my composure. "I-I-I…" I had to stop and hold my breath just to refrain from laughing.

"What is it, Zachary?" she asked, oblivious to my near breakdown.

She must have been either immune to my immaturity or just plain used to kids gawking at her over-the-top attire. Regardless of which, I spit out a brief statement about not having a gym uniform with me. She took the news surprisingly well. That seemed out of character for her. Was she actually going to cut me, Mr. I'm-From-Downtown-Pittsburgh, some slack? Her calm demeanor suggested that she would.

"Not to worry, Zachary," she replied, seemingly pleased I had come unprepared. "It's okay. I won't count it against you. It is your first day, after all…" she paused, then added, "you know what, Zachary? I have an idea. You can use a loaner for today. Now, go to my office and grab an outfit from my brown hamper. There should be plenty of gym shirts and trunks to choose from."

"If it is okay with you, I'd rather just sit out today and—"

"I insist, Zachary," she replied, pulling her frizzy hair into a ponytail. After tying it off with a pink hair tie, she glared at me for a second before shouting, "NOW GO!"

"Dammit," I grunted under my breath making my way over to her office. Now, because of my foster parents, who had promised to pick my uniform up for me, I had to wear someone else's old, nasty uniform that probably reeked of BO. My nostrils flared at the thought.

After entering the office, stocked with—surprise, surprise—more plants and gnomes, I spotted the brown hamper off in the far corner of the room. Within seconds, I snagged a large maroon T-shirt that, on closer inspection, seemed clean enough. That was about the time I noticed there was a problem brewing—a major one. I couldn't locate any trunks. I began tossing the shirts all around like a crazed thrift store shopper, searching for a single pair of shorts. Finally, after sorting through the entire hamper, shirts pooled all around my feet, I found a lone pair of once-maroon shorts, which were now a faded pinkish color. The problem was not necessarily the color, although that didn't help. The real problem concerned the size of the old, faded shorts. The barely legible label read: *XS*. Just my luck. I had the pick of the litter when it came to shirts, but for the shorts, I was stuck with the runt.

Distraught, I took my aggression out on the shirts, hurling them back into the hamper with excessive force. I should have just left them strewn all over the floor, but responding in a passive-aggressive fashion wasn't my style. If I was going to do something—ask Dante—there'd be nothing passive about my actions. Holding the ridiculous outfit in my hand, the tiny, pink shorts concealed by the much larger shirt, I made my way into the locker room.

Fortunately, by the time I entered the dank, urine-smelling locker room, just about all of the other students had already changed and were making their way out into the gymnasium. There was only one other kid still changing. Wedged between an open space between two sections of lockers, the rotund young man removed his sweater, replacing it with his gym shirt in one swift motion. If he was embarrassed about his physique, which I assumed he was (why else would he be the last one out of the locker room and corked in between two sections of lockers?), he probably would have felt much better about himself had he stuck around just a little bit longer. Being the fat kid paled in comparison to what I had in store for myself—pink daisy duke shorts. Sliding my shirt on, I glanced at the shorts and contemplated feigning sickness to get out of wearing them. In the end, not wanting to piss Maddows off too much on my first day, I grudgingly squeezed into the humiliating shorts.

Checking them out in a mirror, I was horrified at my reflection. There stood a boy, two inches shy of six feet, sporting an entirely new look. Some people prefer boxers, some prefer briefs, and some even prefer a combination of the two—boxer briefs. I was taking the third preference to an entirely new level—briefs over boxers. Trendsetter, I think not. An ill-equipped imbecile who was about to become the laughing-stock of gym class, undoubtedly. The shorts were so tight, so *snug*; nothing was left to the imagination.

I had two options: embrace what was unquestionably a fashion *faux pas* or sag the crap out of tight fitting pink shorts. Choosing the latter made the most sense. Entering the gymnasium, I held my head low and ignored the snickering that was coming from all directions. Death never seemed so appealing.

"There's a spot right here for you," Ms. Maddows said, pointing to a space right in front of where she was standing.

It wasn't getting any better, only worse. Now, in addition to having to wear the ridiculous outfit, I was stuck parading my sagging daisy dukes in front of the entire class. Even the obese kid from the locker room was laughing. I had officially made my presence known at Stone Creek High. If kids were not already talking about me, they soon would be.

"Thanks for the loaner uniform," I said, masking my disdain.

"There weren't any larger shorts in the hamper?" she asked, glancing down at the tight pink shorts. "I could have sworn there was a bunch of larges in the hamper earlier this morning. What in the world could have happened to them?"

I couldn't believe what she was implying. Had Ms. Maddows *sabotaged* me? Had she noticed that I was without a uniform and took an off chance that there wasn't one stowed away in my locker? If so, she was right on the money.

Her mood elevated, evidenced by the smirk painted across her face, Ms. Maddows flashed her coffee-browns at me and then blasted a deep breath into her pink whistle. Standing mere feet away, the intensity of the whistle rocked my eardrums. All laughter ceased—or so it seemed to me as my ears no longer functioned properly.

"ALL RIGHT, CLASS, TIME FOR WARM-UPS. COUNT OFF WITH ME," she screamed, her voice carrying through the entire gymnasium.

Whether I wanted to or not, I found myself counting off with her as loudly as humanly possible. To be honest, I was actually terrified not to follow her orders. Who knew what would be in store for me had I not? I'm not embarrassed to admit that Maddows definitely got the best of me.

After finishing the calisthenics and prepping the gymnasium for the activity of the day, Ms. Maddows paired the class off into teams for badminton. I was teamed up with a kid named Jason Storms, who went on to inform me that Ms. Maddows lost her mother to breast cancer, thus her obsession with the color pink. Her outfit was still extreme, but since it was for a good cause, I felt it was grossly inappropriate to ridicule. As for everything else about Ms. Maddows, all bets were off.

A crazy thing happened next. I actually found myself enjoying a Maddows-taught class. I also discovered a newfound talent. Badminton, of all things. Of course, I probably could have done even better if my tight, sagging shorts did not restrict some of my mobility. After winning three straight matches, forgetting all about my reservations regarding my appearance, nothing mattered more than crushing my opponent. Next in line was a team composed of the obese locker room kid and a tall, lanky fellow with a bad complexion and droopy eyes. It was payback time. I was respectful enough not to laugh at fat kid's protruding abdomen and gynecomastia so he deserved to get spiked on, preferably in the mid-region. That would certainly wipe the smirk off his gluttonous face. Ready to get the match started, I tossed the birdie in the air just as Ms. Maddows blew on her damn whistle again.

"OKAY, CLASS, TIME TO CLEAN UP! YOU HAVE THREE MINUTES. SO GET MOVING," she screamed like a drill sergeant.

Everyone, except for me, sprang into action. I would like to believe I was purposely being defiant, you know, standing my ground, but that wasn't the case. Unlike the rest of the worker bees, who already knew their roles in Maddows' matriarchy, it was my first day on the job so I expected a little slack. Maddows saw differently.

"WHAT IN THE WORLD ARE YOU DOING, ZACHARY?" she shouted, her turkey wattle neck jiggling with each scream. "GET A MOVE ON IT."

And I did.

"Ms. Maddows means business," Jason whispered to me while carrying the badminton net over to the supply room. "It's best just to do what she says. You don't want to experience the wrath of Maddows. Trust me, it's not pleasant. She made a kid wet his pants last year. And that's only scratching the surface of what she's capable of."

Leering down at my shorts, I could relate. I had experienced her capabilities firsthand.

Out of my loaner uniform, I approached Ms. Maddows. "Do you want me to throw these back in the hamper or take them with me and have them washed?"

"You know what, Zachary? Why don't you just go ahead and keep those. You know…in case you ever need them again."

"Okay, thanks," I replied, one hundred percent certain it would never come to that. There was no way Zack Treadwell would ever come unprepared again.

"Very well, now get back in line. I have an important announcement to make before class lets out."

Like an obedient soldier, I complied. Standing in line with all the other docile troops, I listened as Maddows rambled on and on about the importance of maintaining a healthy lifestyle, respecting your parents and teachers, and staying away from cancer-causing carcinogens. She became so engrossed in her monologue that it seemed nothing could stop her, not even the final bell. Afraid to bear witness to the wrath Jason had spoken of, my feet stayed grounded as did everyone else's. Ms. Maddows eventually wrapped up her announcement—five minutes after the bell had rung—and everyone darted for the exit.

On the way back to my foster parents' house, sitting all alone in the front of the bus, I reflected on my first day at Stone Creek High. Ms. Maddows and the pink daisy duke shorts fiasco aside, the day had not been a total disaster. I was aware that there may be repercussions for the shorts in days to come, but at least there was an entire weekend to help cool things off. If the kids at Stone Creek High were anything like me, the filtration process would begin immediately, effectively erasing all the useless information learned throughout the day. Regardless, even if no filtration occurred, which was perhaps likely considering the hilarity of the situation, I was beginning to feel optimistic that Stone Creek High was going to work out for me.

Arriving back at the Baniaks' split-level home, Susan greeted me at the door. "How was your day, Zack? I finally picked up your uniform!"

I smiled, let out a quick chuckle, and shook my head as I entered the house.

"What is it, Zack?" she asked curiously, the sun gleaming off her tinted glasses.

With no other outlet to voice my frustration and utter embarrassment, I laid it all on Susan. She laughed, apologized for failing to pick up my uniform sooner, and made for some good company. In a surprising twist, Susan informed me that she actually attended high school with Ms. Maddows. She went on to add that she was a colossal shrew, even back then. I listened in pure enjoyment as she ragged on about Ms. Maddows, and proceeded to tell story after story of Ms. Maddows being Ms. Maddows. For the first time since relocating, I actually felt good about the move. I was far enough away from my old life, and the nightmares associated with it, to start anew. And that's exactly what I planned on doing.

Chapter Two

Notes

The next few weeks zipped by with only minimal reminders of my eventful first day. A few kids called me Daisy, a few others called me Pinky, and some even asked to see the infamous shorts. After the joke had finally run its course, in about a week-and-a-half's time, I went back to being the quiet kid who kept to himself. Eventually it got to the point where I was like a ghost amongst the living. I just seemed to glide by, unnoticed, invisible to all, including myself. At least that was the case until something out of the ordinary happened. I found a strange note in my locker.

Zack,
If you're interested, there are a couple of
us going to the park after school. If
you'd like follow along, just meet us out
front next to the bike rack.
Nick T.

To be honest, I had absolutely no interest in meeting up with them. Nick may have shared a class with me, but other than that, I knew virtually nothing about him. In fact, I couldn't even recall ever speaking a single word to him. Besides, the whole note passing thing seemed a bit childish to me anyway. Hadn't the emergence of social media effectively wiped out that practice years ago?

It wasn't until after contemplating my alternative options that I decided to reevaluate my initial decision. The thought of vegging out in front of the television didn't seem all that alluring either, so I decided why not. If anything, it would at least get me out of the house for a little bit—something my sun deprived skin desperately needed. Plus, as a secondary perk, maybe I'd finally hear how "The Girl with the Pierced Clitoris" ended. That last part was a long shot.

Moments before the final bell rang, doubts about meeting up with Nick and his friends began creeping in. The cold, hard facts were right there, front and center. I barely knew Nick, had no idea who any of his friends were, and it wouldn't be the first time traveling down that *path less desired*. Contemplating my options, either to go or continue my perpetual reign of boredom, I decided there was no viable reason not to give it a shot. Even if Nick and his friends had ulterior motives, I could handle myself. Ask Dante.

BRRRIINNNGGGG! The bell echoed loudly through the gymnasium. Already finished with her daily monologue, Ms. Maddows waved us away.

Stepping outside, I immediately spotted Nick and his friends hanging out over by the bike rack. To his left was a kid I had never seen before, and to his right was the *fat* kid from gym class. Strike one. Nick's judgment was obviously skewed. Yeah, as immature as it was, I still held a grudge against the fat kid for laughing at my pink shorts.

"Hey, Zack," Nick said, waving me over, his white backpack slung over his shoulder.

"Hey," I replied meekly.

"I'm Nick, as you probably already know since you had the pleasure of reading from my notebook, the imbecile located to my immediate left is Mike Jeposi, and that's the infamous Alex Vunpuffles," he said, gesturing to each of his friends in turn.

I shook all of their hands, Alex's pudgy and sweaty hand a little more forcefully than necessary, and nodded towards the walkway. "You guys know the area so I'll follow you."

"All right, let's go then," Nick said, taking the lead.

After only four steps into our voyage to the park, I heard an unusual metallic clicking sound. It almost sounded as if someone had a nail embedded into the sole of their shoe. Hoping to eliminate myself as a suspect, I stopped for a moment to inspect my shoes. They were slightly worn with dried chewing gum embedded in the treads, but that was about all.

"Hey, do you guys hear that sound?" I asked after catching up with them. "It sounds like a nail or something. You guys might want to check your shoes."

Mike and Alex instantly burst into laughter, the roll under Alex's chin jiggling like a tub of vanilla pudding. Nick didn't even acknowledge the question. He just kept on walking down the street with his white backpack slung tightly around his shoulder, the metallic clicking following his every step.

"What's so funny?" I asked sheepishly.

"There's your culprit..." Alex replied, pointing towards Nick, his greasy skin glistening in the bright sun. "Come on, Nick, tell Zack about the thumbtacks!"

Nick shook his head, obviously annoyed. There was definitely more to the story—much, much more. But what?

"Don't be shy, Nick," Mike pressed, his light brown eyes filled with amusement. "Just tell him about your OCD. He's going to find out anyway."

Nick suddenly stopped, spun around, and stared me straight in the face with his deep-set dark, brown eyes. "Since I know they won't shut up about it until I tell you..." Nick glared sharply at Alex and Mike, "I might as well just get this over with. I have this thing with counting. It's stupid, and I know that. But I can't help it. For whatever reason, it calms my nerves. The thumbtacks just aid my compulsion. They make it so much easier to count my steps, especially in crowded areas. So now that you know, can we please drop the subject?"

I nodded, afraid to say anything else on the topic.

Mike did not share my reservations. Smiling, he hurled himself onto me, throwing an arm around my shoulder and nearly gouging one of my eyes out with his sharp, spiked hair. "Zack, if you think the counting thing is weird, you should see his room. Come on, Nick, tell him about your concept room—"

"That's enough," Nick barked, throwing his slender arms up in the air, briefly exposing the bone white underside of his protruding abdomen. In contrast to the triplets Alex was seemingly carrying underneath his brown and red rugby shirt, if I didn't know any better, I'd say Nick was in his second trimester. Having never noticed his poorly defined mid-region before, it caught me off guard. Compared to the rest of his physique, which was on the frail side, his sizable gut seemed out of place. In only his teens, Nick looked liked the aftermath of decades of poor dieting and heavy drinking. But who was I to judge, it wasn't like I was the poster child for healthy living. "Let's go. We're never going to make it if we continue at this lethargic pace," he concluded, whipping his body around and picking up the pace.

With Nick's emotions flaring up, it seemed like the perfect time to change the subject. "So what's it like to live around here?"

My diversion worked perfectly. As we continued on our way to the park, Nick, Mike, and Alex gave me the rundown of the school and general area. They filled me in on the different cliques, told me which teachers were cool, which ones were not, interesting facts about Stone Creek, and then went into grave details about the girls they found attractive.

Alex was in love with a girl named Tina Sheyvors.

"Dude!" he said animatedly, "she's 5'6'', thin as they come, a natural redhead, has sexy green eyes, and the most amazing legs I have ever seen. She plays soccer all the time, and actually takes an advanced yoga class. She's...perfection."

"Why don't you ask her out?" I asked, warming up to the kid I once despised. He didn't seem so bad after getting to know him a little better.

"Yeah, right, like Alex would ever ask her out," Nick said bluntly. "He'd rather bore us with a never-ending bar-rage of Tina facts than actually do something about it."

"Shut up, Nick. You know why I can't ask her out."

"Why?"

"Well, Zack, our friend Alex here thinks he has BDD," Nick said, slapping Alex in the gut.

I glanced at Nick with my head cocked to the side. "BDD?"

"Body Dysmorphic Disorder," Nick replied. "Alex thinks he's morbidly obese. Overweight...yeah. Obese... I'm not sure about that. Technically speaking the criteria's very stringent for someone to be classified as morbidly obese."

I suddenly felt extremely bad for referring to Alex as "the obese locker room kid." In fairness to Alex, I wouldn't have really considered him obese. It just came out of me when he laughed at me for the pink shorts. He was definitely out of shape—there was no denying that—but morbidly obese was a stretch.

"At least I'm not a frotteur...Nick," Alex lashed back. "And for your information I don't think I'm morbidly obese. I'm overweight and there's no way Tina would go out with a fat ass like me."

"Frotteur?" I asked, cocking my head to the other side.

Mike wasted no time cuing me in. Scratching a large patch of dried skin on his forehead, presumably a bad case of psoriasis, Mike told me all about how a frotteur is a sexual deviant who engages in the fetish of rubbing up against an unsuspecting person for sexual pleasure. He went on to add that Nick does it all the time.

Not amused, not in the least, Nick shook his head with a wryly smirk. "Since Zack wasn't there, I feel obligated to once again set the record straight. I am not a frotteur, nor have I ever practiced the act of frotteurism. Mike and Alex both know, although for some strange reason will never admit it, that I was pushed into that poor, old lady last summer. Furthermore, my genitals did not make contact with, or rub against, any part of that woman's body. End of discussion. Now can we please pick up the pace? At this rate it'll be dark by the time we get there."

"He totally dry humped her," Mike whispered in my ear. "He's just embarrassed to admit it."

As we turned down Cleveland Street, which I was informed was the halfway mark, the discussion shifted back to the topic of girls. Nick did not contribute much to that particular conversation. He just seemed to agree with whatever Alex and Mike said. Mike, on the other hand, had no qualms about discussing who he thought was attractive. In fact, he seemed to be in love with just about every girl at school. Unlike Alex, who was terrified to approach the woman of his dreams, Mike did not share his inhibition. Nick and Alex talked all about how Mike spent the better part of his days networking with all of Stone Creek High's finest. When he wasn't talking to girls face-to-face, he was glued to his phone constantly exchanging texts and Facebook messages. Using past and present yearbooks, Mike *friended* at least three-fourths of the female student body at Stone Creek High. An impressive feat motivated purely by raging hormones and unrivaled horniness.

He bragged, "I've been rejected so many times, I've lost count. I understand most people would be embarrassed to admit that, but at least I had the balls to try. Plus, I've had two serious girlfriends so far. Lynn and Stacey Fargas. Let me tell you, Zack, that's two more than any of these tools have had. While they're standing there all tight-lipped, afraid to make a move, I'm out there making things happen."

"Wait a minute…you dated sisters?" I asked, putting two and two together.

"Twins actually!"

"How in the world did you pull that off?"

"Well, I dated Lynn last year for about two months before she dumped me for flirting with another girl. Then, during the summer, I dated Stacey for about two months before she dumped me for the same reason. Twins are weird."

"What about you? Anyone catch your eye yet?" Mike asked.

"I've noticed some cute girls here and there, but I haven't really talked to anyone yet. I've kind of been keeping a low profile…"

"Yeah, we've noticed!" Nick, Mike, and Alex responded in unison.

In a desperate attempt to sound normal, I mean who purposely chooses to avoid any significant social interactions, I blurted out, "I've just been trying to get acclimated to the area first. You know, test out the waters before jumping in."

Alex and Nick seemed to understand, or at least pretended to. Mike, on the other hand, appeared completely lost. "I'm not following you," he replied, sounding sincere. "When it comes to meeting chicks, what's there to get acclimated to? You see someone hot. You do whatever it takes to seek her out. End of discussion."

Fortunately, for my sake (I had no clue as to how to reply to Mike's simplistic logic) Nick came to my rescue. He stomped on the gas, took a sharp right, and steered the conversation away from my personal choice to live a solitary lifestyle.

Jumping back into a previous topic, Nick further explained the group dynamics at school, interesting factoids about West Virginia (including a brief history of the infamous Mothman), and how they all came to be friends. Although some his "fun facts" were trite, I did learn a few interesting things about my new surroundings. While Nick was busy talking about his own personal theory regarding the Mothman, Mike and Alex made it obvious that they had no interest in what he was talking about. Trailing a few feet behind, they began hurling small pebbles at the back of Nick's head. Ignoring the minor distraction, at least for the most part, Nick kept on talking only stopping every so often to threaten bodily harm to Mike and Alex if they didn't stop. Which, of course, they didn't.

Shortly before arriving at Stone Creek National Park, the largest forest in the area, Nick informed me that the recreational section of the park was not our final destination. He had somewhere better to take me. I asked him where, but he refused to say. Then after passing up several hiking trails and heading straight into the belly of the surrounding woods, I finally demanded to be told where we were headed. After all, following a strange group of teens into the harsh wilderness was a recipe for tragic consequences. Sizing them up, I eased my worries knowing full well that none of them stood a chance against me. Even outnumbered three to one, I felt confident in my abilities to defend myself.

"Don't worry, it's really cool," Mike assured me, now scratching a whitened and scaly knuckle. "It shouldn't be too much longer."

I wasn't fond of his choice of words. *Shouldn't* instilled a lack of confidence that they had any clue of where they were going. From personal experience, getting lost in the harsh wilderness was not fun. As a boy, I used to walk into the woods purposely trying to get lost. At the time, I was convinced I enjoyed the challenge of finding my way back. It took me years to realize that wasn't the case. Not at all. Much older and wiser, I've come to recognize that it was most likely an unconscious ploy to escape from my life and the pain associated with it. If I couldn't find my way back, maybe, just maybe, I could start over and forget everything that transpired on that fateful spring day.

Dwelling on my past brought back painful memories of the worst day of my existence. All the depressing and gruesome details of my parents' horrific and traumatizing deaths began invading and taking over control of my every thought. Not wanting to get too depressed or shut down in front of potential new friends, I attempted to divert my attention.

"Are you sure you guys know where we're going?" I asked, crossing yet another creek by way of a fallen tree. "You *are* aware that it's extremely easy to get lost in the woods, aren't you?"

"Why, are you getting scared?" Alex said mockingly. "You think there are Zomb—"

"Shut up, Alex!" Nick growled.

I stopped dead in my tracks, halfway across the creek. "What were you about to say?" I asked, taking the final few strides with little care of falling. "Come on, let's hear it!"

Alex looked confused as he backed away from me. He quickly glanced at Nick, then Mike, and then back at me. "Are you being serious?"

"As a brain attack," I said, jumping down from the tree and closing the distance between him and myself. "I want to know exactly what you were going to say."

He looked at me sideways, one eyebrow raised. "I don't know…just something stupid about zombies. Why?"

To anyone else the comment may not have hit so close to home. For me, it was like having my nails filed down with a cheese grater. All the fights, the moves, the nightmares, all stemmed from that one simple word—zombie. My paranoia, which had subsequently fizzled out after getting to know them better, sprang back to life. It posed a very important question: Did they bring me in the middle of nowhere just to ridicule me? I hoped it was an overreaction on my part, but if the past is any indication of the future, it seemed unlikely. I had been in this exact position more times than I cared to recall. As for Alex, the perpetrator of the egregious offense, I just wanted to punch him right in his fat, greasy face.

Clenching my fists, I turned to Nick, no longer caring what any of them thought about me. "Your boy is out of line. He's REAL lucky I made a promise to stay out of trouble. If not…well, I think you know exactly what would be happening right now."

I abruptly turned away and began making my way back to the park. I made it twenty feet before stopping. Annoyed, I waved Nick over. Enraged, yet embarrassed, I reluctantly admitted that I needed help finding my way back to the street.

"He didn't mean anything by it, Zack. He was just fooling around. How could he possible know that talking about zombies would incite you?"

"He shouldn't know. No one should. But judging by your actions, it seems as if you had an inclination. Don't think for a split-second I didn't take notice of you trying to cut him off. So…Nick…mind telling me how you know so much about me?"

"Look, Zack, now's not the time or place. Why don't we just put this little misunderstanding behind us and forget it happened. I assure you Alex meant nothing by it. He was just joking around. Besides, we're nearly at our destination."

"You know what…why don't you just point me in the right direction and I'll find my own way back."

"Zack, come on, can't we…" Nick suddenly paused, shook his head, and starting walking. "All right, if that's what you want, I'll respect your wishes. Follow me. It's easier if I just show you." There was defeat evident in his voice.

Nick then shouted to Mike and Alex for them to keep on going and that he'd catch up after escorting me back to the street. On the way back, my nerves calming down a bit, it finally dawned on me that Nick might have actually been telling the truth after all. Maybe Alex didn't mean anything by his comment and he *was* just goofing around. Even if that ended up being the case, one thing was certain, it was too late to turn back. I had made an ass of myself, and it was just easier to cut my losses and call it a day. Besides, I didn't need friends. I had never had any in the past so why start now.

After returning to the park, Nick tried to smooth things over again. Like I did the first time, I blew him off, showing no signs of wavering. At that point, all I wanted to do was return to seclusion, courtesy of the Baniaks' small second floor room. As welcoming as they had been to me, I still didn't consider their house my home—probably never would. In my mind, a home is a place you share with loved ones, not people who ship you out once the going gets tough. Even if the Baniaks had done right by me so far, it was only a matter of time. Would they also send me packing if someone's nose just happened to get broken? Probably.

Arriving back at the Baniaks' house, the moment I stepped foot inside the house, Susan blindsided me. With deep concern etched in her slightly skin-damaged face, Susan asked me about the incident in the woods. Apparently, my good friend Nick, God knows how he got Susan's number, felt it necessary to call her up in an attempt to do damage control. Shrugging my shoulders, I told her not to worry and that it wasn't a big deal—just a "little misunderstanding," so to speak.

Changing the subject, I asked Susan what was for dinner. With a big smile, she clapped her freckled hands and told me that oatmeal ravioli's was on the menu for supper. I nearly barfed in my mouth after hearing that bizarre concoction.

***

The next day, out of pure embarrassment, I made it a point to avoid Nick, Mike, and Alex as much as possible. Mike, who wasn't in any of my classes, was the easiest to avoid. Alex and Nick were another story. They each shared a class with me. Knowing that it would be impossible to elude the two of them indefinitely, I did the next best thing. I treated them as if they didn't exist. To my surprise, neither Nick nor Alex made any attempts to smooth things over. That stung a little. Even if I was an oversensitive psycho, who almost threw down for a stupid comment made about zombies, I still thought Nick would make another effort. He did call Susan, after all. Alex, on the other hand, I expected no such thing. He's not the one that should have been apologizing. I was.

A week later, just when the incident was starting to feel like a distant memory, I found yet another note in my locker. I thought of tossing it straight into the trashcan.

However, I couldn't quite bring myself to do it. Maybe somewhere deep in my subconscious there was a part of me that still yearned for acceptance. I unfolded the note.

> *Zack,*
> *We need to talk. Just you and me. No one else. Meet me in the same spot out front*
> *–Nick*

I thought back to that day in the woods and how Nick seemed to know intimate details about my past. If there ever was a time to find out how he was privy to such information, a one-on-one session seemed like the perfect opportunity. This time I wasn't going to let him off the hook so easily. That much was for sure.

***

"Follow me. I need to show you something," Nick shouted the moment I stepped out the front door.

Running up to him, I crossed my arms and stared at him intensely. "Wait, before we go anywhere, first tell me how you know so much about me?"

"Just follow me and I'll explain everything later."

"That's not good enough for me. I want to know now."

"Zack, I promise I'll tell you everything. But I *need* to show you something first. It'll all make sense after you see it. Trust me!"

I looked at him with a doubtful expression tattooed across my face.

"Come on, Zack," he pleaded. "I was hoping to get to know you a little better before I sprung this on you, but you left me no other choice. You just have to trust me. It's something that you, and only you, need to see."

I rolled my eyes. "Fine, but it better be worth it."

Similar to the previous week, yet at a much faster pace and with much less talking, Nick brought me back to the same park, the same woods, the same place where everything had went down. Except this time, as we made our way through the dense wilderness, it didn't seem as if we were headed in quite the same direction. In fact, it seemed as if we were going in a completely opposite direction.

"Not this again," I muttered under my breath.

"What was that?"

"Would it kill you to give me some type of idea of where we're headed?"

"Look, all I can tell you is that it's a place not even Alex or Mike know about."

"Then why are you showing it to me and not them?" I said, stating the obvious. "You guys seem to be attached at the hip."

"They're good guys and all, but they wouldn't understand the significance of what I have to show you. Besides, they don't know how to keep their mouths shut—especially Mike."

"And how do you know I will," I challenged him.

"That's easy. Even though Maddows constantly calls you out on your claim that you're from Pittsburgh, your stance has never faltered. In fact, half the class is convinced you are, even though you have one of the thickest Jersey accents I've ever heard."

"What are you talking about? What accent?"

Nick stopped and faced me. "Maddows is no dummy and neither am I. We both know where you're really from. But that's not important right now. Aside from your accent, which you conceal quite well by never talking to anyone, I have undeniable proof, which will all be explained in due time. Now, can we please pick up the pace? We have quite a hike ahead of ourselves."

He wasn't lying about that either. In addition to the thirty minutes it took to get to the park, it took another forty-five minutes of hiking through the rugged terrain before we arrived at our final destination. At first glance, nothing seemed particularly out of the ordinary. At an elevation of a few hundred feet, we were standing on the edge of a rather high cliff. In the ravine below, there were countless trees, shrubs, and rocks jutting out in all different directions. The spot definitely had a nice scenic view to it, but other than that there wasn't anything that caught my interest. Why had he brought me there? What was so important for me to see? I still had no clue.

"I'm a little lost here, Nick. Unless rock climbing is on the agenda, nothing's making any sense to me?"

Pulling binoculars out from his bag, Nick spent a few moments adjusting the focus before handing them over to me. "Look exactly where my finger is pointing, okay?"

I nodded, putting the binoculars up to my eyes. Things were starting to get interesting.

"Do you see that huge boulder covered in beard moss? The one the size of a small Volkswagen."

"Yeah, I see it. What about it?"

"Good. To the right of it you'll see some old, withered bushes that have seen better days. Do you see them?"

"Uh huh."

"Excellent. You're almost there. Now look right beside them, just to your right. If you look closely, you'll see what resembles a camouflaged vault door. Just look for the vault wheel, its camouflaged as well, but if you stare at it for a minute you should be able to spot it. Do you see it yet?"

As if I was studying one of those 3D stereogram posters (the ones where you almost have to look at it cross-eyed just to see the hidden image), after staring at it for a minute straight, the vault wheel finally popped out at me. It was there, just as he said it would be. My interest was definitely piqued.

"Okay, I see what you're talking about. What's the significance? What am I looking at?"

"Well, Zack, what you're looking at is a door leading into a highly secretive military lab. Aside from myself, and the people involved, you're the only other person who knows of its existence."

Chapter Three

Memories

I looked at Nick with shock and confusion, then put the binoculars back up to my eyes for another peek. It shouldn't have been there, but there it was, a steel vault door, probably titanium steel if I had to guess, built into the entrance of an underground cave.

I glanced at Nick with an inquisitive frown. "How do you know that there's a secret military lab behind that door? I mean, couldn't it just be an old mine shaft or something?"

"Maybe in the past it was, but not anymore. I'll explain everything once we get to my house." Gesturing towards the ravine, Nick added, "It's not wise to be around here during the day."

If he was implying that there could be surveillance cameras all around watching our every move, then I couldn't have agreed more. Getting arrested for spying on a secret military operation was the last thing I needed in my life. That would be a swift recipe for me having to find a new home—one with barred windows and limited visitation privileges.

"Come on," Nick growled. "We need to get moving. Like I said, it's not smart to be here during the day."

He didn't give me a chance to respond. Plucking the binoculars out of my hands, Nick threw them back into his backpack, and took off. Maneuvering through the woods with ease, I struggled to keep up. The rest of the way to his house wasn't much different. Nick kept up the same frantic pace, he had impressive cardio considering his non-athletic physique, all the way back to his house. With his feet clinking and clanking against the asphalt, sounding like a tap dancer in a foot race, Nick dodged every question I huffed his way. He stayed true to his word, not discussing anything until we got back to his house. Not even the weather.

When we finally arrived at his house, envy tore through me. Light blue stucco, well landscaped, and toys strewn across the front lawn, it reminded me of my parents' home. They looked nothing alike, but Nick's house felt like a home—a real one—a place where a kid could feel as if he or she belonged. For me, I couldn't remember what that felt like.

Reaching for the doorknob, Nick turned to me and said, "Zack, my parents are big dinner people. They make it a point to eat as a family every night. Before we even step foot inside my house, be prepared to stay for dinner."

"That'll be a blessing," I replied, then proceeded to cue Nick in on my current meal situation.

Repulsed at what he had just learned, Nick assured me that his mom's cooking was the best. I remember thinking the same thing about my own mother.

Moments before entering Nick's house, I did something completely out of character for me. I actually texted Susan to let her know of my whereabouts and my expected return time. Clicking the send button, I couldn't help but to think what was happening to me. That wasn't the Zack Treadwell way. After all, I was the type of kid who got into fistfights and was kicked out of more schools than I cared to keep track of. Calling your foster parent to tell her that you would be a little late usually didn't fit into the particular mold.

"Come on, Zack. I'll introduce you to everyone. Smells like dinner's almost ready."

Oh, it did. I savored the undeniable scent of roasted pork. I couldn't wait to eat.

Before taking a seat at the table, Nick did the honors of introducing me to his mom, dad, and younger brother Hank. Excluding Hank, who just made farting sounds when I went to shake his hand, Nick's mom and dad seemed very friendly.

"Well it's very nice to meet you, Zack," Nick's mother, Teresa, said. "Nick tells me that you're new to the area."

"Yeah, I just moved here not too long ago. It's nice here. I like it so far."

"Well, again it's very nice to meet you, Zack. Now, would you please excuse me, I need to tend to my chops. Nicholas will you please be a dear and grab a plate for Zack."

"Come on, grab a seat," Nick's dad, Richard, said, gesturing at the seat beside him. "Would you like a beer? Nah...you don't look like the beer-drinking type....shots it is! We'll have to drink vodka, though. Nick and Hank finished off the tequila last night!"

"Oh dear, stop messing with the boy," Teresa said, entering the room carrying a large bowl of mashed potatoes. "That one's such a jokester."

I didn't know what to say. It didn't sound like he was joking to me.

"I'm just messing with you, Zack," he said, his voice deep, slightly gravely. "Come on, let's hunker down and get ready to eat. My wife makes the best pork chops around, or at least that's what I've been instructed to tell everyone."

Teresa shot a look at Richard before the both of them erupted in a light-humored laughter. She promptly left the room smiling. Moments later, Nick reappeared holding a plate, utensils, and a can of soda. Following a step behind him, Teresa entered the dining room carrying a large, sizzling plate of seasoned pork chops. I began to salivate at the smell, something that was a rarity of late.

Gobbling down my food in only a matter of minutes, I briefly contemplated tearing into the scattered bones. Noticing my immense hunger, Teresa glanced at my near empty plate and smiled. "Would you like seconds, Zack? I made plenty."

"Absolutely," I said, slopping more and more food onto my plate.

"Wow, it seems like you haven't eaten in years," Teresa joked, watching me stack a tower of pork chops on the eastern region of my plate. Filling the entire western region, and even spewing over into pork chop territory, were sizable mounds of mashed potatoes and applesauce.

"He hasn't," Nick said.

We shared a glance and started laughing. Teresa gave us a "boys-will-be-boys" look and we laughed some more. It felt good to have an inside joke with someone. I couldn't remember the last time I had one. Actually scratch that—I had never actually shared one with anyone before.

After dinner, I thanked Nick's mom and dad for the wonderful meal. Nick then led me upstairs to his bedroom. Ever since the day I met Nick, Mike, and Alex after school, I had anticipated this very moment. I wanted to see once and for all what Alex and Mike had been alluding to in reference to Nick's room. Up until that point, all I knew was that Mike and Alex were, for some reason or other, extremely amused by Nick's room.

To say Nick's room caught me off guard was a colossal understatement. Mike and Alex could not have been more right. His room was without a doubt off the charts. Not only was everything neatly organized, which was no surprise considering his OCD, but it also appeared as if Nick had a 24-hour cleaning crew at his disposal. People living in bubbles would be jealous. In fact, not only was his room immaculate, but everything, and I mean *everything*, was pure white. *This must be what it's like to go to Heaven*, I joked to myself staring in astonishment. From his white carpet to his white walls, light fixtures, curtains, and furniture, everything bore the same exact shade of white. There was even a plain white poster hanging from the wall.

Examining his sterile looking room in awe, I thought about my own, which was already on the verge of being condemned. To think of it, I couldn't even remember the color of my rug—or if I even had one—it was covered from wall to wall with clothes and all my junk.

"Clean much?"

"Funny, Zack," Nick retorted in a dry, serious tone. "Make all the jokes you want—Alex and Mike do all the time."

"I think it's kind of cool, Nick. But, I'm sorry, I just don't get it."

"Don't apologize, Zack. You see, my room used to look like your average teen's room—minus the clutter or filth—my OCD wouldn't allow it. But I got bored of it. I wanted to do something different. So, when my parents gave me the okay to remodel, I developed what you see here—" Nick waved his arms around the room, "—my concept room. Its designed to induce creativity and increase productivity. I'm not sure if it really works. I feel that it does. I've been much more productive since creating it, but that could all just be a placebo effect. You know, I'm more productive because I think I should be. Regardless, I've grown fond of it and have no plans of altering it in anyway."

"What's that all about," I said, pointing towards the plain white poster hung by matching white thumbtacks.

Nick laughed. "Oh, that. Well, Mike and Alex bought it for me for my birthday last year. They intended it to be more of a gag than anything else. But after pinning it up, I came to like it. In fact, I feel as if it absorbs the essence of my room."

I walked over to his desk and slid my fingers across his white laptop computer.

"Matching everything was the hardest part," he added. "I had to special order just about everything in here just to make sure they were all the same exact white. Believe me, it was a pain in the ass. But it was worth the effort. I couldn't have been happier with the results."

"So is this where 'The Girl with the Pierced Clitoris' was born?" I asked, remembering the plain white notebook from that first eventful day in class.

"As a matter of fact it was. That was just something I put together after reading *The Girl with the Dragon Tattoo*. I'm glad Maddows stopped you when she did. It's not very good and was only a rough draft. I'll let you read it if you want. But first things first, let's get down to business. You have some questions and I have some answers. So bomb away."

Finally! I thought.

"Okay, let's start right from the beginning. How do you know so much about me?"

"I'll show you," Nick said, holding up a finger. Then without saying another word, Nick walked over to his closet and pulled out two, as you would have guessed, white behemoth-sized scrapbooks. After flipping through several pages in the first scrapbook, he handed me an article. "Here, read this," he instructed, his eyes staring at me intently, "it'll explain everything."

Zombies ate my parents

By CRAIG REZNICK
Stone Creek Press Staff Writer
In a tragic story, a five-year-old boy
lost his mother and father to an alleged...

***

I didn't have to finish reading the newspaper article, now yellowed with age, to know how it ended. The article, which stirred painful memories from my past, was all about me.

It happened on a peaceful, sunny afternoon just as my family was getting ready for a small barbecue in our backyard. The sun was shining as brightly as ever, and I was with my heroes, my mom and dad. My dad, wearing his favorite grease-stained grilling apron that read in faded bold letters, **World's Greatest Griller**, was stationed at the grill; while my mother, clad in a beautiful pink and white sundress, her blonde hair silhouetted in the intense sun, set the picnic table. My parents, who loved eating outdoors, shared the philosophy that if the weather was nice enough, we were eating outside. To this day, and not surprising considering the trauma endured, eating outside always makes me nervous. Even the faintest smell of food grilled outdoors induces flashbacks from that fateful day.

I was seated at the picnic table chugging a cold glass of lemonade, waiting as patiently as a small boy can for his food, when it happened. Watching my dad flip the burgers, I loved watching the flare-ups, the bigger the better, an alarmed expression swept across my dad's freshly shaven face. I followed his gaze and saw what was troubling him. Ascending towards us up the small incline in our yard were four sickly, almost inhumane-looking people. My mom, who had just refilled my glass with fresh lemonade, maneuvered herself protectively in front of me. Peeking out from behind her—the creepy looking people piqued my curiosity—terror finally tore through me as they closed the distance between us.

As long as I live, the terrifying images of those four people, if you could call them that, will forever be tattooed in the forefront of my brain. Etched with a colorful array of reds and blacks, I will never forget their grotesque appearances. From their deathly pale skin, to their bulging veins, pallid eyes, and gelatinous, black cherry colored substance that seemed to be oozing out of every orifice—they personified death. I can't even watch a zombie flick without the images of their grotesque faces appearing inside my head.

My mother, God rest her soul, instinctively heaved me over her shoulder and bolted towards the house. With my head bopping up and down, I watched in horror as the intruders began sprinting towards my father. I tried to scream to my father to tell him to look out, but could only muster faint groans with my mother's shoulder digging deeply into my abdomen. When we reached the backdoor, my mother hurled me to the ground and swung the door open. There was no time to be gentle.

"GO, ZACK!" she screamed hoisting me to my feet. "GO INSIDE AND LOCK THE DOOR BEHIND YOU! NOW!"

Tears streaming down my face, I pleaded for her to join me, but she had other plans. She was going back for her husband. Seconds later, bellowing screams erupted from the backyard. First my father's, then my mother's. Terrified of the horrors lurking beyond the door, with trembling fingers, I nervously locked the deadbolt. I will never, ever, forgive myself for my cowardice. By locking that damn Godforsaken door—I choose myself over them. Realistically there wasn't any I could have done to help, but it still felt as if I let them down. I didn't even think to call the police or run for a neighbor. I watched instead as the horror unfolded before my tear-welled eyes.

Glancing out the window, ready to run for the door and unlock it if the moment presented itself, I prayed someone would come to my parents rescue. They did come—just too late. Peeking out from the lower right-hand corner of the window, my eyes locked on an almost unspeakable act. Hunched over in groups of two, the intruders were busy gorging into my parents' bloodied and raw abdomens with animal-like ferocity. They were actually consuming them, tearing off chunk after chunk of flesh and gulping them down faster than a pelican swallowing a live fish. There was blood everywhere, and even though my parents' bodies were convulsing, seemingly alive, I knew they were gone. Unable to bear the gruesome sight any longer, I collapsed to the floor and buried my face in my hands.

The police arrived on the scene shortly later, guns drawn and ready to take my parents' assailants down. I didn't just want to watch my parents' killers gunned down—I felt compelled to watch. They deserved to die, and with my tragic loss, I earned the right to watch. Leering out of the very same corner of the window, with pure contentment in my heart, I watched as the police opened fire on my parents' killers. My only regret, still to this day, was not being able to partake in the justified slaughter.

Following the incident, an investigation was conducted to determine whether or not the police used excessive force. Count the amount of bullet wounds and you'd know why. But if you weren't there to see it, it'd be impossible to fully comprehend how the extreme measures were necessary just to take them down. Unlike me, who would have kept on shooting out of pure hatred and vengeance, the officers had no choice. My parents' killers just wouldn't go down. It didn't matter how many times they were hit, bodies peppered with bullet wounds, they kept pressing forward. I began to worry that the officers would meet the same fate as my parents. Fortunately, it never came to that. The *monsters* who stole my parents from me eventually slowed, then ultimately stopped altogether after another rain of bullets came pouring down on them. Even if I wasn't on the front lines seeking out my payback, which still stings to think about, the officers deserved to be recognized for their tenacity and determination to get the job done. If it takes sixty-five bullets per monster—so be it. For me, if I had gotten my hands on them, sixty-five would have seemed like child's play. No charges were ever filed against the officers—too many witnesses collaborated the officers' accounts.

Probably the thing that terrified me the most about the assailants was their incredible pain tolerance, or lack of one. It was as if they were immune to it—like zombies you'd see on TV. If bullets didn't faze them, nothing would. Stuck in that particular mindset, convinced my parents' cannibalistic murders were zombies, in the aftermath I told the reporters exactly what was on my mind. Virtually inconsolable, I screamed that zombies had eaten my parents, thus setting in motion future turmoil for myself. Why couldn't I have just kept my mouth shut?

Holding back tears, I dropped the article on Nick's nightstand and asked to use his bathroom. I needed some time to regain my composure.

"Sure, Zack, it's the second door on the right, just down the hall. Take as much time as you need."

Collapsing behind the door, just as I had done at my parents' house on that day, my emotions overtook me. I hadn't cried like that in years. The sheer presence of the article induced a vivid flashback of the most traumatizing day in my life. In terms of a defining moment—that was mine. The loving son, with all the potential in the world, lost his innocence on that day and would never be the same. My parents were not the only ones that died on that particular day. The Zack Treadwell of today is a just a mere exo-skeleton of his old self. On the outside, he may look the same, but underneath is a different and much more charred and blackened, story.

When my parents' blood finally soaked away, I found myself a prisoner of the system. I spent the next few years going from orphanage to orphanage, never quite fitting in, before hitting up the foster homes scene. If I thought the orphanages were bad, they paled in comparison to some of the awful conditions found in some of the foster homes. Some were good—most were not. In so much pain, I didn't care either way. Even when I had a good thing go-ing—Jesse and Dana Gilchrist—ruining it was a natural progression. A psychologist would peg it a self-destructive pattern, and I would know I'd seen my fair share of them throughout the years. Whatever the root cause was, one thing was certain, it's never easy to deal with loss and change—not to mention both at the same time.

As for my struggles in Jersey—kids are ruthless. As if it was divine intervention—the *Bully Gods* at work—my misguided comment about zombies being responsible for my parents' deaths followed me all throughout school. The cruel and sadistic nature of the harassment nearly destroyed me. Suicide crossed my mind once, or several hundred times. I even futilely tried it a few times—unsuccessfully of course. One day, many years ago, I just got sick of be-ing targeted and turned my inner pain outwards. Instead of withdrawing into my depression and feeling sorry for my-self, I began retaliating. Hence, Dante's shattered nose and my near throw-down with Alex. So accustomed to letting my fists fly first and suffering the consequences later, it was a miracle that a thin red sauce wasn't added to Alex's greasy complexion.

Tired of reminiscing over my past, I staggered to my feet and stared into the large oval mirror above the porce-lain sink. As would be expected, my eyes were bloodshot and welled with tears. I couldn't return to Nick's room looking like that. So, with hopes of killing some time, I dropped *trou* and attempted to take care of business. With the exception of a small, marble-sized light brown nugget, it was a failed mission. I guess the monstrous dump that clogged a toilet at school earlier in the day must have flushed out my system. The janitors at Stone Creek High can thank Susan for that one. After washing my hands and rechecking my face to ensure the blotchiness had faded, I headed back to Nick's room.

Chapter Four

Revelations

"Hey, Zack, I know it must have been real tough on you," Nick said the moment I reentered the room. "That's why I waited to approach you. Are you okay?"

"Yeah, I'm fine," I replied wryly. "Honestly, that explains a lot, it really does. But what does my past have to do with the secret military lab in the woods? I'm not seeing the connection, Nick."

Nick gestured for me to sit down on his bed. "Did you ever watch the *X-Files*?"

"Yeah, I've seen some episodes. Why?"

"Well," Nick took a seat across from me in his white computer chair, "I used to be a huge *X-Files* fan, would catch reruns on TV all the time. Anyway, one day I came across that article," Nick pointed at the newspaper clipping, "and decided to cut it out. As dumb as it sounds, I used to keep any articles that pertained to the unexplainable, convinced like Mulder and Scully, it was an X-File that needed solving. I, of course, planned to solve all of them in due time. Back then, aside from your article, which was from a legitimate source, most of the ones I collected came from those silly, fake magazines. But none of that is important now. What is…is that I found yours…and the subsequent ones that followed."

"What do you mean? There were others?"

"Your parents attack wasn't an isolated incident, Zack. There were other attacks—plenty of them. The articles may not have referred to them as zombie attacks, as yours did, but the details were eerily similar: unprovoked attacks, cannibalism, murder, unresponsiveness, excessive force, and deadly assaults. There was a pattern developing and I was going to figure it out what it was. Those scrapbooks," he said, pointing at the two monstrous binders, "contain every reported incident I could get my hands on. It took me years to put those together. Sadly, those scrapbooks brought me no closer to the answers I was seeking. That was…untill I found the lab."

He was finally going to talk about the lab and how it related to me. I couldn't wait to hear what he had to say.

Nick leaned in closer, lowering his voice. "It was a freak occurrence that I even stumbled across it. I could go into an array of details describing how I found myself lost in the woods on that particular night, but the general gist of it was that I did. I was eleven at the time, terrified I'd starve to death when a helicopter whipped by. I thought it was a search team, rescuing me after my hellish eight-hour trek through the woods—boy was I wrong. What I saw…"

Just then, Hank busted into the room, naked with the exception of a lone Spiderman sock tied around his head. All eyes on him, he marched his four-year-old body into the center of the room and began dancing. Nick did not seem amused by his little brother's performance. He shouted at him to leave, which he of course didn't do. Nick's father, Richard, arrived on the scene to save the day. With well-timed precision, as if Hank was a poisonous snake, Richard snagged Hank by the arm and pulled him into his clutches.

"I DON'T WANNA BATH," Hank wailed, kicking his feet in all different directions. "I HATE YOU, DADDY!"

Hoisting him under his arm, Richard glanced at us and smiled. "If you think Hank's bad—you should see Nick in action. He's not as easily distracted by his killer dance moves," he joked exiting the room.

"HA...HA...HA! Very funny, Dad. We were sort of in the middle of something."

"Yeah! So...was...I," he said, gesturing at Hank.

Nick watched with annoyance as his brother squirmed his naked body in his father's arms. When Richard and Hank finally exited the room, Nick slammed the door shut and shook his head disapprovingly. "He does that at least three to four times per week. My grandma doesn't help matters either. She actually likes his dancing, if you can believe that, and is always encouraging him to keep on at it."

"He doesn't appear to have any stage fright if you know what I mean. He might have a future in exotic dancing—if you catch my drift."

Nick laughed. "You're right about that. So anyways...I hear the chopper off in the distance and decide to give chase. I kept thinking my nightmarish ordeal was over. Never, not even for a split second, did it register in my brain that the chopper could have been out there for an alternative purpose. I mean, honestly, who would.

"Minutes later, I spotted the chopper in the ravine, and like an idiot, I ran over to the edge of the cliff and began waving my arms up and down like an overexcited imbecile at a ballgame. I shouted as well, loud as possible in fact, but the deafening chopper drowned out my screams. I'm lucky for that. If not, who knows what would have become of me."

"What did you see?" I asked, my fingers gripping his soft, white comforter.

"It was dark, and I didn't have my binoculars with me, but as clear as day, I saw heavily chained people being escorted out of the chopper and directly into the cave. It was crazy, Zack. And judging by their attire—military—I decided my presence was no longer necessary."

"What do you think they were doing with those people?"

"I wasn't sure at that point. I had my theories, just no facts. Those came later."

"You went back?"

Nick nodded. "A bunch of times. It took me a few weeks to find the spot again, a little longer to perfect the route, but once I did, all bets were off. I'd find a comfortable spot to hang out and wait until they showed up. It was always the same pattern. They would arrive by air, usher the heavily chained people into the cave, do whatever they did with them inside, seal the door off, and take off. A 'drop off,' which I came to call them, usually didn't take longer than twenty or thirty minutes."

"What did they look like? The ones in the chains, that is."

"See for yourself," he said, pointing to the thicker of the two binders. "I took pictures. The quality isn't the best, but you can get the general idea of what was going on."

I opened up the binder and began shuffling through page after page of notes, newspaper clippings, diagrams, and sketches, before finally locating the photos. The pixelations in some of the pictures left much to be desired, especially the zoomed in shots; nevertheless, I was able to put a visual to Nick's description of what he witnessed all those years ago. With its blades still spinning, the black, military-style helicopter sat next to the opening of the cave.

Inside, and all around the chopper, were men decked out in full riot gear, machine guns trained on their *captives*.

"Here use this," Nick said, pulling a magnifying glass out from his desk drawer. "The clarity is much better with the originals, but as you can see, it's still hard to see anything. God, I wish I had a better camera. Even with a night vision feature, nearly all of these pictures are garbage."

Using the magnifying glass, I carefully examined the pictures. I nearly dropped the coaster-sized magnifying glass after noticing the similarities between the captives and my parents' assailants. It was hard to tell just from the pictures, but in contrast to shots of the military men without their helmets on (pictures taken with the vault door securely locked); the captives' skin appeared much more pallid. In addition to their mostly ragged appearances, the captives also had dark shading all around their eyes and mouths. I could almost picture a dark puss-like goo oozing out of their orifices. Without needing any more evidence to convince me that the captives had whatever ailment or condition my parents' attackers had, I finally understood the connection.

"Do you know what this means?" I asked, my heart racing, hands beginning to tremble.

"I do…and there's more."

Just as Nick finished this last sentence, gentle footsteps were heard approaching Nick's room. Eyes wide, Nick frantically gestured for me to hide the scrapbooks. Bolting into action, I leaped off the bed and slid the binders under it just as his mom entered the room. Left in a precarious position, what the heck was I doing on Nick's soft, white carpet? I had to think on my feet—or more appropriately—stomach. Then it happened. My brain took over. My arms pushed up, then down, in a repetitive, continuous motion.

"Oh, I'm sorry, did I interrupt?" Teresa asked apologetically.

"No, Mom, we just decided it'd be cool to compete in a push-up contest. I'm not even going to bother trying. Clearly, as you can see, there is no way I'll be able to beat Zack. He's an animal. What number are you even on, Zack?"

"47..48...49....50....." I said, before collapsing to the floor. I had really only done about five or six push-ups.

"Wow, Zack, that's impressive! I don't think Richard's ever done more than 25 in one sitting. You should be proud of yourself. Anyways, I brought up some cookies and milk. Zack, would you rather I go down and get you a protein bar?" she joked with a big smile sweeping across her angular face.

"No, the cookies and milk sound great," I replied, raising myself to a standing position. "Besides, I think I burnt off enough calories. Thanks for everything."

"No problem at all," Teresa said, placing the tray on the nightstand. "What's this?" she asked, picking up the old newspaper clipping.

I wanted to smack myself for being such an idiot. I completely forgot to put the article back into the scrapbook.

"Zombies Ate My Parents," she read aloud brushing her shoulder length brown hair out of her face, her expression changing almost instantaneously.

Thinking quick, Nick snatched the article out of her hand before she could read any further. "Quit being nosy, Mom? If you must know, it's for a school project. Ms. Maddows wanted us to find an interesting article and act it out in front of the class. And you know me, if I'm stuck presenting something in front of the class, I might as well have some fun with it."

"Well, I don't personally think that's appropriate for school, but I won't interfere. You better know what you are doing, Nicholas. I do not...and I repeat...do not want to get another call from your school. Understood?"

"Of course, Mom. Now, quit your snooping and let us get back to work," Nick said playfully.

"Very well. Just bring the dishes and tray down when you're done."

Teresa then exited the room without saying another word. Nick and I both looked at each other, presumably thinking the same thing—the cookies. In the grand scheme of things, even if his mom had read the article and learned the horrific details of my past, I'm fairly certain that was as far as it would have gone. Other than feeling sorry for me, she would have had no reason to be alarmed or concerned. But just to be on the safe side, especially with the plot brewing inside our heads (it was in mine), it was best to keep everything, and I mean everything, highly classified.

With his mom and little brother out of the picture, Nick proceeded to dissect his theories of what had been transpiring for the past ten years. He laid out a theory that the government was secretly covering up what he referred to as a "zombie-like" virus through containment and deception. Using his log, something he had started and has continued to use since the discovery of the lab, Nick was able to loosely (loosely in his view because he did not have the capacity to watch the drop off point 24/7) correlate an alarming number of "drop offs" that coincided with reported instances he was able to locate through various online sources. Visiting the drop off point several times per week, a few hours at a time, it was a sure bet that if Nick witnessed a "drop off," he would be able to find a relatable article the following day. Eventually, after getting caught sneaking out one night, Nick was forced to develop a new system of detecting "drop offs." Although not as accurate in his opinion, especially during the winter months, Nick routinely visited the drop off point in broad daylight. Using his trusty binoculars, Nick would look for any signs that a helicopter had landed (e.g., circular patterns in the grass, footprints, debris, to name a few), log his findings, and return home. He still occasionally visited at night; it was by far much more thrilling to witness an actual "drop of" than to evidence hunt, but going so few times over the past few years he rarely lucked out. Using a combination of both methods, Nick revealed "in his professional opinion," that there hadn't been a "drop off" for quite some time—well over a year.

In terms of the origins of the "zombie-like" virus, Nick had his theories but no irrefutable proof. He felt that it could have been man-made (homemade or abroad), a natural phenomenon, or even extraterrestrial. Based off his personal observations and research, Nick laid out a few undeniable facts concerning the infected: they were highly contagious, incredibly dangerous, and predisposed to cannibalism. Hence, the extreme measures taken to contain the growing problem. Nick also theorized that the government had an elaborate cover-up going on to avoid widespread panic and knowledge that a "zombie-like" virus even existed. He thought it a bit ironic that the Center for Disease Control and Prevention allegedly developed a "Zombie Apocalypse Plan." Positive the CDC were in cahoots with the government—they were a government agency—Nick felt that if the rumors were true, it was nothing more than a reverse psychology ploy. After all, if there really was a threat looming, the government certainly wouldn't make its contingency plan public, now would it? The mysteries surrounding *Area 51* comes to mind in those regards.

After concluding his discussion on all his personal theories, Nick paused and chugged the rest of his glass of milk. Watching him gulp down the white liquid, I couldn't help but to ponder the choice of beverage. Had Nick's mother chosen that particular drink with his *concept room* in mind? If so, it fit perfectly with the decor.

"Why do you think the 'drop offs' stopped?" I asked, studying his log entries.

"I'm not sure what's going on, but as far as I can tell there hasn't been any activity going on down there for well over a year now. I can speculate all I want, often do; however, it does no good. Without any physical evidence, it's all just guesswork. If we're lucky, maybe the government's *extreme* measures eradicated the threat before it really got going. And if that's the case, let's hope it stays that way."

"So what now?"

"I think you know the answer to that question."

I nodded. "We find out the truth."

"You got it."

"But how? It's not like we can just knock on the vault door and someone will let us in."

"Not sure. But when there's a will, there's a way. So are you up for the challenge?"

"HELL, YEAH!" I shouted. "Of course, I am."

"Good! Then the next thing we need to focus on is finding a way inside. It won't be easy, that much I can guarantee."

Thinking about his cohorts, I felt compelled to ask if they would be involved. "What about Mike and Al—"

"No way," Nick interrupted, "absolutely not. Their great guys and all, but I'd rather ask my grandmother to help. The last thing we need is Mike posting incriminating evidence all over his Facebook page and Alex complaining about his hair and 'white-crap' every two seconds."

We both erupted in laughter at Mike and Alex's expense. Even if I didn't understand his comment about "white-crap" at the time, I still found his summation of the two spot on.

"Speaking of Alex and Mike," Nick said after the laughter ceased. "I completely understand why you flipped your lid, but you might want to consider—"

I waved my hand for him to stop. "—giving them another shot?"

Nick nodded empathetically.

"It's no excuse, but do you know how many times I've been harassed over the years for a stupid comment made when I was five?"

"Judging by your reaction, I'm assuming it was a lot."

"It was! So when Alex said the 'Z' word, I just flipped out, plain and simple, convinced you guys were no different. The craziest thing is that one of you guys actually knew of my past. I mean what are the chances?"

"Pretty high. Everybody seems to be up in everyone else's business in Stone Creek. Why would you be any different?"

I laughed at Nick's sly comment. "Well since you put it that way, I guess it makes sense."

"I don't know how everything will transpire, but I do know one thing for sure. When we're finished with that lab, everyone who ever doubted you is going to feel like a real ass."

The certainly hit the spot. "So when do we start?" I asked, anxious to blow the vault door off its hinges and expose the military cover-up.

"How about tomorrow? We can meet up after school and jump right into it. Sound good?"

It did.

Chapter Five

The Project

The following day we met in the schoolyard before racing all the way to Nick's house. After ghost riding our bikes into a thick bush in Nick's backyard, we sprinted all the way up to his room to start formulating our master plan. Once inside the confines of Nick's concept room, Nick handed me a white folder entitled "The Project." Opening up the folder, I saw that Nick had taken the time to formulate a detailed outline of how we would expose the "zombie conspiracy," which is what he started referring to it as. Looking over his outline, which looked professionally crafted, I was left feeling inept. In contrast to his diligence, I had done absolutely nothing related to the project. I wondered if Nick was the type of student who knew ahead of time what to expect on the first day of school, and hence came prepared.

Reviewing his outline, and all its intricacies, I suddenly began to feel overwhelmed at the prospects of such a daunting mission. How could I, slacker incarnate, feasibly hold up my end of the bargain? I was also having a difficult time envisioning how we would be able to sneak into the lab undetected. It seemed an unattainable goal.

"Earth to Zack," Nick said, waving his hand in front of my face.

"Sorry, I was just thinking of how impossible it's going to be to find a way inside."

"I know exactly how you feel, Zack. Felt exactly the same way when putting the outline together. It's the reason I left that section relatively vague, only alluding to a 'way in,' without going into any specifics. But let's not get ahead of ourselves just yet. We still have a whole heck of a lot of planning to do."

"Speaking of planning, how do you feel we should proceed?"

Nick smiled and then dove into a detailed explanation of what he felt was our best approach. "PHASE ONE!" he said, raising his voice. "We learn as much as humanly possible about the cave—and then learn some more. We need to know its name, its origin, how to pinpoint it on a map, basically everything about it and the surrounding woods. This phase will also entail formulating a general strategy for gaining entrance into the cave/lab."

That should be fun, I thought to myself. *Two kids sneaking into a heavily fortified military lab. What could possibly go wrong? Only everything!* I was beginning to think we were crazy for even contemplating such a risky endeavor.

"PHASE TWO!" Nick announced, now holding up two fingers. "We dig deeper and deeper until we find rock solid evidence to identify who's involved in the cover-up, and uncover just how high up the conspiracy goes. It goes without saying that this will be the most challenging aspect of our plan, bearing in mind the difficulty of obtaining such information and the risks involved. But it is a vital component all the same. When we're ready to expose the cover-up, we need to know who should be held accountable."

More research, I thought. "The Project" was beginning to sound more and more like a *project* than anything else. I couldn't help but to feel a little disillusioned at all of the hard work and effort the project would entail.

"PHASE THREE! Once we have—"

Nick suddenly stopped talking after hearing a knock on his door. "Is everything all right in there?" his mother asked gently.

"Everything's fine, Mom," Nick said, rolling his eyes. "We were just working on another presentation for Maddows' class. I'll try to be quieter."

"That's okay, dear. I just came up to tell you that we're eating early tonight. Will you be able to watch Hank for a little bit after dinner? Your father and I would like to go out car shopping."

Nick shook his head, mouthing the words, "I'd rather die!" Then, in a calm and collected voice, he said, "Sure, no problem. Just make sure he's bathed before you go. I don't want any part of Hank's bath time."

"Your father is already getting him ready for one. We shouldn't be too long. Your father just wants to window shop. Will Zack be staying for dinner?"

"Of course, Mom. Now can we get back to work please?"

"Certainly. Dinner will be ready in about ten."

Nick shook his head, mildly aggravated. "Okay, so as I was saying, once we have a list of possible suspects and have a solid plan for how to get inside the cave, we figure out the necessary tools, supplies, and expenses needed in order to accomplish that part of the mission. We will need to be reasonable when it comes to the money part. I don't know about you, but I certainly don't have stacks of cash lying around. With that in mind, our best bet is to be practical and use items we can either borrow or possibly rent. You with me so far?"

I nodded. He was dead on about the money part. I probably didn't have thirty bucks to my name. I had an inheritance, enough to pay for college and some other minor expenses, but like the secret military lab, it was sealed off in a secure vault, not to be touched until my thirtieth birthday or for when I enrolled in college. Academically speaking, the former seemed a more plausible scenario.

"Okay, good. Phase four!" he whispered, holding up four fingers. "Plain and simple, we gain entrance into the cave and get as much video and physical evidence as possible. This will undoubtedly be the most grueling and dangerous portion of the mission. So we'll need to plan well and take every possible precaution to make sure everything goes according to plan. There is absolutely no room for error in this phase."

He was certainly right on the money about his assertion about the complexities and risks involved in phase four. If, and it's a big *if*, we were fortunate enough to gain entrance into the cave/lab, the dangers involved were unimaginable. Not only would we have to worry about military personal trying to gun us down, but we would also have to worry about the hordes of cannibalistic zombies trapped inside. The project seemed more and more like a suicide mission than a plot to expose the government's wrongdoings.

"And last but certainly not least, phase five," Nick concluded, holding up five fingers. "If we are able to successfully accomplish phase one through four, we've officially hit pay-dirt. We take whatever evidence we uncovered and stick it to them—and *hard*! We show the world what the government has been hiding inside that cave. So what do you think?"

I thought his, no, *our* plan, was about the dumbest thing two disillusioned teens could embark on. Nothing about the plan sounded feasible. Not even remotely close to it. I still couldn't wrap my brain around how we were going to find a way inside. The front door was out of the question, that is, unless Nick had some "white" sticks of dynamite hidden in his room. That left the *mysterious* alternative route, which could only be one thing—tunneling inside. I didn't even want to begin thinking about all the work associated with digging a tunnel of that magnitude.

"Sounds great," I said, masking my doubts. "Can we eat now? I'm famished. The Baniaks served bean with bark soup this morning."

"Bean with what?"

"Don't ask. Even talking about it is making me nauseous."

Laughing, Nick led the way downstairs where we enjoyed yet another delicious Tinderson meal. Afterwards, we hung out in the dining room watching television while Hank ran around screaming at the top of his lungs. The screaming was beyond annoying, but it sure beat out his nude dancing—that much was for sure. We called it a night after Nick came within an inch of murdering his brother with the same shoelace Hank removed from one of Nick's shoes. There was never a more perfect time to leave. If he really did end up killing Hank, which seemed likely, I didn't want to be charged as an accessory.

***

The next day I endured another brutally boring day of school before racing over to the public library to meet up with Nick to get started on the *thrilling* geography research. Two hours later, it became abundantly clear that the two of us working in tandem wasn't going to happen. Instead of doing the research, as we had planned, we wasted valuable time goofing off, talking, and gossiping about our classmates. Realizing we had failed to put a dent in phase one of "The Project," we called it a night. Nick returned to his amazing family life, while I headed to my stomach's worst enemy—the Baniaks' house of indigestion.

***

The next several attempts went just like the first. We'd spend more talking and joking around than anything else. After an incident involving a world atlas being used as a flying disc, which nearly got us expelled from the library, we mutually decided to split the workload and go our separate ways. Phase one and three went to me, with phase two going to Nick. As for the remaining two, we would collaborate when, or if, it got to that point. Initially, it seemed as if I got the raw deal, two phases as opposed to one; however, the phases designated for me paled in comparison to the complexities of phase two. I wouldn't even know where to begin on that particular phase.

When asked how he planned to complete the arduous task of finding out who was involved in the cover-up, Nick refused to tell me. Annoyed, I asked him again, this time more forcefully. "Come on, Nick. Just tell me what you have in mind."

Leering at me expressionlessly, Nick gestured over to one of the elderly librarians struggling to place a large, dictionary-sized book back on the shelf, and whispered, "Now's not the time or place, if you know what I mean."

"You think she's involved and was sent to spy on us?" I asked playfully.

Nick rolled his eyes. "No, you dummy. I just don't think it's wise to talk about..." Nick lowered his voice, "...'The Project' when people can be listening in on our conversations."

"Do you think that mechanism in her ear is really a listening device and she's recording everything we're saying...hey, where are you going?" I asked after Nick abruptly stood up.

"Phase one and three is all you, buddy. I'm going to get started on my own phase. Talk to you later."

And then I was all alone with no distractions—a productive combination. After aimlessly roaming around the library for 10 minutes it became evident that I needed professional help, and lots of it. So I did the only thing you can do when in such a predicament. I asked the poor, old librarian for help. The same one Nick was all paranoid about. The elderly librarian, whose purplish, fluffy-hair matched her tight leggings, was as patient as a brain surgeon. With her tutelage, I was able to locate several local history books loaded with information about Stone Creek and the surrounding woods. Although helpful, it took me the better part of an hour to find anything useful inside the books.

As it turned out, the cave in question, known as Timmonds Rock, was at one point a popular landmark in the area. Apparently, during the prohibition period, the Timmond family, notorious in the area for an array of underground enterprises, used that particular cave to bootleg all types of booze. Their underground endeavor proved profitable for the Timmonds, so much so, they actually purchased the land all around the cave and named it after themselves—hence, Timmonds Rock. Eventually, due to poor business ventures, unpaid taxes, suspicious deaths in the area, and extensive legal issues, the state reclaimed the land. Then in the early '60s, the state made an unpopular decision to seal off the cave because of reports that it was structurally unsafe. Most locals theorized that it had more to do with underage kids using the cave to drink alcohol and abuse drugs than anything else. Regardless of popular opinion, the cave's only entrance was boarded up and left alone for decades. Of course, the book didn't mention this, but I knew it didn't stay that way forever.

After reading up on the history of the cave, taking meticulous notes throughout the process, a method for gaining entrance into the cave was beginning to materialize. From all the descriptions of the cave, and dimensions provided, I guesstimated that the inside of the cave was roughly the size of a winding football field. How many "infected" people could that house? I wasn't sure; however, if humane treatment wasn't an issue, it was probably a substantial number.

With the history of the cave out of the way, I shifted my attention to mapping out an alternative route to the cave—one that didn't include rappelling. This proved to be a rather simple task. All it took was locating the perfect map for everything else to fall into place. Of course, a library novice such as myself wasn't able to stumble across the coveted map all on my own. I had a little help from the ancient librarian that reeked of cheap perfume and cotton balls.

"Oh, you are no bother to me, young man," she said, in a raspy voice. "Follow me. I know exactly what you need."

Following directly behind her, the librarian tooted some farts that smelled of prunes on the way to the atlas section. As it turns out, instead of hurling atlases at each other, it would have been wise to open at least one of them up.

"Here you go, sonny," she said, handing me the atlas. "This is the same atlas the forest rangers use. If you can't find it in here, you probably won't have any luck looking anywhere else. Is there anything else I can help you with?"

"No," I said. "You've been more than helpful."

And she had been. The sheer act of asking for her assistance undoubtedly cut my research time in half, if not more. When the right books are placed neatly in front of you, and not strewn all over the floor, it's much easier to get the job done. With the perfect resource in hand—the atlas was a godsend—I mapped out the alternative route. In comparison to the entry point from the park, the one Nick commonly used, the route I mapped out had us entering from the other side of town, specifically adjacent to Warton Street. It was the perfect landmark for me, symbolic as well. You see, before *IT* all happened, I lived on a street with an eerily similar name—Wharton Avenue.

Now that a route had been laid out, and I knew just about everything there was to know about Timmonds Rock, the next part was devising a way inside. My brainstorming session was brief. There wasn't a lot to think about or contemplate. The simple fact remained, unless we tunneled in, there was no way of gaining entrance.

That allowed me to shift my focus away from the cave and onto the subject of digging. Initially, I became discouraged after reading the recommended digging tools for a tunnel of that magnitude: a jackhammer or explosives. Neither were viable options. They were both way too loud for the purposes we would need them for. No, if the tunnel was going to happen, we needed discreet tools such as a sledgehammer, rock hammer, chisels, railroad spikes, and an electric drill. In comparison to the jackhammer, which could get the job accomplished in about three-fourths of the time, the alternative method was a much quieter option. Backbreaking work, something my body would surely pay for down the road, but a much more serene method for tunneling into the cave. Thinking about the general layout of the cave and the descriptions Nick provided from his espionage missions, I wasn't too worried about the amount of noise produced throughout the process. According to Nick's account, the cave was presumably filled to capacity with hordes of "cannibalistic zombies," whose grunts and groans would undoubtedly drown out any noise we generated—or at least that is what I hoped would end up being the case.

With the basic plan set in motion, the next task was to compile a list of all the essential tools and supplies, including ones designed to break through rocks. After jotting down the last item, satisfied with my work, I left the library proud of myself for completing both phases in the span of four hours. I wondered how Nick was doing in regards to phase two, uncovering the chief conspirators.

***

The next day, Saturday to be exact, using my list, I ransacked Bill's garage in order to determine what tools we could borrow and which ones would need to be purchased. As it turns out, his garage was loaded with all types of tools. I couldn't believe it. It seemed as if he had a tool for just about any type of project you could think of, and then some. After rummaging through his garage, it was a relief to see that there were only a few items that still needed purchasing: railroad spikes, a rock hammer, new gloves (his were old and nasty looking), and stone cutting drill bits. Sure, Bill had tons of drill bits, probably stone cutting ones as well, the problem being it was impossible to decipher which ones were what. Apparently, over the years, the black toolbox where he stored them had become a sort of melting pot for all the different types and sizes. Before exiting Bill's garage, several other tools caught my attention. Adding them to my list entitled, "Bill's Tools & Supplies," I scribbled down the following items: a hatchet (for defensive purposes only), flashlights, a tent (to conceal the dig site and shelter us from the elements), plywood (to be used in conjunction with dirt to camouflage the tunnel), a pick-axe, and a steel digging bar.

With all of the essential information in hand, I decided to take it a step further and organize them on the computer. You know, attempt to make them look professional—similar to Nick's impressive outline. After messing around with the margins, line spacing, and hanging indent for the next few minutes, I quickly became discouraged and gave up. Nick would just have to deal with reading my horrendous penmanship.

All done with my designated phases, at least as done as it was ever going to be, I tried unsuccessfully to get in contact with Nick. He didn't answer any of my calls or texts. Assuming he was entirely immersed in phase two, and didn't want to be bothered, I left him alone figuring he would call me when he was ready. With nothing else to do in terms of "The Project," I was at a crossroads: should I veg out and watch television or do my homework. In the end, I made the right choice by deciding to watch the complete season of yet another stupid reality show. I hadn't intended on watching the entire nine hour marathon, but after the first episode I was hooked.

The show's premise was to take eight chronically homeless people and have them live inside the confines of a huge mansion with eight B-movie stars. As with most reality shows, there was a competitive element to make the show more entertaining. In this particular show, each team (consisting of one homeless person and one movie star) competed against rival teams in an array of competitions. It was beyond funny. In the end, Homeless Bob won alongside his Baywatch bombshell. The prize for each: Homeless Bob won the house, while the Baywatch bombshell's favorite charity received a sizable donation.

Before going to bed that night I texted Nick one final time.

Zack: *Where are you? Haven't heard from you since you stormed out of the library. Everything OK? Did the librarian reveal her undercover status and arrest you?*

An hour passed before he replied.

Nick: *Very funny, Zack. Everything's fine! Been hard at work. Meet me in the park at 6:00 pm tomorrow! We have a lot to discuss!*

Zack: ☺

Nick: *Huh?*

The smiley face was no mistake, but he didn't need to know that. A simple "OK" would have to suffice from that point on. I let my fingers do my dirty work.

Zack: *Sorry! Hit the wrong button. I'll be there. Did you find anything out?*

Nick: *I'd rather tell you in person if that's okay?*

Zack: *Gotcha, the librarian is probably already monitoring our phones, right?*

Nick chose not to reply, ignoring every subsequent text message sent his way.

***

The next day, I met Nick in the park at exactly 6:00 P.M. He had his white backpack slung over one shoulder and a flashlight in each hand.

"So what'd you find out?" I asked impatiently.

"Go ahead and lock your bike up next to mine. We're going to the secret hideout. I'll tell you everything once we get there."

He was, without a doubt, the king of leaving you in suspense. It seemed like he couldn't say anything to you unless the timing was perfect. It drove me crazy. In contrast, I was the complete opposite. If I had something important to reveal, on the rare occasions that occurred, I couldn't wait to spill the beans.

"Come on, Nick," I pleaded. "Can't you just tell me here? Do we really have to go all the way to the secret hideout?"

"Yes, actually," Nick replied, "it's cold as a polar bear's nuts out here, and I'd prefer to disclose what I found out in the privacy of my hideout with a nice fire going. Sound reasonable?"

It was cold out, I gave him that much. But then again, what did he expect? It was the beginning of November and we were in the mountains. I began to wonder why he couldn't unveil his big "reveal" in the privacy of his arctic looking, yet warm and cozy room. I shrugged my shoulders apathetically and followed him into the woods.

It took a total of thirty minutes to make it to the secret hideout, which turned out to be quite impressive. Nick, Alex, and Mike had evidently put a great deal of time and effort into the construction of it. There was a small area set up for a campfire with three tree stumps encircling the pit, a weathered picnic table off to the side, and a poorly crafted wooden clubhouse large enough to house at least four to five people. That wasn't even the best part. The entire hideout, which was roughly about fifteen feet in diameter, had an abundance of trees and thick bushes surrounding it, keeping it relatively hidden inside the dense forest. It could have easily passed as thick overgrowth and nothing more. As for the hideout's entrance, there was a small gap, about the size of a manhole, that you had to crawl through just to get in. It left me wondering how they got all of their crap inside.

"Wow, Nick, this place is amazing. Did you guys set this place up all on your own?"

Pointing at the poorly constructed clubhouse, Nick nodded, saying, "Does it look like we outsourced?"

We shared a quick laugh as his expense and moved on.

"How'd you get all this stuff inside here? I mean, aside from the rabbit hole we crawled through, it's like the Cubs ivory wall in here."

"All I'll say is that it was a colossal pain in the ass. Think Stone Hedge, only on a much smaller scale."

I assumed he was implying from his Stone Hedge reference that they had used some type of pulley system or something along those lines. Regardless, it wasn't anything important enough to insist he elaborate on. Of course, had I insisted, I'm certain he wouldn't tell me until the timing was just right. That seemed to be his *modus operandi*.

After starting up a fire, Nick patted the tree stump next to his. "Here, take a seat. Alex usually uses this one, so if it smells a little funky you know why."

I promptly sat down and retrieved all of my documents and maps related to "The Project." Before passing them over to Nick, I briefly glanced over them to ensure that everything was in order. Then as Nick astutely studied my notes, the maps, and the list of supplies necessary for the task at hand, I laid out my plan for gaining entrance into the cave. Nick didn't seem too surprised by my tunneling scenario.

My plan was as simplistic as they come. Locate the perfect spot and then dig a tunnel descending downward, as if we were installing a sunroof. Digging the tunnel in this fashion served two purposes: one, with safety as our primary concern, it would allow us the opportunity to peek inside the cave with little worry of getting attacked by a zombie, or whatever the heck they were. And, two, using Bill's tent as a decoy, we'd be able to conceal what we were really up to and, as an added bonus, it'd shield us from inclement weather—a virtual must. Anyone passing through would see a faded, green tent, and not the tunnel that was slowly forming below. In my opinion, it was a great idea.

Nick stared at me blankly for a few seconds before tossing another piece of wood into the fire, sending ashes of smoke shooting up in the air. It almost appeared as if he was disappointed. Doubt began rearing a familiar face. Maybe my plan was not as good as I originally thought.

"Good work!" he finally said, relieving all my worries. "Have you located a spot to dig yet?"

"Well…no…not exactly. But there's a reason," I half lied. I had started working on it, then figured without actually seeing the terrain, it was impossible to pick out the precise location. Plus, measurements would also be necessary to ensure we were digging in the right spot—specifically above the rear of the cave. I proceeded to cue

Nick in on my rationale, telling him all about my plan to inspect the area first.

"Don't you think it'll be extremely risky to walk all the way over to the front of the cave to get our measurements? I mean isn't there a safer way?"

"We can always buy a dog leash," I said, thinking on my feet. "Then if we get caught lurking too closely to the front entrance, which I'm sure is under some type of surveillance, we can plead ignorance and say we lost our dog. Why would anyone doubt that story?"

"It's risky...but could work. Now, let's say we venture all the way to the front of the cave, how do you propose we measure our way back. I mean aside from the leash, we can't exactly walk around with a surveyor's wheel, can we?"

Still thinking on my size 11's, I kept rolling. "We have two options. One, we buy a pedometer and measure our strides walking on similar terrain. Or two, you do what you do best and you count your steps on the way back. As long as we keep our strides consistent, we should have no problems mapping out the length of the cave."

Nick glared at me. "So is that what I am to you—a walking pedometer!"

I laughed shaking my head. He hit the nail on the head. If there ever was a person that fit that bill, it was surely Nick and his trusty thumbtacks. With my basic tunneling plan out there in the open, I then delved into all of the supplies we would need to complete the arduous task. There were definitely going to be expenses, that was unavoidable, but most, if not all, of the additional supplies were absolutely necessary. If our mission was to gain entrance into the cave, cutting costs was not the way.

"What's wrong?" I asked, noticing a troubled expression setting across Nick's pale face.

"That's a lot of money," he replied meekly. "Money neither of us has. I'm pretty sure my dad has some things we can use, but not all of them. Is there any way we can start before we ultimately purchase all of the extra tools and supplies?"

I wanted to say, "*Of course we can! In fact, let's start tomorrow.*" But I knew better. In addition to learning all about breaking through rock, I also read passage after passage related to ideal digging conditions. Winter did not fall into that specific category. With the ground frozen solid, especially at that elevation, starting the tunnel in November would be a grueling nightmare, to say the least. We would probably get discouraged before we even put a dent in the earth—literally.

"In my expert opinion," yeah, I had nominated myself the definitive expert on subject, "we shouldn't even consider starting the dig until spring."

"SPRING!" Nick shouted. "That seems a bit far away, doesn't it? I was hoping to get this project started pronto."

"Yeah, but if it's going to get done right, our only option is to wait. The simple fact remains, the longer the tent's up, the likelier we'll get caught. With that in mind, we need to dig that damn tunnel faster than a hungry badger smelling the irresistible scent of baby rabbits."

It's amazing how all of that information seemed to channel right through me. I remembered reading all of it, but had never formulated those specific guidelines all together—thus, finalizing my plan. They all seemed to unite at just the right moment. My parents would have been proud—minus the extremely dangerous and illegal mission we were embarking on.

"Dammit," he muttered. "I was really hoping to get started way sooner than that."

Nodding sympathetically, I replied, "Well, if anything, it'll at least allot us the opportunity to save up for additional supplies and tools, which will ultimately make the process that much easier."

Nick still appeared moderately disheartened.

"So how did phase two go for you?" I asked, changing the subject. "Did you find anything useful out?"

Nick shook his head, staring at me wide-eyed. "Not even a single name, Zack. I can't believe it. I thought I'd at least come up with something. But there was nothing I could get my hands on."

"Didn't you say you knew someone that could help out?"

"Yeah...my cousin, Louie. He's a complete ass and I hate whenever we have to go over to his house, but he knows his way around computers. All day long, all he does is eat, play video games, and hack into systems just for the fun of it. I wouldn't be surprised if he gets nabbed for cyber crimes one day. Anyways...we made a trade off. I offered to do a research paper for him in exchange for his services."

"So did he chicken out when you cued him in on our project?"

"Not at all! He just couldn't hack into any systems with useful information. And, I'll be honest, Zack, it wasn't for a lack of trying. I practically lived in his room all weekend, and let me tell you, that's not a good thing. To put it in perspective, he's in his third year of college, he barely attends classes, and when he does, he's usually hyped up on some type of energy drink or a combination of his mother's anxiety pills. Plus, he barely, if ever, bathes."

"Wait, did you say he's in college?"

"Yeah, he goes to Stone Creek University."

"And *YOU'RE* going to write a paper for him," I asked, unable to mask my surprise.

"As crazy as it sounds...I am! He's the type of person that does just enough to get by. So if it means having your younger cousin, who's still in high school, write a paper for you, he's all for it, especially if it allots him more time to game."

"Is he still going to make you write it even though he didn't deliver on his end?"

"Not sure, but honestly, I'd feel weird if I didn't. After all, some of the things he was doing weren't technically legal, if you know what I mean."

I did. I knew exactly what he meant. I also understood the ramifications of what he and his unhygienic cousin, Louie, were doing. If caught, who knows what would become of them. Think about it. The government clearly has no qualms about stowing away the "infected" inside Timmonds Rock. Would they treat Nick and his cousin Louie any differently? Who knows? I didn't even want to think about what the consequences could possibly be—zombie chow, perhaps?

"Aren't you about worried about getting caught?"

"Not really. Louie was smart enough to bail before he dug too deeply. He may be socially inept and smell like a locker room, but he knows his stuff. And more importantly, he knows how to cover his tracks."

"Even so, Nick, what you did was insane and highly illegal."

"And what we have planned isn't?"

He had a point there. Our entire plan revolved around breaking into a military lab in order to expose a well hidden, and highly classified, secret. Therefore, it made little sense to rag on him for getting the process started sooner rather than later.

Nick tossed another piece of wood into the fire, sending another flare up of smoke and ash. I had to look away, a flashback from my last family picnic surging through me.

"It was a calculated risk that didn't pan out," Nick added. "It's frustrating, but I'm not going to sulk about it. It's time to cut our losses and move on."

"So…what's next? Where do we go from here?"

"Hold on a sec," he said, pulling his phone out of his pocket. Then, after fiddling around with it for about a minute, he handed it over to me. "Check it out. I wasn't completely useless this weekend. I went ahead and began developing a website we can use when we're ready to expose the cover-up. It's in its infancy right now, and I'm aware it still needs plenty of work, but it's definitely coming along. Let me know what you think?"

It was difficult to absorb the full essence of the website on his phone's miniscule screen; however, from what I could see, it looked amazing. It had information about the "zombie-like" virus, links to newspaper articles, his personal eyewitness accounts of all the "drop offs," pictures from the before mentioned "drop-offs," and our individual bios (concealed with pseudonyms he conjured). I was Trent Zackwell and he was Rick White. I sort of liked my alias and had no intent of changing it. Morphing my first and last names together had a nice zing to it. As for his, well, I was at a complete loss. After asking, it all made sense. Rick stemmed from his middle name, Richard, and "White" was a play off his concept room.

Probably my favorite aspect of the website was the background. Nick took an enlarged close-up of one of the infected person's pale, blotchy face and used it as the background. With the surrounding background pitch black, it reminded me of the punisher logo, except scarier.

"It's looks great, Nick. When did you find time to work on it? I thought you said you were at your Cousin Louie's all weekend."

"I couldn't show up here with nothing, now could I? I just threw all of that stuff together this afternoon. Once you know what you're doing, it doesn't take all that long."

"Easy for you to say. I wouldn't know the first thing about setting up a website, much less putting one together in an afternoon. It's pretty impressive, Nick."

Nick looked embarrassed. "We should probably go."

I felt likewise. It wasn't late, still early in fact, but the fire was dying out and my toes were beginning to feel numb. Adjusting to the mountain cold was going to take some time.

"All right, you lead the way."

"First things first, though. We have a tradition for how we like to put out the fire. Care to do the honors or should I?" Nick asked, pulling at his belt buckle.

"By all means, you go ahead."

Fifty-eight seconds later, all that was left of the fire was ash, smoke, charred wood, and the faint smell of urine. We then exited through the small opening and made our way back through the woods. Before going our separate ways, we set the ever-important dig date. Since spring was roughly four-and-a-half months away, we decided to start the dig the Friday leading into our spring break. That way we could start fresh on that Friday and get a solid ten days of digging under our belts before school started back up. With luck, and a tremendous amount of hard work, to quote Morrison: "Break on through to the other side," may not have been out of the realm of possibility.

Chapter Six

Break Time

With slightly over four-and-a-half months to kill, I decided that if my relationship with Nick was going to flourish, making things right with Alex and Mike was priority number one. I had ample opportunities to do it on my own—Alex was in my gym class, after all—yet, I couldn't force myself to go through with it. I just couldn't muster the courage to do in on my own. I eventually turned to Nick for assistance. He met with the two of them, smoothed things over, and before long, we were all hanging out again, no questions asked. From that point on, the four of us were inseparable.

Things went great for the next three months. Nick and I would still hang out independently of Alex and Mike, usually doing something related to "The project," but those sessions were few and far between. From time to time, I also worked at Bill and Susan's independently owned and operated business, Bill & Suzie's Jacuzzis, to earn extra cash for "The Project." Their business, which was doing quite well, sold top-of-the-line jacuzzis and their patented add-on device appropriately coined the Jacuzzi Uzi. Invented by Bill, the Jacuzzi Uzi was designed to make it feel as if tiny air bubbles were being shot right into your muscles at varying speeds ranging from gentle to deep tissue massage. To sit in a tub while the Jacuzzi Uzi was set on full blast was like having a thousand tiny, little fingers simultaneously massaging all your muscles while in the comfort of a warm, cozy tub.

Hanging out with the guys on a regular basis, I got to know them much more intimately. He wasn't bullied as far as I knew, but he certainly fit the bill to a T. He was overweight, neurotic, and had a peculiar and silly sounding last name: *Vunpuffles*. When Nick first introduced us, I remember wanting to beat-up his entire lineage for having such a ridiculous last name. Okay, I take that back, only the paternal side that bore the name in question. I'm guessing the main reason he was left alone had something to do with his personality. Not only was Alex really down to earth, but he also had an amazing sense of humor. It didn't hurt matters either that he didn't take crap from anyone. I know it's a little insensitive to make fat jokes, especially to someone who's overweight and has body image issues, but there's an unwritten rule that makes it all right when the perpetrators are friends. Plus, it helps when the target, a rather *large* one at that, can absorb it, laugh, and lash out with an equally devastating insult of his own.

Mike was a little different. He was fun to hang out with, but deep down had some real *issues*. It seemed as if his only mission in life was to try to embarrass and humiliate everyone around him. He wasn't happy unless someone else was left miserable or humiliated, or a combination of the two. It didn't take long for me to figure out that you always had to be on your toes whenever he was around. Like a target in prison, you never knew when, or from what direction, the shank was going to come. Oh, did I say "shank," I should have said, "prank." Yes, truth be told, Mike was a master at the art of pulling off pranks.

There was one time when Mike was making prank calls, an area of expertise for him, and after about his fifth or sixth call, he dialed a number, then quickly passed the phone over to Alex. Under his tutelage, Mike encouraged him to proceed. Although slightly wary, prank calling was not one of his strengths, Alex took the phone and began rambling on about something that made no sense. Unbeknownst to Alex, or any of us for that matter, it turned out that the person Alex was pranking was his own mother. That's how Mike rolled. He wasn't exactly trustworthy, but in the end it usually made our nights all the more entertaining.

As for Nick, he was another beast all together. While Alex and Mike enjoyed having fun, Nick was more reserved and laid back. *Shocker*, right? He seemed to enjoy everyone's company, yet at the same time, often appeared as if he was lost in his own thoughts. Who knows, maybe he was busy counting in his head or something. Jokes aside, Nick was the definitive know-it-all of the group who flaunted his talent every opportunity he was allotted. He didn't care who he called out. I heard story after story of Nick calling out parents, teachers, and even the principal of the school.

There was one instance where Nick landed himself in the principal's office for insubordination, familiar territory for him, and he proceeded to systematically demonstrate for the school's principal, Mr. Ladel, how the designated textbook in his European History class was grossly flawed and filled with inaccuracies. Mr. Ladel, a ruthless tyrant, who had a long track record of suspensions and expulsions, actually thanked Nick for his concern, impressed with Nick's astute observations regarding Stone Creek High's existing curriculum. But then turned around, true to his reputation, and informed Nick that he would have no choice but to get used to the inaccuracies—or suffer the consequences.

So was he a dedicated student, a budding sociopath, or just a know-it-all who enjoys the sound of his own voice? Beats me, all I knew was that he was a good friend. Okay, truthfully—he was my best friend.

As for me, for the first time in my life my true personality began to emerge. As it turns out, I actually had a decent sense of humor. Who knew? I certainly didn't. Regardless, it was an amazing feeling to make people laugh— even if it was the same three people over and over. I could honestly say that a sense of happiness began to slowly creep into my tortured life.

About three months into our freshly formed circle, Mike came running up to Nick, Alex, and me, wearing an up-to-no-good smirk on his face. "Dudes, I just heard there's going to be a huge party at Rick Kent's house this Friday. I used to be real tight with Rick back in the day and I think I can get us in. Except for you, of course," Mike pointed at Alex, "you smell kind of funky."

"I wouldn't get my hopes up," Nick chimed in. "Isn't he like a football god now playing for Trinity High? Besides if Alex can't go because of his god-wretched stench, I don't think I'd like to go either."

Alex just stood there discreetly attempting to smell his *pits*. After giving each a deep whiff, he cupped his hands around his mouth and attempted to smell his breath. Alex then looked lost in thought—as if he was trying to figure out the last time he changed his underwear. I was aware that they were just playing off his neuroses so I stayed muted and played along with the gag.

Mike grabbed Nick by the shoulders and rocked him back and forth for a moment. "Do you know how many hot chicks are going to be there? Trinity girls! I'll crash the damn party if I have to. So are you in or are you guys going to stay home and play with your Legos?"

Hearing the words "hot chicks" was all the convincing my adolescent mind needed. Even if we were stuck on the outside looking in, I wanted to be there. But first, I wanted to have a little fun. "Look," I said, turning to Mike, "I'd love to go…I really would…but I already told Bill and Susan I'd play bingo with them next Friday. I think Bill's ranked 24th in the state. Bad timing I guess. See you guys later."

I then turned around and began making my way down the hall.

"You're just messing with me right," Mike shouted. "You're not really playing bingo on Friday, are you?"

Laughing, I turned around and faced Mike. "Of course I'm screwing with you. Do you think I'd want to miss out on an opportunity like that?"

Mike look relieved. "Then it's settled. I'll track Rick down and won't take 'NO' for an answer."

Nick didn't say much on the topic. If we were all going, so was he. He didn't seem like the partying type, but then again, who was I to talk. If Rick gave us the "okay," it'd be the first real party I ever attended.

Busy checking his shoes in case he stepped in something foul, Alex finally broke his silence. "Guys, do I really stink, 'cause I don't smell anything. My breath probably isn't the freshest, but I know for a fact I changed my underwear *and* used deodorant today. Or, was that yesterday…" Alex paused, "…no, it was today. Come on, are you guys screwing with me, or what?"

We all broke out into a cackling laughter, reaffirming his skepticism.

Later that day, I received a call from Mike. "WE'RE IN, ZACK! I ran into Rick after school, and he said it'd be fine if we all came—even Alex."

Maybe it was a coincidence. Maybe he did just happen to run into Rick. However, if I were a betting man, my money would be on Mike forcing that *chance* encounter to materialize. I pictured Mike patiently stalking Rick, waiting for the perfect opportunity to "randomly" bump into him.

"That's awesome."

"I don't know about you," he said, talking so fast it sounded like he was about to blow a gasket, "but I'm going to work my butt off to get in shape for the party. I'm going to start doing crunches, lunges, push-ups…anything and everything to get in shape. Just wait, Zack. I'm going to get buff for the party."

"Are you off your meds, Mike? Doing push-ups and all that other crap for three days isn't going to make you buff. You'd be lucky to even see the slightest improvement in your physique."

"Whatever, Zack! What do you know? The last time I checked you weren't some type of fitness expert with credentials to dole out advice."

I ignored his last comment. "You need me to call Alex or Nick to break the good news?"

"Already gave them the heads up. Oh…and guess what…"

I was afraid to ask. "What, Mike?"

"I'm going to the store tomorrow to buy some flavored lu—"

"BYE!" I interrupted abruptly hanging up the phone. I hadn't intended on being so rude, but in the same sense, I really didn't want to hear what Mike had planned for his extracurricular activities at the party. Sometimes it's best to end on a high note. We were in!

Okay, it was a bit hypocritical considering my antics with Mike; however, without giving it another thought, I hurled myself onto the floor and began doing push-ups. It had been a long time since I had seriously done push-ups (not counting the incident at Nick's house, which was more out of necessity) so going in my goals were set high. Too high. Fifty in a row seemed reasonable—didn't it? After all, wasn't that how many I allegedly did at Nick's house?

Nineteen push-up's in, my arms felt like Jell-O and my chest, shoulders, and triceps were on fire. When your muscles burn like that there's only one surefire way to extinguish the flames—stop what you're doing and rest. So that's exactly what I did. I collapsed to the floor, rolled over to my back, and waited for the burn to fizzle out. Several minutes later, muscles feeling moderately rejuvenated, I gave it a second go, this time opting to complete a total of 100 repetitions through sets of 10. After finishing the push-ups, arms and chest feeling rubbery and fatigued, I jumped right into completing sets of crunches, sit-ups, and something called a "burpee," which further destroyed my chest and arms. Although sore for the next few days, I forced myself to complete the same exercise regimen every night leading up to the party.

Finally, the night of the party had arrived. I should have felt exhilarated at the prospects of attending my first real party—but I wasn't. Anxiety began rearing its timid head. The simple fact remained that going to a social event, such as a high school party, was uncharted territory for Zack Treadwell. I wouldn't consider myself overly shy, although some would beg to differ, but socializing was just not my thing. I was the type of kid who mostly kept to himself, not the type to mingle with complete strangers, especially ones of the opposite sex. Doubt began to creep in as to whether or not I should even attend the party. I mean what's the point of going to a social event if all you're going to do is stand in the backdrop and not say anything to anybody? Didn't make much sense in my opinion; yet in the same sense, I knew it was too late to back out—so why fight it. I had made a promise to Mike, after all.

I thought of seeking advice from my foster parents, they surely looked the partying type, yet hesitated. You see, they had this annoying habit of always trying to turn everything into an analogy. One time, when asked about the process of obtaining a passport, traveling abroad seemed vastly appealing to me at the time—still does—Bill and Susan went on a tirade about migrating birds from the Philippines. Mildly annoyed, I tuned them out, went to my room, and looked it up online. Don't get me wrong, my foster parents aren't stupid. They're actually pretty intelligent people. You just wouldn't know it by looking at them. They exude cluelessness.

Opting not to ask them for advice, I reminded them of the plans for the night. I told them about the party (there was no point in lying—everybody in town already seemed to know about it), and how we all planned to spend the night at Mike's house following the party. Trudging out the door, I overheard Bill and Susan mentioning something about a caterpillar metamorphosing into a butterfly. Typical Bill and Susan Baniak talk.

Arriving first at Mike's house, he only lived about a mile away; I let myself in through the side door. When it comes to a teen's room, *location* is everything. Naturally, it goes without saying, that no one wants the room adjacent to their parent or guardians' room, unless of course, the teen in question has some real deep-rooted mommy or daddy issues. As for Mike Jeposi, who could care less for his parents, he hit the jackpot of bedrooms. His room, conveniently located all the way in the basement, as far as possible away from his parents' love nest, even had its own private exit. What teen wouldn't want that? He could come and go as he pleased, and in the event he wanted to sneak somebody in…a girl perhaps…there were no obstacles to overcome. It's fair to say I was envious of his pad.

Announcing my entrance into his room, Mike came waltzing out of his bathroom wearing nothing but puppy-dog boxers. "Chicks dig puppy dogs. Oh yeah, Zack, chicks dig the dogs."

I shook my head and laughed.

"Dude, I'm still getting ready so why don't you take a load off and watch TV or something. Nick and Alex should be here in a little bit."

I took Mike's advice and turned on his flat screen. It may sound weird, but instead of actually watching the television and his seemingly endless variety of channels, my eyes found themselves drawn to Mike as he prepped himself. It wasn't anything sexual. Not by any means. It was just fascinating to watch him get ready for his night on the town. He put deodorant on his armpits, which was normal, then proceeded to put it on his feet, stomach, chest, and bottom—basically everywhere. Then after trying on nearly every shirt in his wardrobe, Mike finally settled on a navy blue polo shirt, the same one he had tried on at least three times. Once dressed, it was cologne time. He sprayed himself everywhere, and I mean *everywhere*. I indulged myself with a few spritz while Mike spent the next twenty minutes messing around with his hair and applying makeup. Yes, Mike Jeposi wore *makeup*. You see, my suspicion was right, Mike had psoriasis, and in an attempt to rid his face of the whitish, scaly patches that formed around his nose and forehead, he would vigorously scrub his face till it was beet-red. Then in order to rid his face of the ripe tomato look, he'd generously apply dabs of concealer wherever necessary. He was pretty good at it too. You'd only suspect he was wearing some if you looked closely enough.

By the time Nick and Alex arrived, Mike was engrossed in doing his hair all over again. It apparently didn't come out right the first few hundred times. I probably spent a solid thirty seconds on my slightly pushed forward hair. Gel was involved, but nowhere near the handfuls of product that was caked in Mike's hair. By the time he was finished, I was afraid to go near his head, his short spiked hair looked deadly to the touch.

Taking over command of Mike's room, I let Alex and Nick in. "Mike's still getting ready so you might want to get comfortable," I said, pointing to Mike's brown futon. "He just finished doing his hair and is now busy plucking his eyebrows."

"Shut up," Mike shouted, "I'll be done in a second. Besides, chicks go wild for guys who manscape. It's the new in-thing. Don't you know anything?"

Who knows, maybe he was onto something. I had heard the term *metrosexual* mentioned once, or a few hundred times on TV.

When Mike was finally finished *dolling* himself up, we decided to play pool to kill some time before we left for the party. Yup, that's right, in addition to the killer location, the private bathroom and exit, Mike had the luxury of owning his very own pool/ping pong table. Could the kid get any luckier?

"You guys ready to go?" I asked after prematurely sending yet another eight ball into the corner pocket—losing the fourth straight match for my team consisting of Nick and myself.

"This is going to be so great," Mike shouted. "I can't wait to get there. It's not supposed to start for another twenty minutes, but by the time we get there it should be in full swing."

Right as we were about to head out the door, Alex abruptly ran into Mike's bathroom and began checking himself for "white-crap." I laughed thinking back to Nick's comment about Alex complaining about "white-crap" every two seconds. For a normal person, "white-crap" is nothing more than the dry skin that forms on or around your nostril region. It commonly follows a cold, the aftermath of a gang of mucus absorbing tissues repeatedly ravaging a person's raw and reddened nose. Once the attack is over and the smoke, or more appropriately snot clears, you're left with a tender, irritated nose that will eventually sprout tiny, little flecks of dry skin. In Alex's case, unlike a normal person who deals with the minor annoyance from time to time, he couldn't go five minutes without thoroughly inspecting his face. It got extremely annoying at times. I mean, who really cares! It's just dry skin—get over it.

"If there wasn't any 'white-crap' ten minutes ago, there wouldn't be any now," Mike shouted unsympathetically.

"Besides," I chimed in, "if you have to look that closely just to see them, I don't see how anyone else will notice if you have 'white-crap' or not."

Turning away from the mirror, Alex stared at me with his cold grey eyes. "Oh, they'll notice, Zack. They always do."

I sincerely doubted that, but if it improved his confidence who was I to discourage the practice. By bicycle, it took us roughly forty minutes to reach Rick's house. Or should I say palace. The Kents' residence was nearly three times larger than every other house on the street. Shaking my head in disbelief, I asked, "What the hell do Rick's parents do for a living?"

"They invented some type of exercise equipment called the Glute-Boots," Mike replied. "It turned out to be a real hit and the money has been pouring in ever since. They even had a cheesy infomercial for it. I tried using the damn things years ago, but I thought the boots were just crap." Mike abruptly stopped and turned to us with a serious expression plastered across his face. "Don't tell Rick I said that. The last thing I want to do is piss him off and get us all thrown out of the party."

If the roles were reversed, I'm fairly certain Mike would make it a priority to disclose that particular tidbit with Rick and his entire family. However, in contrast to Mike's ruthless and cold-hearted nature, the rest of us didn't particularly enjoy hurting other peoples' feelings.

Our actions didn't always convey that attitude, but on a whole, we were nowhere near Mike's level.

"Don't worry, Mike," I said, patting him on the shoulder. "I have no interest in getting you, or anyone else for that matter, kicked out tonight. I just want to enjoy the—"

"Whatever," Mike blurted out, "let's hurry up and get the party started."

Bearing in mind we could clearly hear that the party was going on in the backyard, we respectfully rang the front doorbell. Rick's dad answered the door with a wide grin. "How's it going guys?" he asked before recognizing Mike. "Oh...hey, Michael. Long time no see. How are your folks doing?"

"They're doing fine, Mr. Kent," Mike replied. "I'll tell them that you said hi."

"Great to see you again," Mr. Kent said, grasping Mike by the shoulder. "The party's out back. Come on, I'll show you the way."

Mr. Kent then took the lead and we all followed closely behind as he maneuvered through his immaculate home. I was impressed. The Kents' house looked like something you would see in a magazine: marble floors, fancy furniture and curtains, a sparkling chandelier hanging from the cathedral-like ceiling, sculptures, paintings, and every top of the line appliance you could imagine. Having lived in some of the roach and bed bug infested dumps I had grown up in, the Kents' house was the polar opposite. I felt weird even being inside—terrified my sheer presence would somehow tarnish the flawlessness of the house.

Just as we reached the door leading to the backyard, Mike glanced at me for a split second and smiled a devilish grin. "Oh, by the way, Mr. Kent," he said, pointing in my direction. "This is Zack Treadwell and he's new in town. He didn't want to put you on the spot or anything, but he told me that he would love to check out your Glute-Boots."

After hearing the words "Glute-Boots" mentioned, Mr. Kent's face lit up. His blue eyes gleaming, he slid open the back door and gestured for Mike, Alex, and Nick to enter the backyard. "Go enjoy the party. Zack will catch up with you guys in a little bit."

Mike Jeposi had struck again.

"It's nice to meet you, Zack. I'm Lonnie. Come on, I'll show you the way to the gym."

We walked approximately five feet before he abruptly stopped. "You know what, Zack? I have a better idea. Why don't you wait here for a minute and I'll be right back."

Glancing over towards the backdoor, towards freedom, thoughts of making a break for it crossed my mind. It was an appeasing, very alluring impulse—just not one I could pull off and feel good about myself in the morning. In addition to it being flat out rude, Lonnie's smile made it impossible. He seemed so proud that someone as young as me was actually interested in his masterpiece. Returning to an empty hall would just devastate him.

Opting to wait for his return, I stayed grounded until Lonnie reemerged with his gorgeous wife, both clad in matching neon yellow exercise outfits. In contrast to Mike's egregious claim that the Glute-Boots were utterly useless, if Lonnie and his wife used them religiously, Mike's case would have been blown out of the water. Looking at least 10 years younger than his 45-year-old body, Lonnie was in exceptional shape. In addition to his bulging biceps, broad shoulders, and chiseled pectoral muscles, Lonnie's perfectly formed six-pack poked through his skin-tight shirt. With his gleaming white teeth, soft blonde hair, and square jaw line, Lonnie looked more like a Hollywood star than a father and successful businessperson.

His wife, whose outfit fit just as tightly, sent a wave of discomfort and anxiety coursing through my body. Plain and simple, she was beyond stunning. In her forties as well, she didn't look a second over 25. If it was even possible, her hair was blonder, her eyes were bluer, and her angular face was more striking than her husband's. Whether it was a natural tan or not, it was still wintertime, after all, her bronzed, smooth skin glowed. In terms of her physique, she had a better body than just about any of the scantily clad Maxim model's Mike had taped to his walls and ceiling.

"Allison, this is Zack Treadwell. Did I say that right, Zack?"

I nodded.

"...And, Zack, this is my beautiful wife and best friend, Allison."

While shaking her hand, my eyes stayed locked on hers, terrified to get caught looking anywhere else. That would come later. My raging hormones would make sure of it. Holding Allison's hand, Lonnie led the way to the gym, which was located in their massive finished basement. Once inside, it was easy to see how the two stayed in such great shape. The gym, which was the size of a large basketball court, was stacked with an array of state-of-the-art equipment and free weights. From the countless exercise machines to bikes, treadmills, rowing machines, rock climbing walls, and a resistance pool, the gym had it all, and then some. Even if the Glute-Boots worked as advertised, the two of them appeared as if they outsourced—and quite often.

"This is my masterpiece," Lonnie said, waving a hand around the gym. "I spend probably at least two to three hours a day in here. If you think that's a lot, Allison's down here for at least three times that."

Wow, I thought. *That's seems a bit excessive if you ask me.*

"Stop it, Lonnie! You're going to make Zack think I'm some type of fanatical workout fiend."

Lonnie laughed, then pulled Allison in for a kiss. "Sorry, couldn't resist, sweetie!" Turning to me, he said, "She's not that crazy. She works as personal trainer right here in our lovely gym. It's the perfect gig for her. She gets paid to work out with people all day. She's good at it too. We have stacks of photo albums to prove it. But you're not down her for that so let's get down to business. Mike tells me that our Glute-Boots product has piqued your interest. Is that so?"

I forced myself to nod. A regrettable response. For the next twenty minutes, I found myself trapped inside a late night *infomercial*. Using the same diction he presumably used in his own advertisements, Lonnie flooded my brain with as many Glute-Boots facts as he could think of. To the satisfaction of my raging hormones, he even had his wife demonstrate all of the different exercises. That was my favorite part. Especially, since it allotted me the perfect excuse for staring at his wife's amazing body. And, by name alone—Glute-Boots—my eyes were keyed in on one particular area. It was a memorable experience to say the least. Towards the end of his presentation, Lonnie became so emotional, so absorbed, he actually broke down and began crying, which only brought out the blue in his eyes that much more.

Shortly after Allison completed the last exercise, a real shame if I may say so, Lonnie turned and faced me. I thought he was going to call me out for my eyes being glued to his wife's "glutes," even though he kept pointing at them and asking me if I could see the muscle striations through her tight exercise shorts. He didn't. Not at all. Instead, he put me on the spot. "All right, Zack, you're up. What are you about a size 10 or 11?"

I'm what, I panicked. *No one ever said anything about actually having to try the damn things out.* Things suddenly went from bad to worse. And there was only one person to blame—Mike. I was going to murder him.

"An 11, I guess."

Lonnie then ran over to a supply closet and grabbed a box of Glute-Boots. Running back, he handed them over to me and patiently waited for me to try them on. Not wanting to offend Lonnie or Allison, I tossed open the box, set aside all of the karabiner hooks, threw the boots on, and laced them all the way to the top. To my surprise, the boots were actually very comfortable. If they didn't look so ridiculous with all the steel rods embedded throughout the boots (from where the karabiners could be harnessed), I probably would have worn them out.

With the boots on, Lonnie put me to work. In addition to the selected workout regimen, which destroyed my legs and glutes, the boots had other uses as well. Weighted down, the metal made sure of that, the boots were also designed to be used in everyday use to further sculpt and tone your legs and gluts. Plus, as I later found out, they could also be worn while doing your cardio—if cardio wasn't hard enough already. As for the selected workout regimen, the boots came stocked with the Kents' very own patented astro-cables, which obliterated your muscles and promoted strength and growth by increasing the ever-important positive and negative resistance as you worked out. On the boot itself, the steel rods were conveniently placed all around the sides, the top, and even had some built into the heel of the boots, making it possible to hit every conceivable target area. Using the karabiner hooks, you could attach the cable to the hook and then use either a central lock station (could be purchased separately) or with any pulley machine at the gym. You could even attach the astro-cables to each boot and annihilate your inner and outer thighs.

After Lonnie and Allison walked me through every conceivable exercise, Lonnie patted me on the back and handed the box over to me. "Here, Zack, they're yours."

I was shocked. Unless it was some type of marketing scheme, you know, trying to branch out to the younger generation, I couldn't understand why he'd give them away—especially to me. I did sweat in them...excessively...but that was no reason to part ways with such an expensive product. It felt wrong accepting such a generous offer. "I'm sorry, but I can't accept this..."

"Oh, don't worry about it, Zack. Besides, we have a new model coming out this spring. These will probably just collect dust anyway, that is, until the bargain hunters start buying them all up. Happens every time a new model is released."

"Still, it seems a bit much to accept as a gift."

"You know what, Zack. Why don't you start coming over on the weekends to exercise with us. We'd love the company, wouldn't we, hun?"

Allison nodded.

"My business card's in the box. So if you're up for it just call and we'll set up a time."

It was easy to see that they were not going to take "no" for an answer, regardless of how hard I tried. Coming to terms with that reality, I relinquished control and accepted their kind gift. Lonnie and Allison couldn't have been happier. Still wearing a joyous smile, Lonnie escorted me to the backyard. It was a long time in waiting.

Lugging the large box labeled, "Glute-Boots," under one arm, I coyly entered the backyard. *High school kids are above finding the humor in someone walking around with what are essentially "Ass-Boots,"* I thought sarcastically to myself. *Yeah, just like the pink shorts fiasco...*

Making my way through the enormous backyard, covering up the shoebox as much as possible, no one initially noticed that anything was out of the ordinary. Unfortunately, for the sake of my self-esteem, my luck didn't last. As soon as I began making my way through the hordes of partygoers, reminiscent of my eventful first gym class, kids began taking notice. The pointing and laughter quickly followed suit. The trashcan suddenly seemed like an optimal solution to my problem.

"Hey man, nice glutes!" someone yelled from the crowd.

Glute this, glute that, you name it and I heard it while roaming through the backyard in search of my friends. Locating them did little to end the abuse. In fact, it gave rise to an even more brutal display of adolescent torture. And that was before Mike even showed up on the scene. In typical Mike fashion, he was off doing what he does best— harassing every pretty girl at the party.

Running over to get a better look, Nick and Alex began convulsing—they were laughing so hard. Holding his protruding gut, which was giggling like a tub of green Jell-O, Alex waved at Nick to stop. "Mike's going to die when he sees Zack with those," he said, wiping away a tear.

Nick nodded in agreement before the laughter took on an entirely new level. Going from loud boisterous cackles, the laughter fell deeply into their chests, only evident by their seizure-like convulsions and reddened faces bulging with veins. Not even seconds later, as if he had a sixth sense for things of that nature, Mike appeared virtually out of nowhere. As expected, the instant he saw me, his eyes widened and his upper lip began to twitch. Taking notice, Nick and Alex's laughter made sure of it, a small circle of partygoers formed around us, prepared to join in on the festivities.

"It's not that funny," I barked. "So anytime you guys want to knock it off would be fine with me."

Swiping the box out of my hands, nearly salivating, Mike opened it up and began inspecting the boots. "Oh, you're putting these on, Zack."

"Just give me the boots and knock it off," I ordered. I was beginning to get pissed. "Come on, Mike, you've had your fun, now quit it."

"Just try them on, already!" he insisted, his temperament changing from light-hearted to solemn. "What's it going to hurt? Besides, if you do, I'll shut up about it for the rest of the night."

"PUT THEM ON! PUT THEM ON! PUT THEM ON!" the mob cheered, led by Nick and Alex.

"I'm not putting the boots on—and that's final!" I screamed, quieting the mob.

"Why, what's wrong with the boots?" An unfamiliar feminine voice asked from behind.

I swung my head around, and the moment my eyes locked with her gleaming blues, it felt as if someone had taken a sledgehammer to my abdomen. Completely caught off guard, I stood there speechless, jaw agape, staring at the most attractive, most stunning person my eyes had ever had the pleasure of seeing. She was so beautiful the image of Allison Kent bent over an exercise ball doing cable kickbacks vanished from my memory bank. How had I not noticed her, and her silky blonde hair, striking blue eyes, and tight frame, earlier? Oddly enough, she reminded me of Allison—just a younger and more stunning version.

"There's nothing wrong here," I said, forcing myself to talk. "I mean with the boots that is."

"I'm just messing with you," she said, smiling, her thick, luscious lips captivating my attention. "Lighten up, already."

Wake up was more like it. Similar to an unattended computer, my brain went into sleep mood, unable to function without a little stirring. I wanted to say something, anything, but was incapable of even formulating a single word, much less string a few together to form a complete thought—commonly known as a sentence. Where's back-up when you need it? You know, someone to jump in and go to bat for you. Unfortunately, with the crew I hung out with, the only time they had your back was when they could *de-pants* you and make things worse.

"Hey, Mike, who's your new friend," she asked, raising a thin, blonde eyebrow to me.

"Oh, this guy," he said, pointing in my direction. "This is Zack. He just moved here a couple months ago. Stone Creek actually recruited him to play on the marching band. He's a three-time junior piccolo champion, you know."

"That's funny. I didn't even know schools recruited people to play on the band."

"Neither did I. Till I met Zack, that is. Isn't that right, Zack?"

I must not have been listening to a single word he was saying because my head started bopping up and down. *Recruited by Stone Creek's marching band—check. Three-time junior piccolo champion—check.* That all sounded just about right, didn't it? Okay, no it didn't. Not at all. But at the time nothing was registering in my head. He could have told her I was a sexual deviant on the national sex offender registry and my head still probably would have went up and down.

"Nice to meet you, Zack," she said, extending her hand, "I'm Tiffany."

"Don't leave her hanging," Mike barked, snapping me out of my transfixed state. "Snap out of it, already."

My brain finally stirring itself out of the sleep mode it was in, I reached for her hand and shook it gently. Her hand felt warm to the touch, yet rough in some areas. The roughness left me wondering if she was a gymnast. Naturally, as would be expected for someone my age, that roused images of her clad in a tight leotard jumping up and down on a trampoline. Was it appropriate to visualize her in such a fashion? Probably not. Was it something I could control? Possibly. Was the vivid image bouncing around in my head pleasurable? Without a doubt.

Without uttering another word, probably freaked out by my bizarre demeanor, Tiffany pulled her hand away and started walking off through the mob. Could I blame her for leaving so abruptly? Nope. It wasn't as if we were striking up much of a conversation, and I was the only idiot at the party walking around with "Ass-Boots." *Wow, talk about first impressions.*

Then, just as she was about to be engulfed by the slowly dispersing mob, she stopped, turned around, and locked eyes with me. "I see my parents were very generous to you. They don't give their merchandise away to just anyone."

She's a Kent: were the words that shot through my head. Now it made perfect sense why she resembled Allison so much. She was her daughter. That was my in. If nothing else, we now had something to talk about— something to break the ice. It was a novel idea, one that may have worked too; however, in the end, I just stood there and watched as she continued walking away.

The mob now completely gone, I turned, and shouted with excitement, "Did you guys just see that?"

"See what?" they replied in unison.

"She gave me the eyes."

Mike shook his head. "Zack, I don't mean to pull the stool out from beneath your feet, but she's *not* into you. Trust me, I know. Not to be mean or anything, but she's way too hot for you...or any of us for the matter...except for me maybe."

Under normal circumstances, I would have accepted what Mike was saying outright, yet something *synapsed* inside me. I knew what I had seen. Tiffany Kent communicated to me through her eyes, loud and clear, that she was intrigued by me. And nothing Mike, Alex, or Nick could say would make me think any differently— naiveté in its purest sense.

Moving past the Glute-Boots and Tiffany Kent encounter, I learned what the guys had been up to while my legs were being destroyed in the Kents' personal gym. Alex and Nick had spent the majority of the time stuffing their faces while Mike bounced around from girl to girl in a desperate attempt to hook up, land digits, or a combination of the two. So far, he'd come up empty in regards to both pursuits. I also learned that Rick's party, virtually unheard of in my opinion, was a clean one. There wasn't a drop of alcohol to be found. It made sense when you really thought about it. Not only was he the star quarterback at Trinity High School, as a sophomore no less, but he was also already fielding offers from several impressive Division I colleges. That said, tarnishing his image probably wasn't in his best interest. Plus, his parents were still home and they didn't seem the type to encourage unhealthy habits— let alone illegal ones.

I briefly met Rick, and go figure, he recommended I try out for Stone Creek's team next year. *Maybe, I will*, I thought walking away. Then, before the idea really grabbed a hold of me, I overheard him saying the exact same thing to a scrawny teenager wearing a Stone Creek High Varsity Rifle Team letterman jacket. I later learned from Mike that Rick encourages just about every guy he meets to go out for their school's football team. It stung at first, but if that was his gimmick, so be it.

The four of us eventually found ourselves engrossed in a game of two-on-two volleyball. As we played, my thoughts shifted towards my newfound obsession—Tiffany. Did she play volleyball? She was a little on the short side, but that didn't mean anything. I could just visualize her tearing up the court, clad in those extremely tight fitting, skimpy shorts. It suddenly began to feel real hot on that chilly late fall night. Then out of nowhere, I heard a familiar voice shout over to us. It was Tiffany asking who was winning.

"Tied up, ten-a-piece," Mike replied, kicking his feet in the sand, prepping himself for the next serve.

That was all it took for me to lose my focus on the game. Glancing over in Tiffany's direction, I watched as she whispered something into one of her friend's ears before they both started giggling. I wasn't sure if it was a good laugh or a bad one. Realistically, it could have been either. They could have been secretly making fun of me, hopefully not the case, or sharing a laugh in that special way when one or both of them is interested in someone in particular—call in subtle flirting. I convinced myself it was the latter—and with good reason. For the second time that night, there was no denying that she was leering at me in that special way—this time suggestively biting her lower lip.

My attention entirely absorbed on Tiffany, I didn't notice the volleyball whizzing at my head until it was too late. The ball smashed me right in the face, sending Mike and Alex into a howling laughter. Falling backwards, it wasn't the blow itself that made things bad—Mike's spike was on the weak side. The aftermath is what did me in. The slightly deflated volleyball caught me dead on the nose, welling up tears in my eyes, the first sign of the impending mucus storm. Ten sneezes later, hunched over on all fours with a string of snot almost touching the sand, it was becoming painfully obvious that I was ruining any shot I may have had with Tiffany. Why in the world would she ever consider hooking up with someone like me? An "Ass-Boots" carrying, face spiked on, mucus-harboring nightmare. I was a walking disaster.

"Damn that looked like it hurt. Are you okay, Zack?" Nick said, pulling a wad of napkins out of his pocket. "Here take these and clean yourself up."

Mike and Alex were not as sympathetic. While cleaning the cocktail of sand and snot off my face, they cackled like immature hyenas, enjoying the moment for as long as it would last. I didn't know it at the time, but Alex caught a small glimpse of my sneezing fit on his phone. That particular video later became a minor YouTube hit amongst the students at Stone Creek High. The legend of Zack was growing.

Could anything go right for me? I thought not, especially after glancing over at Tiffany and her friend, both laughing hysterically. There was no doubt in my mind what type of laughter that was. Annoyed, but trying not to show it, I got back to my feet, grabbed the volleyball, and muttered, "Come on, let's play. Game's not over yet."

After the laughter subsided, which took much longer than it should have, we finished the game, Mike and Alex proving victorious. I just couldn't get my head back in the game, aside from using it to stop the ball, that is. In high spirits following the win, Mike disappeared once again to focus on priority number one—girls. Tiffany and her friend also vanished. My guess was that any glimmer of interest dissipated after the volleyball incident. Therefore, that left Alex, Nick, and me to our own accord. We ended up on the basketball court where we played game after game of H-O-R-S-E. His volleyball triumph must have done wonders with his confidence because it seemed like just about every ten to fifteen minutes, Mike would come waltzing back bragging that he had landed digits. We, of course, likely out of jealously, continuously asked him the same question over and over: "What's his name?"

Mike wouldn't even bother responding. He was too "in the zone" to care about trivial jokes. He'd stick around for a second, tell us all about her, and then in a flash he'd be gone, off to try to land more numbers. Although his primary goal for the night was to hook up, Mike abandoned that quest after realizing that obtaining as many phone numbers as possible would serve him better in the long run. To him, attempting to hook up was too much of an investment—time better spent increasing his network. In his world, if he was lucky enough to obtain a number, the more, the merrier, he'd have all the time in the world to seal the deal.

Shortly after midnight, the party finally started to die down. With the exception of Mike, who was busy sorting through the scraps of girls still left at the party, the rest of us wanted to leave. We eventually had to drag Mike out against his will. On our way out, I spotted Rick waving goodbye to a bunch of his guests. Glancing down at the Glute-Boots box, I felt compelled to thank Rick for allowing us to attend his party.

"Zack, right?" he asked, as I approached.

I nodded.

"Hey thanks for coming," he said, his hand outstretched. Squeezing my hand with his powerful grip, he added, "Have you given a thought about playing next year? I've heard Stone Creek could really use the help."

"I'll definitely consider it," I said, tightening my own grip in an attempt to negate his muscular superiority over me. It didn't work. His bear claws were just too big and powerful. "Anyway, I just wanted to thank you for letting us come. And, I thought I'd offer up my assistance with the cleaning tomorrow, if that's all right with you."

"Nah, man, that's all right. We got that covered, bro, but thanks..." Rick paused as his eyes drifted down and keyed in on the Glute-Boots box. "Hey, where did you get those?"

You can't get anything past the Kent kids, now can you? I thought laughing to myself. It was wishful thinking in the first place to believe that Trinity High's star quarterback (a position known for a keen sense of awareness) wouldn't notice the massive box of Glute-Boots. Earlier in the night, hoping to avoid having to explain the Glute-

Boots to yet another Kent, I wisely used Alex's large frame to obstruct Rick's view of the box.

"Oh, these," I said, jiggling the box, "your parents gave them to me after putting on a demonstration of how to use them. They wouldn't take no for an answer."

Rick laughed. "That's my parents for you, all right." He looked lost in thought for a moment before continuing. "I get it, now. Because of my parent's generous offer, you feel obliged to return the favor, right?"

I shrugged my shoulders. "Yeah...that and...the backyard's a complete disaster."

"Look, if it makes you feel better, by all means. But if you wake up with a change of heart, don't sweat it, we got it covered."

After thanking Rick for his hospitality, I raced to catch back up with my friends. Already peddling down the street, they were too impatient to wait for me, I watched as the three of them disappeared around a corner. Approaching my bike, it finally dawned on me that I might have had an ulterior motive for asking to help clean up. That motive came in terms of a person—in particular, Tiffany Kent. There was no guarantee that she'd be home the following day, much less involved in the cleanup project; however, if she was, it was worth a shot. Heck, I'd do garbage duty for a week at the Kent's luxurious mansion if it meant catching another glimpse of her.

Jumping on my bike, balancing the humongous Glute-Boots box on my knees, it became abundantly clear after about two blocks that there was no way I was going to catch up with my friends. The thought of ditching the boots for the second time that night briefly crossed my mind. Again, that just felt wrong. In the end, Mike's wish came true. I tossed the box next to a neighbor's garbage can, tied my sneakers and the astro-cables around my bike's handlebars, placed all of the karabiner hooks in my pockets (designating one to be used as my new personal keychain), and strapped the Glute-Boots on my feet. I felt like a complete idiot riding around Stone Creek with the boots on. Fortunately, Mike and the rest of the guys weren't around to see.

Arriving at Mike's house, a total of fifteen minutes after they made it back, I quickly jumped off my bike onto rubbery legs. The boots worked as advertised. Lonnie was right—they did add an extra element to your cardio. Although exhausted, barely able to lift a leg up, I managed to muster up just enough energy to take the boots off before entering Mike's house. After all, hadn't I already met my quota of humiliation for one night?

Chapter Seven

Distraction

Even though my body yearned for rest, and felt utterly drained the next day, I willed myself to rise to my feet on little sleep and make my way back over to Rick's house. Not wanting to smell bad, or be seen wearing the exact same clothes as the night before, a quick pit-stop was in order. That, of course, meant having to throw the Glute-Boots back on and torture my aching legs some more. Back at the Baniaks' dwelling, struggling to pick out the perfect outfit for the occasion, a flashback of Mike getting ready the previous night flashed before my eyes. Most people dress down when spending an afternoon cleaning up filth. But then again, most people don't clean in the presence of someone like Tiffany. I had to look my best—overdressed or not. And, with my limited wardrobe, that turned out being a long sleeved black polo-shirt and dark-green cargo pants. Now, all fresh and clean, next on the agenda was to go ahead and get all sweaty again riding up and down all the hills en route to the Kents' palace.

Arriving forty-five minutes later, a nice casual ride to reduce sweating, I parked my bike on the side of their house and rang the bell. "Wow, you're motivated, Zack!" Lonnie said, answering the door. "I didn't expect to see you so soon. Come on in!"

"Actually, Mr. Kent, I'm not here to workout. I thought you could use an extra hand with the backyard."

"That's a nice offer and all, but it's really not necessary, Zack. We got that covered. It's a sort of tradition for us. The family that cleans together...you know...you get the point. Well, anyway, since you're here, did you want to get a quick workout in while we knock out the cleaning?"

I shook my head. "I was raised to believe that if you contribute to a mess, you should help clean it up. So if it's okay with you I'd rather pitch in and help out."

"All right, if you insist. But let's make one thing clear. If you help with the cleaning, it's mandatory you stay for dinner."

"Deal!" I replied, any inhibition over accepting meals long gone by that point.

"Are you sure you don't want to go and get a quick workout in, first?" he asked, flexing his veiny biceps.

"Honestly, my legs are killing me today. I rode the entire way home in the Glute-Boots last night and this morning! You weren't kidding when you said it adds an extra element to any cardio workout. And I think I know what that element is—pain!"

Lonnie laughed for a moment, enjoying my joke. As he walked me through his house, towards the backyard, it was easy to see he was beaming with pride. I took him as the type of guy who never tired of hearing about how amazing his product is—even coming from a fifteen-year-old boy with a limited exercise background.

"Hey, Ally, Zack's going to help out today," Lonnie shouted after leading me into the yard where Allison, Rick, and...*Tiffany* were all hard at work.

"That's wonderful," she replied, waving at me with a bright smile.

Rick briefly glanced up, acknowledged my existence, then went right back to work. He seemed motivated to get the job done efficiently and fast. He probably showed the same mentality on the football field. No games, no fooling around, nothing but a willingness to complete the task at hand. In football that means orchestrating a scoring drive and putting your team in a position to win the game. In terms of the "task at hand," it meant ridding the backyard of all debris, recyclables, and furniture that needed to be stowed away until the next bash.

"Think fast," Tiffany shouted, heaving a ball of garbage bags at my face.

I easily caught the two large garbage bags. I was already having a better day. If it had been the night prior, I probably would have somehow suffocated on them.

"Recyclables go into the white bag, garbage into the black one," Tiffany explained. "Any questions?"

I shook my head. Her directions were as simplistic as they come. How could I possibly screw that up? Then again, we were talking about me.

Glancing around the yard, it was astonishing just how much trash was blanketing it. The majority of the rubbish consisted of bottles, cans, paper plates, crumbled and stained napkins, empty cups, food, and even though smoking was strictly prohibited, cigarette butts. The garbage was strewn all over the ground, on tables, chairs, all over the basketball and volleyball courts, and even in the heated pool that some guests braved the elements and used the night before.

Please, God, let Tiffany clean the pool out, I thought, or rather prayed, to myself. The sun was shining, steam seen rising from the heated water, so why not. Somebody had to clean it. Why not Tiffany? Even if she bundled herself up in a thick bathrobe before and afterwards, catching a glimpse of her in a bikini sent my imagination into hyper-drive.

"Quick, Zack, think of a distraction," I mumbled to myself, my hormones taking over the control deck.

Surveying the amount of work involved, an excellent diversion, a thought crossed my mind: *Should I start with sit-ups or crunches?* Obviously a joke, I wasn't going to ditch the Kents. All the same, it sure seemed like a better option than the alternative.

"Where should I start?" I asked Lonnie.

"The whole yard's a disaster, Zack, so pick a spot and have at it."

"He can take my section, Dad. I'll clean out the pool," Tiffany announced tossing her garbage bags aside.

Dear God, yes, I thought to myself. *You really came through for me this...*

Then, to my disappointment, instead of running inside and throwing on a bathing suit, Tiffany retrieved a long, blue skimmer from the pool house and began the painstaking task of cleaning out the pool. Realizing Tiffany would not be taking a dip anytime soon, I lost myself in my work.

When it came down to it, cleaning the yard wasn't that bad. It didn't hurt that I had spent a majority of my life in orphanages or in foster homes, where daily cleaning responsibilities were a constant. You wanted food in your stomach and a warm place to sleep, you cleaned, and cleaned, and cleaned, and then cleaned some more. You didn't have a choice. In terms of the "hierarchy of needs pyramid," cleaning was located just below the physiological level—the basement, per say. Until all the cleaning was out of the way, no other needs were met.

It was an unusually warm late February day, making my outfit selection regrettable. A long sleeved black shirt is just about the worst thing you can wear on a bright, sunny day. But with last night's disaster engrained in the forefront of my mind, ignoring the discomfort was my only option. After all, it was my best shirt and I had a girl to impress. Of course, similar to the night before, things didn't appear to be panning out for me. Regardless of how sly I tried to be, it seemed every time I'd casually glance over at her, you know, to check her out, she'd catch me in the act. Then, like a curious yet timid creature, my eyes would immediately shift away from hers. It was pathetic to say the least. After the fourth consecutive time of getting caught in the act, I devised the perfect solution: don't look anywhere in her direction. As much as I hated that particular strategy, it proved effective.

After about two hours of nonstop work, it appeared as if everyone was ready for a break. Allison was just the first to suggest it. "Hey, Lon, I'm going to grab some cold drinks. Is there anything you'd like?"

"Cold water's fine."

As Allison was leaving to get the drinks, I caught her making a subtle gesture to Lonnie. Not even a moment later, Lonnie walked over to Rick and whispered something in his ear. The two of them then heaved their garbage bags aside, folded up a long folding table, and and began lugging it inside the house. With Allison, Lonnie, and Rick all gone, leaving only Tiffany and myself in the backyard, my suspicion was aroused. Had Allison orchestrated everything? It seemed farfetched, but when it came to the Kents you couldn't rule anything out. The family that cleans together...

"So...tell me why you're really here?" Tiffany asked, approaching me from the rear. "Cause if you came here just to see me...be warned...I have a boyfriend."

Her forwardness caught me off guard. "No!" I replied, unsure of what I was even saying "no" to.

"No, what!"

"No, I didn't come here *just* to see you. Your parents were so nice to me yesterday. It seemed like the right thing to do."

"So I had nothing to do with why you're here."

"I wouldn't go that far," I replied, slowly steering off course. She had a way of doing that to me.

"Oh...I see," Tiffany smiled, "so you did come here to see me!"

Frustrated and realizing she wasn't going to drop the issue, I came clean...well, sort of. "Okay, truth be told, the reason I'm here is multifaceted. On one end, your family's generosity was the catalyst for developing the initial idea—you know, payback for the expensive boots. And on the other end of the spectrum, I thought it'd be cool to see you again, and maybe say more than just a few words the second time around."

I surprised myself. Actual words floated out my mouth and produced what are commonly referred to as sentences. It was a great feeling. I'm not sure if it had something to do with the fact that she had a boyfriend or not—a heart-crushing development—but in the same sense, it sure did alleviate some of the pressure. I didn't have to worry about making myself look like a fool. Unless I wanted to try to steal her away, the friend-zone was the only place I was headed.

"Multifaceted? Catalyst?" she asked, edging even closer to me. "Sounds like someone's been hanging around my parents a little too much."

Just when things were getting interesting, Allison re-entered the backyard balancing a tray of cold beverages on her shoulder like a cocktail waitress. Tiffany immediately turned away from me and ran over to help. The timing was good and bad. On one hand, it bought me time to think of what I would say next; and on the other, it saved me from inappropriately flirting with someone in a serious relationship. I didn't consider myself particularly good at flirting, couldn't remember the last time I engaged in the practice; however, Tiffany had a way of opening me up. Flirting was surely the next thing to find its way out of my mouth.

Grabbing the tray out of her mom's hands, Tiffany gently placed it on the table. She then turned back to me and waved me over. I took the seat right across from her. Moments later, Lonnie and Rick joined us at the table. Allison did the honors of pouring the drinks. Throat parched, I chugged mine in one big gulp. Refreshed and ready to get back to work, I jumped to my feet. Thirty-second breaks was something I had grown accustomed to taking.

"Hey, kid, love the work ethic, but take a breather why don't you," Lonnie said, gesturing for me to sit. "Besides, we'd like to get to know you a little better. What brings you to West Virginia, Zack?"

Sitting there silently for a few moments, I contemplated which version of my life they should hear. Should I go with the depressing version or the extremely depressing version? There were no alternatives. I decided to go with the former—there was much less blood and violence involved in that particular account. With all ears on me, I told the Kents about my parents untimely departure (purposely leaving out all of the gory, cannibalistic details), about the gruesome conditions in some the foster homes and orphanages, and about my difficulties fitting in at school. Not wanting to sound like a budding sociopath, I decided to leave out the parts where I may have overreacted in the past (e.g., Dante's broken nose). I concluded my monologue by telling them how Bill and Susan came to be in my life; and how, for the first time, things were looking up. I was making friends, doing well in school, and most importantly, staying out of trouble.

Overwhelmed with emotions, Allison, who was sitting right beside me, pulled me into an embrace. "Oh, you poor thing," she said, tears welling up in her eyes. "I feel so sorry for you. If there's anything we can do, please don't hesitate to ask."

"Yeah, Zack, anything you need, we're here for you," added Lonnie.

What I needed in that particular moment was to have the focus shifted away from me. Things had gotten way too uncomfortable and emotional by that point. A change in subject was in order. "The yard isn't going to clean itself, now is it?" I said, rising to my feet.

And with that, we all went back to work—well, almost all of us. Tiffany was nowhere in sight. She didn't mention anything to anyone, just sort of disappeared as soon as we got up from the picnic table. Maybe she had to be somewhere—perhaps on a date with her boyfriend. The same boyfriend who was too good to help out with the cleaning. That hurt too much to think about. Needing yet another distraction, I lost myself in my work again; something learned many, many, years ago.

Fifteen minutes later, while scooping up a clump of dried vomit (a cocktail of beans, chunks of hot dog, and some type of orange goo), Tiffany reappeared, her eyes looking a tad puffy and red. It didn't take a genius to figure out why she had left. She had been crying, and unlike her mother who openly cried in my presence, she apparently didn't want me to see it. I decided it was best to avoid eye contact. There was no point in making her feel any more uncomfortable that she already was.

In all, working as a cohesive unit, it took us roughly four-and-a-half hours to clean up the entire yard and restore order back to the Kents' property. We then sat down for a delicious vegetarian entrée that Lonnie and Allison prepared together. After dinner, Tiffany pulled yet another one of her disappearing acts. This time I caught her in the act. With Lonnie going on and on about the history of the Glute-Boots, out of the corner of my eye, I watched as Tiffany quietly rose to her feet and vanished down the hall. I had expected her to return, and when she didn't, I decided it was time to head out. I couldn't wait forever. And, besides, it wasn't like I had a shot with her anyway. Her boyfriend spoiled that plan.

With a belly full of health food, I thanked the Kents for their hospitality and asked them to say goodbye to Tiffany for me. On my way out, Allison informed me that Tiffany's never been much of a "goodbye person," then winked at me suggestively. Was the wink supposed to mean something? Did she know something I didn't? I wasn't sure, and unless I took Lonnie up on his offer to start working out with him, it was something I'd probably never find out. Especially, after learning that Tiffany also attended Trinity High School with her brother.

Okay, that settles that, my brain was formulating a plan as I headed towards my bike. *Get in good with the parents, start building a solid rapport with them, and maybe, just maybe, the floodgates will open up and I'll find out what Allison thinks she knows about her daughter. Is a breakup looming on the horizon? Please, God, let that be the case.*

Lost in my thoughts, my heart nearly stopped in my chest after hearing a loud "PSSSSSST" sound coming from somewhere nearby. I immediately froze, fearing it was some type of poisonous snake. I didn't know a lot about the area, but it was common knowledge that West Virginia housed its fare share of rattlesnakes. Terrified there was a highly toxic predator sending out its final warning signal before striking, I attempted to coerce myself into action. "Okay, don't panic, Zack, all you have to do is—"

"Who are you talking to?" Tiffany asked, popping out from behind a large boxwood bush.

"Oh, thank god," I said, a sense of relief surging through me. "I thought you were a rattlesnake."

"A rattlesnake!"

"Yeah," I replied, slightly embarrassed. "You freaked me out with that weird hissing sound you were making."

"What sound?"

Oh, no! Panic began settling back in. *There really is a snake...*

Tiffany then burst into a deep guttural laugh. "I'm s-s-sorry," she laughed. "I'm j-just me-messing with you. There's no snake, Zack. Not around here, at least."

"Well that's a relief. For a second there, I thought I'd have to save us both."

"Here," Tiffany said, handing me a neatly folded piece of paper. "Thanks for coming over. I can tell my parents really like you."

Before I could even respond, she disappeared back through the side door. I immediately opened up the note, so fast I nearly tore it in half.

> *Zack,*
> *It was so sad to hear about your parents. I couldn't imagine losing mine. I didn't mean to run off, but it was a lot to take in all at once. Sorry for giving you such a hard time. I was just trying to be diffi-cult. I'd also like to apologize for lying to you. I don't have a boyfriend. Had ONE—but he turned out to be a real jerk. Even though we didn't get to talk much, the few minutes we did was nice. If you'd like to talk more...well...call me (999) 685-0376.*
> *—Tiff*

Everything was finally beginning to make sense. Allison was in on it all along. She must have read Tiffany's body language and decided to play matchmaker. That's why she orchestrated the alone time in the backyard. You know, give us some time (but not too much—Tiffany was only fifteen) for us to get to know each other. That would also account for the wink—a subtle gesture made to hint at the idea that there was more to Tiffany's disappearing act than meets the eye. If those were her intentions, I'd never know for sure, it certainly worked in my favor.

Elated, I jumped on my bike and sped the entire way home. After showering off all the sweat and foul odors, thinking the entire time about what to talk to Tiffany about, I nervously dialed her number and waited for her to answer. She picked up after the first ring. By the end of the phone call, which lasted three hours, we had made plans to see each other the following weekend. I had hoped we would be able to see each other sooner, but with Tiffany's hectic schedule, jam-packed with schoolwork, club meetings, and all of her other extracurricular activities, the following Friday was the only day that worked for her.

Leading up to our first official get together, we talked on the phone every night for an average of 104 minutes. When Friday finally arrived, to put it bluntly, I was a wreck. I couldn't figure out what to wear, what to say to her, and most importantly, how to conduct myself when in her presence. Should I try to hold her hand? If the moment presented itself, should I place an arm around her shoulder? And finally, at the conclusion of the date, should I go all in and attempt a goodnight kiss? I was at a loss. I wanted to do all those things, and more in due time, yet didn't want to come off as too pushy. In the end, I felt it was best to just play it safe and wait for her to initiate any physical contact, which unfortunately never happened. Maybe she was just as nervous as I was. Regardless, the closest we came to any type of physical contact was when my finger brushed up against hers while passing a movie ticket over to her. Lonnie picked us up after the date, driving his massive yellow Hummer, ending any shot of a goodnight kiss.

After that day, and at the insistence of Lonnie, I found myself going over to the Kents' house on an almost daily basis. I didn't always get to see Tiffany, her chaotic schedule didn't allow for it, but on a whole I was getting in good with her entire family. As crazy as it sounds, I began exercising with just about everyone in the household. Lonnie and Allison, go figure, guided me through their patented Glute-Boots workouts two times per week. Rick had me for another two, exclusively doing exercises that targeted what he referred to as "essential" football muscles. And Tiffany got me on the weekends. We would usually hit up their parents gym early in the morning, shower separately, a real bummer, and find something to do for the rest of the afternoon. Since we shared a multitude of interests, ranging from sports, movies, music, outdoor activities such as hiking and bike riding, and literature, time flew by while we were together. Okay, the literature part was more of an acquired taste for me; however, that said, if the act of sitting down and reading "Fifty Shades of Gray," impressed her, I was all in. I made sure to keep my copy well hidden from my friends.

Here's the part where things began to get a little complicated. Bearing in mind that everything was going extremely well between us, there was one major problem brewing. It wasn't our chemistry—we were so cohesive I wouldn't have been surprised if a new element was named after us. No, the problem came in terms of making a move. Although I'd never know this for sure, without asking that is, I felt that she was taking the traditional approach by waiting for me to make the first move. Bad idea on her part. And, for whatever reason, even though rejection was unlikely, I just couldn't will myself to jump over that seemingly risk-free obstacle. The Glute-Boots had significantly improved my vertical leap, but did nothing for me in those regards. My game was pathetic to say the least. Eventually, after weeks and weeks of hanging out together, I decided it was best to wait for the perfect opportunity. Which as it turns out was just around the corner, Tiffany's sweet-sixteen birthday party, scheduled the following Friday.

On my way home from yet another visit to the Kent house, on a brisk Sunday evening, I received what appeared to be an urgent text message from Nick.

Nick: *Call me!!! It's important!*

I immediately called him.

"Hey, Zack," he answered solemnly. "Sorry to bug you, but we need to talk."

"What's up?"

"Mike and Alex are pissed off at you, Zack. They feel like you've completely blown us all off since meeting Tiffany—"

"What are you talking about?" I screamed, feeling under attack. "I stopped by Mike's house last week. Not to mention the fact that I see you and Alex at school all the time. That hardly constitutes blowing you guys off."

"Look, Zack, I get it. I do. She's hot, things are going great for the two of you, and we're all probably just a little jealous. But that's not why I'm telling you all of this. As your friend, I just wanted to give you the heads up in the event Mike or Alex call you out on it. We both know you're not the best when it comes to surprises."

"Then why'd you text me? What's so important you needed me to talk to me ASAP?"

"You know the 22nd is right around the corner, don't you?"

"Uh-huh," I mumbled into the phone, the significance of the date eluding me.

"Well…it's been nearly a month since we went out to the designated dig site…and I just wanted to make sure that everything was still copasetic for us to start this Friday. It's still marked on your calendar isn't it?"

A tidal wave of recollection submersed me in a sea of regret. How could I have forgotten all about "The Project" and the designated start date? There was no excuse for that. To make matters worse, Tiffany's party fell on the same exact day. This presented a major problem. Logistically speaking, I couldn't be in two places at once. I had to choose between hurting Nick, who was the best friend I had ever had, and hurting Tiffany, the girl I was falling deeply in love with. It was not an easy decision to make.

"You forgot, didn't you?"

"Nick…you're going to hate me…but—"

"—you can't come, can you?"

"Let me explain," I pleaded. "Tiffany's sweet-sixteen party is on Friday. I can't miss that. Especially, not with being so close to asking her out. If I miss her party, there's no telling how she'll react. It could ruin any shot I have with her."

"But it's okay to do that with me?"

"No, but can't we start fresh on Saturday. It's not like we'll be able to dig the entire tunnel in one night anyway."

Nick let out a sigh. "You know what, Zack? Forget about the whole damn thing. Forget the tunnel, forget 'The Project,' forget everything…"

"Don't say that, Nick. Like I said, we can start on Saturday and put in a double. Heck, I'll even put in a triple if it makes you happy."

"NO, ZACK," Nick barked. "That won't make me happy. Even if I was to agree and set it back a day, what's next? Instead of working on the tunnel around the clock, which was our initial plan, are you going to need days off here and there to hang out with Tiffany. The reality of the situation is that we had this planned for months—way longer than you've even known her. You know what, Zack. Just forget about it…that's something you're apparently very good at."

Call it displacement, call it my inability to respond appropriately when faced with a troubling situation; regardless of which, what I said next was totally uncalled for. I know many people use this very excuse—but I didn't even realize what I was saying until the last word left my mouth. "Well, since we're being so honest with each other, why don't I just throw this out there for you. Even if we starting digging today with the primitive digging tools we have, we'll be lucky to even scratch the surface by the end of spring break. It's a goddamn pipe dream if I ever saw one. The only way we'll ever step foot inside that lab is if we're caught and thrown in with your so called 'evidence.'"

"Wow...Zack," Nick replied, sounding hurt, "didn't see that one coming. Enjoy the party!"

He abruptly hung up.

Feeling awful for my impulsive words, damage control was in order. I immediately called Nick back to apologize. He wouldn't answer his phone. Not ready to give up just yet, I blasted his phone with text after text, apologizing and pleading with him to call me. He wouldn't. Feeling hopeless and aggravated with myself, I left one final message reaffirming my commitment to "The Project." I meant it to. If I had to go out there and dig the tunnel myself to make it up to him—it was on. When it was all said and done, Nick's friendship meant just as much to me as Tiffany's, if not more so. Pissed off at myself, I tossed and turned in bed all night trying to figure out a way to make things right with Nick. I had to—I had no choice.

The next day, things didn't go according to plan. Both Nick and Alex completely shunned me the entire day. It's funny how the roles reversed. Just months ago, they were the unwilling recipients of my cold shoulder. I didn't particularly enjoy the sudden role reversal. Desperate to put the conflict behind us, I even went so far as to leave a handwritten note in Nick's locker—a symbolic reminder of how he smoothed things over with me. Symbolism or not, my plan failed. After another two days of the silent treatment, I gave up. I figured if he was ever going to drop the issue, it probably wouldn't occur until well after Tiffany's party. Why tear open a gaping new wound when the old one is still fresh and singeing with pain? If that was his thought process, I couldn't blame him for needing some space.

The days leading up to the party passed in a blur. I found it impossible to find peace with all the crap going on with Nick. Even when attempting to force myself to think about something else, my mind always drifted back to the argument we had over the phone. There was no doubt in my mind, I had screwed up; but in the same sense, it was arguable that Nick may have overreacted as well. I mean, would it have been the end of the world to start a day later. Not to mention the fact, he didn't even bother to consider the significance of Tiffany's sweet-sixteen party. It's a once-and-a-lifetime event only missed if hospitalized or deceased—both of which were still only barely acceptable reasons.

The whole "Nick" fiasco, if it ever passed over, left me to conclude one thing: balancing relationships and friend-ships is extremely complicated. If one party is happy, it's almost a sure bet that the other is not. It almost seems like you have to be a *Zen master* in regards to balancing out your relationship scales and engineering effective ways to distribute your time proportionally. I was fully prepared to take that role on, that is, if Nick saw it in his heart to ever forgive me.

The night of the party finally arrived, but you wouldn't know it by my glum demeanor. I tried to call Nick one last time before readying myself for the party. As he had every day leading up to the party, Nick didn't bother to pick up or respond. Decked out in a new wardrobe (purchased exclu-sively for the party), I jumped on my bike and headed over to Tiffany's house. Once there, it suddenly dawned on me that I was still uncertain of how to broach the subject of us becoming an item. It was too burdensome to even think about.

Entering the backyard, like an unexpected wave crash-ing into you at the beach, I nearly lost my balance, the sheer magnitude of Tiffany's sweet-sixteen birthday bash hitting me all at once. The Kents had definitely gone all out, and then some, for the party. In charge of the entertainment was DJ Zole, a popular DJ flown in from New York. Where the volleyball court had once been was a large, newly installed dance floor, filled to capacity with hundreds of screaming teenagers. Above the dance floor, blocking out the view of the basketball court stood a huge retractable movie screen showing live footage of the party. As for the inground heated swimming pool, surrounded by a team of lifeguards, the Kents had splurged on a foam machine. Activated at varying intervals, warm foam blanketed the top layer of the pool, upwards of three to four feet in some sections. After a good spraying there'd be a bunch of hands seen sprouting out of the snow-like concoction, growing as the foam fizzled away. Naturally, as with any high-end celebration, a five-star restaurant catered the shindig and a team of photographers and videographers roamed the grounds like salivating paparazzi. To top everything else off, in addition to the countless flower and balloon displays, life-sized ice sculptures of Tiffany were scattered throughout the yard.

All in all, it was a bit much for me. Having grown up in some of the places I did, where drinking soured milk and eating around mold was the commonplace, it seemed a bit lavish to me. But I wasn't there to criticize the Kents' vision of a sweet-sixteen party. No, I was there for Tiffany. The same person I had just lost my best friend over. It took me about an hour to loosen up and forget all about my external issues, which was a much needed relief as I had been unable to focus on anything else other than my falling out with Nick. As we made the rounds (I made sure to stay close to Tiffany at all times—losing sight of her would be like dropping your wallet into a ball pit), her closest friends and relatives kept asking Tiffany the same question: "Is Zack your boyfriend?"

Every time someone uttered that sequence of words, Tiffany would shake her head and say "no," and then proceed to explain the depth of our friendship. Hearing her say that was like having slices of my heart shaved off with a rusty cheese grater. By the time she reported to her Aunt Grace that we were nothing but "best buds," I had had enough. I didn't want to be her friend any longer. I wanted more. And if Nick never did speak to me again, at least I would have something to show for it. Motivated to ask her out regardless of the outcome, I was about to take her by the hand to find a nice, quiet spot to talk, preferably an area free from the clutches of the paparazzi, when my phone buzzed.

Pulling it out of my pocket, I saw that Nick had finally ended his cruel monastic vow of silence. Relief shot through me. Was he finally ready to accept my apology? I immediately read his text message.

Nick: *YOU'RE NEVER GOING TO BELIEVE WHAT I JUST SAW! CALL ME ASAP!*

I turned to Tiffany, who was engrossed in conversation, and after unsuccessfully trying to sway her attention away, made a quick dash into the house. Once inside, hoping Nick was ready to bury the hatchet, I immediately phoned him.

"Zack, you're not going to believe what I'm about to tell you," Nick whispered into the phone.

"Nick, before you say anything, I just wanted to apologize for my—"

"Don't worry about it, Zack. I was going to call you tomorrow morning and smooth things over, anyway. I know it's a juvenile move, and I probably shouldn't have overreacted as much as I did in the first place, but I wanted you to hurt for a little bit."

"I can't blame you for that. I definitely deserved it. But still, I was in the wrong, Nick. I want you to know that

I haven't given up on 'The Project.' It's going to be grueling work, but I'm up for the challenge."

"Zack, that's all in the past now. You were wrong—I was wrong—everyone was wrong. None of that matters anymore. What I have to tell you is going to change everything."

"All right already, what is it?"

"Well, Zack, I was extremely bored at home so I decided to go ahead and make a trip over to the dig site to drop off supplies—spiting you in the process. After stowing the supplies away underneath the arms of a Norway Spruce, not far from where we planned to dig, I was about to leave when I heard a strange noise."

Norway spruce, I thought. *Does he always have to come off as such a know-it-all?*

"What kind of noise?" I asked, enraged he had gone to the dig site without me. Even if it was entirely my fault, it still stung all the same. We were supposed to go and start "The Project" together.

"I'm getting to that, Zack. Be patient. So I hear this weird creaking sound, similar to an old, rusty door opening and closing, and it freaked the hell out of me. I immediately ducked behind the thick Norway spruce, terrified beyond belief. I couldn't even fathom what the source of the noise was. Then…"

"Then what?"

"This is the part I can't wrap my neocortex around. Right in front of my eyes…I swear to God, Zack, I'm not lying to you…the ground un-earthed itself and lifted to one side."

"No way!"

"Yeah! If you're shocked, imagine how I felt—front row seat, and all. Anyways…then, as if that wasn't bizarre enough, I watched as a tall, lanky man, dressed in all black, climbed out of a hatch, closed it behind him, and then walked off into the night."

"You're messing with me, right? Payback for the party!"

"I swear, Zack. I wouldn't lie about something like that. In fact, have I ever lied to you?"

He was right about that. In all the time I had known Nick, never once had he lied to me. To teachers, his parents, Mike and Alex—but never me. He had never even lied to me in a playful manner. As crazy as his story sounded, if it was coming out of his mouth, it was true.

Realizing the implications, we had an in, excitement and fear rocketed through my system. And if this man, who Nick only described as tall, lanky and dressed in all black, was able to access the secret exit in one piece, we could do the same. There would be no digging, no breaking our backs, and above all else, no fear of hordes of the "infected," cannibalistic zombies trying to maul us. If planned and executed to perfection, we could be in and out of the lab within a span of ten minutes, capturing everything we needed on film. In the world of blowing up a conspiracy, it was a discovery of epic proportions.

"HOLY SH—"

"—IT CAN'T GET ANY BETTER THAN THIS," Nick cried into the phone. "We can blow the lid off of this place by tomorrow night if we really wanted to, Zack."

Hearing the impulsivity in Nick's voice, it suddenly dawned on me that we needed to tread as cautiously as if we were crossing alligator infested waters. Jumping in too soon could land us in jail, or possibly worse…

"Nick, we may have an easy *in*, but we need to be smart about this. Jumping in too soon can prove deadly. We need to treat this like a tactical espionage mission."

"I completely agree, Zack. We can start that tomorrow. As for tonight…"

I could almost hear the synapses firing off in his brain. Nick was about to propose something so preposterous, so impulsive—he had to be stopped. "Absolutely not! Whatever you do, Nick…do not…I repeat…do not step foot inside the cave."

"Relax, Zack! The guy's been gone for about twenty minutes. If he's headed back to town, which I'm certain he was, he won't be back for at least a couple of hours. I'm just going to pop the hatch open and take a quick look inside. That's all. It shouldn't take longer than a few minutes."

"Are you having difficulty understanding me? Under no circumstances should you do something as stupid and impulsive as what you're proposing. Just leave it alone, Nick. We can start a stakeout tomorrow morning if it makes you happy. Just please stay away from the hatch for the time being. PLEASE, NICK!"

"Zack, I'm only going to pop my head in for a few seconds and then leave. I promise."

The tone in his voice said it all. There was going to be no talking him out of it. Whether it was his OCD kicking in big time or just overwhelming curiosity, Nick wasn't going anywhere until he had a little "look-see" inside the cave. Understanding that it was futile to try—he wasn't going to change his mind—I still had to make an effort. After all, somebody had to be the voice of reason.

"What if I met you over there and stood guard while you checked it out?" I suggested, not thrilled with the idea but more comfortable if he at least had a watch out.

"My window of opportunity is now, Zack. By the time you get here, the hour or so it'll take, it'll be way too risky. It's not like the guy put up a sign on his secret hatch door, *'Be back in 2 hours.'*"

Again, Nick had a point. Right now, he had the element of surprise. Wait upwards of an hour-and-a-half and there was no way to know for sure when the guy would return. I had to think of something else to lure him away, and fast.

"Nick, if you do this and someone from inside hears you, it may blow our only chance of exposing the cover-up," I said, aiming below the belt. "How do we know there aren't others inside, and if you go and 'pop' your head in, it won't ruin everything? Even if you are able to outrun them, which is no guarantee, I'm positive they'll increase surveillance and take measures to fortify any exits—secret or not. Are you willing to risk all that just for a peek inside?"

"I'm not, Zack. And you make a great point. But..."

Oh, great, here it comes, I thought.

"...acceptance is a good thing, Zack. Take terminally ill people for instance. When they finally get to the stage of acceptance, it makes a world of difference. They accept the fact that they can't change their fate, embrace it, and move on more contently with what little life they have remaining. So...I'm asking you to accept the notion that regardless of what you say or do, I'm going to pop open that hatch door and take a look inside. Accept it, Zack."

His reference to terminally ill people didn't sit well with me; especially, knowing the potentially lethal ramifications of opening the hatch door—a Pandora's box, so to speak. The hidden dangers were unimaginable. If just one of the monsters got out, who knows the potentially catastrophic consequences of his vacuous action? My parents knew all too intimately how that story panned out.

"Nick, you do realize we can check it out tomorrow, or the day after that, or in a week, month, or even years from now. Point being, it's not going anywhere. What's the rush? Why does it have to be tonight?"

"Most people struggle with denial..."

"Will you quit it already with your stupid *stages of death* analogy? It's getting old."

"The point I'm trying to make is that there's nothing you, or anyone else for that matter, can do to change my mind. If my parents had it their way, my room wouldn't be white. Understand? If I leave without checking it out, it'll eat at me until I do. And, Zack, I can't predict what my overtired and obsessive brain will do at three-in-the-morning. It's much safer if I just get it out of my system now."

I got his point—loud and clear. His OCD, which forces him to walk around with thumbtacks inserted into the soles of his shoes, wasn't going to allow him to go anywhere until his obsession was satisfied. Realizing this, I grudgingly conceded defeat. "Okay, but hurry up. And don't do anything stupid. If anything sounds out of the ordinary, no matter how trivial or minute, get the hell out of there. You hear me, Nick?"

"I will. I'll call you as soon as I'm done. Okay?"

"Wait, you're not staying on the phone with me?"

"No, of course not. I need to completely focus on what I'm doing. If it makes you feel better, I'll keep you posted with texts."

That's better than nothing, I thought. *Although not by much.*

"All right, but I want minute by minute updates."

"I'll do my best, Zack. Talk to you soon…"

"Wait," I shouted, realizing we didn't have a contingency plan set in place. "If I can't talk to you, how will I know if something goes wrong?"

"Holy crap, Zack! I'll call or text you. And if you don't hear back from me in any facet—assume the worst and get help. Simple as that."

Yeah, as simple as that, I thought sarcastically. *Just go for help—meanwhile, you're either being mauled by zombies or interrogated by a slew of soldiers.* Nothing about this arrangement was sitting well with me. I couldn't believe he was actually going to go through with it. Feeling sick to my stomach, I grumbled, "Just make it fast!"

"I will, Zack. And if I'm lucky, and there's enough light, maybe I can snap some good shots for you. Talk to you soon, Zack…"

Nick promptly terminated the call. From there on out, our hands would do all of the talking. When it struck the two-minute mark, and still no word from Nick, panic began to set in. He had already failed to live up to his end of the bargain. Terrified that something unspeakable had occurred in the span of just 120 seconds, my fingers swept across my phone's tiny keyboard.

Zack: *Is evrythin ok? U still there?*

Nick: *Calm down, Zack. I'm just trying to figure out how to open the stupid hatch up. Give me a sec!*

His *sec* took approximately four minutes and thirty-four seconds—but who was counting? In terms of comparisons, people have run miles in less time than it took Nick to provide me with a quick status update. The gut-wrenching tension was twisting and gnawing away at my stomach.

Nick: *Okay, it's open. I can't really see anything—it's a sea of black ink inside!*

Zack: *Okay, Nick, you've had your fun, now it's time to get the hell out of there. You promised! Remember?*

Nick: *I don't hear anything coming from inside. I think the coast is clear. I'm going to take a closer look.*

"That bastard," I barked to myself. "He's going to get himself killed. I have to stop him." I immediately tried to call him, but it went straight to voicemail. I tried again with the same results. Desperate, I went back to our sole means of communication.

Zack: *Nick, shut the damn door and leave, NOW! If you step foot inside there, I'll consider it a betrayal of our friendship and never trust you again. Do you hear m*

I ran out of characters and decided to send my message as is. It was a bit harsh, threatening our friendship and all, but considering my current position, at least an hour away by bike, I had no choice. His safety was my main concern at that moment.

Nick: *Too late!!! I touched down thirty seconds ago. It's dark as hell and there's a putrid stench in the air.*

I must admit, terrified for him or not, my interest piqued. I'd never tell him this, certainly not with all the dangers involved, but I secretly didn't want him leaving that cave empty handed. I mean, he was already there—stupidly—but there. He might as well bring something home with him. I'd equate it to voyaging to the moon. Once there, you need some type of souvenir to bring back with you, even it was only a small pebble or handful of dirt.

Zack: *Nick, you've got to get the hell out. Take a quick snapshot and get your butt moving. NOW!!!*

Nick: *Wait, I think I just heard some...*

Zack: *What is it, Nick?*

Nervously waiting for a response, terror coursing through every fiber of my being, I couldn't wait another second. I needed to know what was going on.

Zack: *Come on, Nick, tell me that you're all right. Please!!!*

Eyes glued to my phone, I began to get a horrible feeling in the pit of my stomach. Why wasn't he responding to any of my messages? Something was definitely wrong.

Panicked, I began sending text message after text message to Nick before giving way to repeated phone calls. Minutes passed, the dread slowly rising with each unreturned call or text. When the ten-minute mark arrived, I knew something bad must have happened. He was either captured or...

It was in that moment I knew what needed to be done. I'd have to go out there and find him. There were no other options. Involving family and friends would be a horrendous nightmare full of criticisms, finger pointing, and raging emotions—something I didn't have the time or patience to deal with. And then there were the police. What could they do? Aside from giving me a lift there, they had no jurisdiction. If the military had Nick contained, which is what likely happened, hopefully what happened considering the gruesome alternative, they would send the cops on their merry way and, with much appreciation, take me into custody. A lose…lose…for Nick and myself. Of course, if Nick was attacked, something unbearable to even think about, their guns could definitely come in handy. Then again, what if there was a third possibility? Maybe cell phone reception was atrocious inside the cave and Nick was still investigating the secret military lab. Meaning, involving anyone else could end up being a costly false alarm. Of the three, I prayed that the latter turned out to be the case. Regardless, I had to act fast.

Panic coursing through my body, I raced into the backyard and frantically searched for Tiffany. My heart pumping steadily in my chest, a constant reminder of all the valuable seconds ticking away, Tiffany was nowhere to be found. Glancing at the time, 9:51 P.M., I contemplated leaving without saying goodbye. She'd have to understand, wouldn't she? Regardless, even if she didn't, there was no time to hunt her down. Then just as I was about to run for the exit, a crazy idea popped into my head. There was one surefire way to lure her out of the sea of partygoers.

With little time to waste, I raced over to the DJ's booth, nearly knocking several people over in the process. He ignored my initial gesture. That didn't stop me, though. I'd raid his booth if necessary. Fortunately, for his and my own sake, it didn't travel down that destructive path. He must have seen the intensity in my eyes because after attempting to shoo me away for the fifth consecutive time, he threw his headphones off and approached me. I laid my plan out for him and wasn't about to take no for an answer.

"I got you, bro," he said, with a slight nod.

After the song ended, DJ Zole hit the *mic*: "If the birthday girl would please make her way over to the DJ's booth, your friend Zack has a special gift for you."

The crowd fell silent, everyone glancing in different directions searching for Tiffany. Then, courtesy of one of the videographers—I guess the paparazzi are good for something—Tiffany's face popped onto the movie screen. The crowd erupted into a bevy of screams, whistles, and applause. Her face immediately turned crimson, and a friend had to shove her just to get her moving. I, on the other hand, didn't need a shove of my own. The second her face popped on the screen, I took off.

After reaching her, I grabbed her by the hand, a first for us, and pulled her in close to me. With all eyes on us, the videographer was catching the entire "special" moment and was televising it for all to see, I retrieved a small, fuzzy black box out of my pocket and placed it into her hand.

"Meet me out front in one minute," I whispered in her ear after kissing her cheek. "Happy birthday, Tiffany!"

"What's wrong, Zack? Is everything okay?"

I shook my head. "I don't know. I'll explain every-thing. I just need you to meet me out front." Gesturing towards the movie screen, capturing everything as it was unfolding, I added, "Now, look happy and wave to the camera."

She did as asked, allotting me the perfect opportunity to slip away unnoticed. Once out front, I nervously watched as the minutes ticked away on my phone. *What the hell is the holdup*, I thought impatiently. *Come on, Tiff, I really need to get moving!*

As if she could hear my desperate plea, Tiffany came storming out the front door looking frazzled. "Sorry," she said, apologetically. "No one would let me leave until I opened up your gift, which by the way I love. Then I had to lie to Jason...the videographer...that I had to run inside to use the bathroom. What's going on, Zack? You look troubled."

"You know my friend Nick, right?"

She nodded. "Yeah, he was with you the night we met. Why?"

"Well…he's in danger and I need to go and find him before it's too late. I wish I could elaborate more, but it's a long story and every second that ticks away could be the difference between life and death."

"Oh, my God, Zack! What's going on?"

"I'll tell you everything later. I promise. I'm sorry our night is going to end this way…especially…" I froze.

"Especially what, Zack?" she asked, edging closer to me.

I licked my lips, smiling crookedly. Without uttering another word, I leaned in and made my intentions perfectly clear. The second our lips touched, any thoughts of why I had to leave in the first place suddenly evaporated. It was as if her kiss caused a temporary amnesia of sorts, turning my brain, previously filled to capacity with panic and pure dread, into a slab of black chalkboard with only one name etched on it—Tiffany. Had the kiss lasted forever, I may never have left. Which may not have been a bad thing. However, the second her soft, warm lips that tasted of strawberries, left mine, it all came crashing back to me. Nick, my parents, the secret lab, the "infected," everything poured back into my consciousness, flooding my hippocampus with an overwhelming sense of despair.

"Especially, when I wanted to ask you to be my girlfriend," I said, gazing deeply into her eyes. "So…will you be my…"

Tiffany smiled. "Of course I will, Zack. You know how long I've been waiting for you to ask?"

"Too long," I replied, then leaned in for a second chalkboard-erasing kiss.

When we finally came up for air, 78 seconds later, Tiffany's expression turned somber. "Go, Zack! Find your friend. Please call me as soon as you can. I don't care how late it is."

"I will," I promised.

Before taking off into the night, I pulled my phone out and checked it one last time. Still no returned calls or texts. Trying to buy as much time possible for my search and rescue mission, I sent out a quick text message to Bill and Susan to let them know that I would be staying at Mike's house following the party. With all the time in the world, or at least until the following day, I took off with the intent of searching every inch of Stone Creek National Park, specifically Timmonds Rock, until I found Nick.

Chapter Eight

Finding Nick

On the brink of exhaustion, heart and lungs ready to give out, I tightened my grip and forced myself to peddle harder. Torturing my body beyond imagine, my legs and lungs burning with every peddle and deep gasp for air, nothing was going to prevent me from making it to Timmonds Rock as fast as humanly possible.

Weaving in and out of traffic, nearly ending up as road-kill on several occasions, I was in the zone. I blocked out the pain...the fear...everything. It was the only way. Like a well-trained thoroughbred, imaginary blinders blocking most of my vision, I was forced only to see the path that lay ahead of myself, nothing else. In record time, twenty-seven minutes to be exact, I made it to Warton Street, which ran parallel to Stone Creek National Park. I remembered the exact trail we used a month earlier when we scoped out the area. It was an old hiking trail, which by *design* or a lack of use, cut off a half-a-mile in. When we last visited, we traveled down the entire path before slipping into the dense wilderness.

Still burning rubber, I turned off the road and headed straight for the winding trail. In my warped mind, desperate to cut down on time, I actually believed finagling the tumultuous terrain on my bike was a good idea. I scooted past jagged rocks, tree branches jutting out from all sides, uneven grounds, and a trail that wound like a spine with severe scoliosis—all in the darkness of night. A quarter-of-a-mile in with no accidents to show for, my confidence grew. I was actually going to make it all the way to the end—an unfeasible accomplishment.

Then tragedy struck. With my eyes glued to the treacherous terrain, I rode face-first into a spiderweb. Not just a strand or two either, which I probably would have just shrugged off. No, my sweat drenched grill buried itself in a web the size of a garbage can lid. Swatting at my face with my left hand while anticipating a highly toxic and painful bite, it never occurred to me, not even for a split-second, to slow down. A disastrous mistake. Still riding at warp-speed, my bike veered off the trail, struck a huge boulder, and sent me hurling through the air like a man shot out of a cannon.

When something like that happens, you don't have time to think. You react. With my mind frozen in a per-petual state of fear, I involuntarily braced myself for the fall. Even with my hands acting as a sort of shock absorb-er, my face still crashed violently into the unforgiving earth. For the next few moments, a mini fireworks show kicked off, sending little sparks shooting all around my head. The spectacle, which didn't last very long, quickly fizzled out and was replaced by a surge of excruciating pain.

The first wave swept over my chest, where my con-fused lungs temporarily forget how to function. No air was going in or out. The best thing to do in that type of situa-tion is to try to relax and focus on taking slow deep breaths. Naturally, that's easier said than done.

Entirely focused on my breathing, or lack of it, I closed my eyes and attempted to resurrect my comatose lungs as a warm trickle of blood began coursing down the side of my head. It worked. Fresh air flooded my aching lungs, solving at least one of my current problems. Slightly disorientated from the fall and subsequent head blow, I mistook the warm trickle of blood as the poisonous eight-legged critter that got me into that predicament in the first place. I immediately sat up, and in a desperate attempt to swat it off my head, began frantically brushing and slapping at the side of my head. Eventually, after making artwork out of the side of my face, an abstract concoction of reds and browns, it finally dawned on me that there was no spider. No, what I had been feeling was a slow trickle of blood gushing from a deep gash wound above my eye.

Using my primitive knowledge of first aid, I sprang into action. My objective: cover the wound and stop the bleeding. Throwing off my blood-stained polo shirt, I removed my undershirt and began tearing it into long strands. I then rolled one of the strands up into a tight ball, placed it over the gash wound, and fashioned the longer strands around it to keep it in place. Once securely tied in place, I applied direct pressure to the wound—a painful yet necessary step. With my bandage in place, I threw my polo shirt back on and staggered to my feet.

Head throbbing, body aching, I forced myself to continue on foot. I didn't even bother stopping to check out my bike. What was the point? I wasn't getting back on it anytime soon. Keeping pressure on my head, my equilibrium slowly returning, I began picking up the pace. In a matter of minutes, I went from a slow zombie-like trudge to an all out sprint down the trail. Reaching the end of it, signaled by a massive fallen oak tree, I slowed my pace and began cautiously navigating the unsteady terrain. I'd be no good to Nick with a bum ankle.

Making the trip that much more difficult, there was a direct line from my feet straight to my brain. It almost felt like I was stepping on landmines, the pain exploding with every footstep. It was unbearable yet necessary. As much as it hurt, stopping wasn't an option. Nick needed me. In addition to the throbbing pain, it didn't take long for me to realize that my bandage wasn't doing its intended job. Hand still held in place, I could feel the cloth seeping with blood. Under different circumstances, blood loss may have been a concern; however, I was not under different circumstances. I was in a position where worrying about my own health took second precedence. When it was all said and done, I knew what was wrong with me: contusions of the face and upper torso, a deep laceration above my left eye, and a likely concussion. Nick's status, on the other hand, was a mystery I hoped to solve by the end of the night. So I kept on moving ignoring the pain, the blood loss, the jagged terrain, and the challenge of locating my destination without a map. That was the worst part. With virtually no light, it was nearly impossible to ascertain if I had gone in the right direction or not.

Having located the dig site several times during the day, it seemed as if I was headed in the right direction. Of course, if I overshot it, even by only a marginal amount, it could take hours if not longer to find it. With that possibility pulsating in my throbbing skull, I carefully scanned the area as I continued on my way. Either luck or my subconscious was on my side—I was the creator of the map, after all—because I successfully located the dig site on my first try. Standing atop the large mound of rocks we had situated above the designated tunnel site, I knew I was in the right place. Without hesitation, I quickly searched the area for the Norway Spruce Nick had spoken of—as if I even knew what a Norway spruce was—eventually finding it off to the left. It actually wasn't as hard as I thought it would be to locate. All I had to do was narrow my search to any trees that could possibly conceal Nick's bag of supplies. And with most of the trees in the area just starting to sprout that proved a rather simple task. There, tucked under its prickly branches were Nick's supplies, neatly stowed away in a large hockey bag. That solved half of the problem. There was still the issue of locating the secret hatch door.

Taking a moment to think back to Nick's description of the secret door, "the ground un-earthed itself and lifted to one side," an idea struck me. Tearing open the bag, I quickly rummaged through it in search of the perfect tool to aid my search. The pickings were slim. He had a few shovels, some garden trowels, a spade, and a...34" pickaxe. I looked no further. The pickaxe was the perfect tool. Not only was it ideal for the purposes I needed it for, but it could also serve as an effective weapon. A duel threat, so to speak.

With the pickaxe in hand, holding it by its steel head, I began thumping it against the ground listening for anything that sounded hollow or metallic. It took nearly thirty minutes of whacking away at the ground to finally locate the perfectly camouflaged hatch door. Covered with a thick layer of moss, if I didn't know it was in the vicinity, I never would have found it. Whoever constructed it—the military was my guess—did an exceptional job on it.

Nick was right. It was a pain in the ass to open. It took me close to ten minutes just to figure it out—far longer than it took Nick. Hidden in the thick overgrowth of moss was a small lever that had to be pushed up and to the side in order to unlock the door. Once unlocked, feeling the weight of the door in my hands, I yanked it open with one forceful tug. That turned out to be a horrendous mistake. The old, rusty door screeched as if in agony.

So much for the element of surprise, I thought sarcastically.

Nervous and horrified that my cover had been blown, worst of all by my own stupidity, I ran back to the spruce tree, crouched behind it, and waited. I would like to say that was all part of my master plan. You know, give it enough time for the dust to settle, that the coast is clear, before making my move. However, that wasn't the case. Not even close. Honestly, I was terrified beyond imagine. I was afraid of the military presence, the uncertainty of what had become of Nick, and most of all, I was petrified of the "infected." I was back to being that frightened little boy peeking out of the corner of the window—in this case, in-between the jagged arms of the Norway Spruce. I couldn't believe the gumption Nick possessed to go exploring the cave on his own. It was nuts.

As for me, I wanted no part of the secret lab. I previously did, but that was when it was more of a pipedream than anything else. Kind of like winning the lottery. You want it to happen, but with failure an almost guarantee, you don't get your hopes up too high. I figured we'd end up quitting sooner or later, most likely after the rocky terrain proved too much of a match for us and our pathetic digging tools. Now, presented with a way in, my body warned me against it. Starting in my stomach, a nervous energy began unraveling and stringing itself throughout my body, leaving tangled and knotted messes all along the way. It almost felt as if the nervous energy was slithering underneath the surface injecting a powerful numbing agent as it expanded, turning my tense body frigid.

Before you go and get all catatonic on me, Zack, remember one thing: NICK NEEDS YOU! A voice, my voice, screamed inside my head. It worked. Feeling began to return to my frozen extremities, readying my body for its natural fight response.

Eyes locked on the secret hatch door, ears tuned into my surroundings, I no longer worried about the "infected" causing me any problems. At least not any immediate problems. From my past dealings with *them*, they didn't strike me as the silent, patient type. Violent, unresponsive, and hungry for human meat, undoubtedly. Discreet and cunning, absolutely not. It didn't mean there weren't any in the cave. It just meant there weren't any in the vicinity surrounding the secret entrance.

As for the military personnel, there was no way to gage their intentions. Trained in restraint and tactfulness, for all I knew there was a team of soldiers just waiting for me to trespass inside the cave. At least if that turned out to be the case, I wouldn't become a nutritious meal for a hungry zombie, or whatever the heck they were.

Surmising that I had no choice but to continue, I slowly approached the hatch door and hurled the pickaxe down inside. It made a dull thud sound after striking the cave floor. I then used my phone to get a better view of the hatch door and the path that led directly into the cave. Seeing as how there were no stairs or a ladder to help ease me down, just a five-foot drop to the cave bed below, I took a slow deep breath and attempted to psych myself up.

"You can do this, Zack," I encouraged myself. "You *HAVE* to do this."

Then without giving it anymore thought, like a daring kid jumping into frigid waters, I leaped down through the narrow passage. After hitting pay dirt, I immediately crouched down, picked up the pickaxe, and poised myself in a defensive position. If anything got within a three to four foot radius of me, human or not, they were going to regret it. Nothing did, that is aside from the strong stench that was lingering in the air. It smelled like a cross between a filthy bathroom and a slaughterhouse. Still using my phone for light, I attempted to scan the area—attempted being the operative word. My phone was great for many things: scanning the web, texting, making and watching videos, taking pictures, and was even an effective alarm clock. What it sucked at, aside from eating away at my monthly allowance and getting me in trouble at school, was using it for something it just wasn't—a flashlight. That said, it did a reasonable job of illuminating the general area around me, five to six feet in diameter. Beyond that, there was a thick fog-like blanket of black surrounding me on all sides.

Glancing up through the open hatch door, the darkness not quite as thick as it was down inside the cave, I fully understood the allure of going to the light. I wanted to as well. But as much as my body craved it, needed it, I was there for a reason. I needed to find out what had become of Nick. Good or bad, hopefully the former, I wasn't going anywhere until his whereabouts were known. Like I had pushed myself getting there, riding my mountain bike faster than it had ever been ridden before, I had to push myself again. This time on foot and through a cloud of darkness filled with unimaginable dangers.

As I took my first few steps forward, sweat leaking out of my pores like a dripping faucet, my stomach lurched, my heart rate accelerated, and my breathing suddenly became labored. I blocked the discomfort out as much as possible and continued moving forward, always poised to strike with my trusty pickaxe. The cave was so quiet all I could hear was the echo of my deep exhalations. From memory, I recalled that the cave wound to the right after about fifty feet, where it then ballooned out like a python after a large meal. Figuring it would be easier to use the wall as a guide, I ran the back of my clammy fingers (the hand holding the pickaxe) across its rough, chilled surface slowly making my way deeper and deeper into the bowels of the cave. Just as expected, the wall began to wind towards the right.

Then, terrified of something lunging at me, my eyes began darting back and forth, up and down, but never as low as my feet. Big mistake. Squinting, studying the inky blackness, I inadvertently kicked something solid, yet seemingly hollow. Scrambling to see what my foot had struck, I carelessly swung my hand sharply to the right, crashing it into the jagged wall. Two things happened next: my hand stung with pain, and after losing control of my phone, which instantly disappeared into the engulfing black fog, I was cast into darkness.

I began panicking. "Please don't be broke! Please! I can't lose you now. Not here, not now."

Panic-stricken and on the verge of a meltdown, I dropped down onto my hands and knees, gently placed the pickaxe beside my foot for safekeeping, and began feeling around the cave floor my phone. Moments later, my hand brushed against the object I had likely struck with my foot. Upon further inspection, it felt smooth and round, and although I had an inkling as to what it was, I tried my hardest to push those thoughts out of my head. I had more pressing matters to attend to—my phone. Still on my hands and knees, swirling up clouds of dust in the process, my fingers finally brushed against a slick surface. Lying completely facedown, the moment I picked it up, a bubble of dim light illuminated the area around me, allowing me to catch my first glimpse of the object my fingers had caressed only moments earlier.

A deep chill ran down my spine staring into the dark pits where eyes once rested. I couldn't believe it. Leering blankly at me was an actual human skull. I wanted to bolt for the exit and never look back. Probably should have, but I didn't. The deadening silence of the cave told me to press forward and find Nick. There was nothing to worry about any longer because, if there was, it would have gotten me already. The simple fact remained that the "infected" didn't strike me as the calculating type that could remain hidden in the shadows waiting for the perfect opportunity to pounce. No, they were the polar opposite, they'd charge at you head on with the ferocity of a rabid grizzly bear.

After taking a few deep breaths to calm my nerves, using my pickaxe as a crutch, I slowly rose to my feet and began moving on, this time with my eyes stitched to the ground. I made it another ten feet before spotting another gravely site—an entire torso wearing what remained of a withered blouse, bones gleaming through the tattered holes. I cautiously stepped over the headless remains, determined to continue pressing forward. Venturing on, there were more and more gruesome discoveries lying in wait. Eventually, it got to the point where walking around the carcasses was unavoidable, and the only way to press forward was by navigating the grossly unsteady terrain. Bones cracked and crumbled under my 150-pound frame as I made my way further and further into, conveniently enough, the belly of the cave. I tried not to stare, out of both respect and fear, but like a horrific accident, it was unavoidable. Ranging in all different sizes (the smallest just breaking two feet in length), tattered remnants of clothes hanging off most of them, and matted hair pooled all around them like sprouting fungi, the sheer amount of skeletal remains was haunting. Some sections of the cave were so thick with death, it was impossible to see the ground below. Most of the remains had completely decomposed; however, there were a few still in the process, accounting for the atrocious stench. Those were the toughest to look at. Aside from the decaying, greenish-black flesh, that almost appeared charred, maggots were busy devouring what was left of the carcasses.

Staring at all that death beneath my feet, Nick's outlook was looking grimmer and grimmer. I no longer worried about the "infected," as there was nothing to worry about. I had an inkling of what was really going on in the cave. Placed inside Timmonds Rock to conceal their existence, experimented on, and ultimately slaughtered, the "infected" were the least of my concerns. No, what I now had to worry about was the military and their apparent cover-up. An operation like this doesn't stay a secret for as long as it has without extensive effort. And anyone who is stupid enough to stumble across it may pay dearly for that mistake. Yet as meek as that outlook was, I trudged forward anyway, holding onto a quickly fading hope that Nick was still alive. If that were the case, and I prayed it was, maybe, just maybe, I could possibly catch the military by surprise and rescue Nick in the process. In the movies, it always seemed to work. If the protagonist has a sliver of a chance at saving the day, no matter how minute or implausible, everything always seems to work out in the end. Understanding real life is much different from the fictional world of movies, it at least provided me with hope—something that was in short supply.

Continuing to navigate the unsteady graveyard, I came to a stop after climbing a mass of skeletal remains three feet in height—forever pinned against a barricade of steel prison bars. Feeling the cold metal in my hand, I glanced down and saw bony arms poking through the bars. Maybe they hadn't been executed after all and had just been left to slowly die in their hellish dungeon. I'd never know for sure, but it seemed a likely scenario.

Following the path of the thick steel bars, I located the sturdy cell door a few feet over to my left. I yanked, pulled, and pushed the door in all directions, all to no avail. It wouldn't budge. Visibility almost nothing, it was barely possible to make out what looked like a cooler door slightly to the right and a steel door just ahead. I tried the cell door one more time before giving up. If Nick hadn't been caught, he had to be somewhere on this side of the cave, possibly camouflaged in the sea of death. Who knows, maybe he tripped over something—a skull perhaps—and knocked himself out. It was certainly possible. Heck, it almost happened to me.

Reserved to inspect the rest of the cave with utmost care, I turned around just as a bright spotlight suddenly turned on above the steel door. Terror ripped through me, surging my body with its natural flight response. Adrenaline working its way to my legs, readying them, prepping them for flight, I dug in, bones cracking beneath my feet, and took off. Sprinting over the uneven terrain, I made it a solid ten feet before tragedy struck. How it happened exactly, I'm not sure. All I know is that I tripped and fell face first into the government's secret bone-yard.

Amazingly, I wasn't seriously injured. Scraped up and terrified, but overall relatively healthy and intact. No gaping wounds resulted from that fall, at least. That didn't mean the fall didn't present a major problem for me and my ploy to get my butt out of the cave. You see, the fall stirred up a waft of dust and bone particles directly into all of my facial orifices. I immediately began gagging, more so with the realization of what foul substances coated the insides of my mouth, nostrils, and eyes. The taste reminded me of the last time I had dental work. Dr. Morris, a man with steady hands and no bedside manner, drilled the crap out of one of my rear molars, sending miniscule tooth fragments all over the inside of my mouth. I remember it taking four gargling sessions just to rid myself of the microscopic tooth fragments.

As nasty as it tasted, my mouth was the least of my concerns. My eyes burning and welling with tears, I began rubbing them incessantly. It didn't help. All it did was push around the now gelatinous gook from one side to the other. In an ideal world, a good rinsing is what my eyes needed. Unfortunately, it wasn't an ideal world, and all I had was the inside of my quickly becoming ragged "new" polo shirt. Sometimes you have to work with what you have. I hoisted myself onto my knees and began using the inside of my shirt to rub my eyes. That was around the time my other problem kicked in. Dust circulating around, and irritating your nasal cavity is never, and I repeat never, a good thing. The storm came out of nowhere, sending a concoction of saliva, dirt, bone particles, and snot in all directions. It was a sneezing fit of epic proportions. Six...seven...eight...nine...sneezes in a row with no signs of slowing down. The volleyball incident paled in comparison. I was beginning to close in on Carlos Perez's (a sickly kid with whom I used to room with) record of 23 straight sneezes. I previously thought that number couldn't be topped. I no longer shared that opinion.

Slightly disoriented from my body's volatile reaction to the irritants, I found myself more focused on my body's overwhelming response mechanism rather than the terrifying fact that a light had switched on. There's no good that can come from a light switching on, especially when you're trespassing inside a highly secretive military base. Still blinded and sneezing uncontrollably, up to 15 at that point, I jumped to my feet with plans of stumbling through the cave, impaired vision or not.

"There's no point in trying to run," a gravelly voice shouted from behind. "It's too late for that."

I turned in the direction of the voice, and painful or not, peeled my eyes open. The intense light from the spotlight felt like someone had taken a razor blade to my over-dilated pupils.

16...17...18...19...my sneezes raged on.

Not wanting to make any sudden moves, I had no idea if a gun was trained on me or not, I desperately struggled to regain control over my eyes. The sneezing was incredibly annoying, but the lack of vision was debilitating. I couldn't do anything. That crippling problem had to be corrected, and fast. It was a painstaking task, one not without its worries, I nearly poked my eyes out several times from the sneezes, but I stuck with it and was finally able to force the rest of the goo out of my eyes. It took another few moments for my eyes to begin adjusting to the sudden change in lighting.

20...21...22...then nothing.

The storm passed, stopping at a whooping 22—one shy of Carlos' record.

Vision slowly coming into focus, albeit still a little hazy, I caught my first glimpse of the man. Silhouetted in the piercing spotlight, stood a tall, dark figure, arms crossed as if it was no big surprise to find me snooping around inside the cave. His mangy hair stuck out in all different directions, presenting him with a disheveled, eerie appearance, reminiscent of a mad scientist. Leering at me like a ravenous vulture, my trembling body begged me to flee. It wanted me to run and never look back. But I couldn't do that to Nick, could I?

"Did you come searching for your friend?" he asked coldly talking a few steps towards the cell door.

Oh, my God, I cried to myself, *he's done something to Nick.*

"H-h-h-ave y-you seen him?" I asked nervously.

"If you are referring to a young man named, Nicholas Tinderson, then the answer is, yes."

"W-w-hat have you d-d-done with him?"

"Come closer, will you. I see that you have something wrapped around your head. What is that?"

Why was he so curious about my bandage? You know what, it didn't matter. What did matter was the fact that he knew where Nick was, and I was going to make sure that the police sorted everything out. I mean what else was there for me to do? My only weapon was the element of surprise, which was clearly blown.

I shook my head. "I'm n-n-not coming any c-closer. It's j-j-just a b-bandage. Why?"

"From where I'm standing it looks pretty bad, possibly infected. Therefore, why don't you come a little closer, let me take a look at it. I am a doctor, after all."

A doctor! What kind of physician could he possibly be? Honestly, I didn't care to find out. "P-p-please tell me what happened to m-my friend, Nick!"

"It seems as if you two have a great deal in common," he said, pointing towards my head, a blackened, jagged fingernail looking like a sharp talon on the end of his long, slender finger. "I came back from a stroll through the woods to find him incapacitated on the ground. He took quite a whack to the head, you know. So severe he's still unconscious. As you can see," he waved his long arms around gesturing at all of the skeletal remains, "I can't exactly call for help, now can I?"

His story seemed plausible enough. Not only did he fit Nick's description to a *T*, but his reasoning also made a great deal of sense. After all, he was clearly an active participant in a massive cover-up that would shock the world if ever uncovered. He probably also had the authority to maintain that secret—regardless of the collateral damage. I should have run for the exit right then and there. Instead, like a complete idiot, reminiscent of Nick's reckless endeavor that got me into this mess to begin with, I edged closer to him. Standing only a few yards from him, I caught my first real glimpse of the creepy doctor.

Standing a towering 6'3", the tall, slender man was dressed in all black, from his old, weathered shoes to his raggedy lab coat. He appeared to be anywhere from his early to late forties, impossible to decipher with all of the grime and bushy facial hair covering his pale, white face. His salt and pepper matted hair, which was pointed in all different directions, looked as if it hadn't been washed in months, possibly years. He had cold, dark eyes that seemed as lifeless as a black slab of coal. Careening down the side of his face, starting from above his left eyebrow, was a long, jagged scar, nearly six inches in length. As appalling as his general appearance was, there was an unbearable stench permeating from him. It smelled unhealthy and putrid, as if he had basked in the decaying mess beneath my feet.

"Don't mind my appearance, young man. I was having issues with the sewage system. And…as lead scientist and only occupant…caretaking unfortunately falls on me, whether I like it or not. It was the primary reason I went for a short walk through the woods. You know…to get some *fresh air*…"

"W-who are you?"

"Well, young man, I am Dr. Arthur Voxolomin. Dr. Vox for short."

Chapter Nine

Dr. Vox

Gesturing towards the mass of bones and decomposing bodies, I asked him bluntly, "S-s-so what now?"

Dr. Vox folded his arms. "You and your friend have put me in a precarious situation. No one is supposed to know about this place. NO ONE!"

That didn't sound good. Glancing over my shoulder, the thought crossed my mind once again to make a break for it. Dr. Vox appeared to be in good shape, could probably run for days, but deep down, I knew I could outrun him. And even if I couldn't, the woods would neutralize any speed or stamina advantage he may have had over me. With endless places to hide, all I needed to do was beat him out of the cave, and I'd be home-free. And, if for some unforeseen reason I wasn't able to outrun him, there was always the pickaxe. Lying on its side, a good fifteen feet from where I was standing, retrieving it would be no problem. I could probably have it in my hands before Dr. Vox was even able to pass through the cell door.

"I won't say any—"

"Shhhhhh—" he said, placing a stained red finger up to his lips. "That's what everyone says. But it's a rarity that someone holds up their end of the bargain."

"Is that b-blood on your hand?"

Quickly glancing at his finger, Dr. Vox wiped his hand off on his raggedy lab coat. "Like I mentioned before, your friend suffered a substantial head injury. He was bleeding quite profusely, so much that applying direct pressure was absolutely necessary. I just haven't gotten around to cleaning myself up as you can see."

"I promise I won't say anything!"

"It's too late for that, Zachary, or would you prefer Zack?"

He knows my name, I thought, terror ripping through me. *How could he possibly...*

"I can see that you're racking your brain trying to figure out just how I know your name..."

I was.

"Deductive reasoning. I found your friend Nick's phone lying on the ground and read through all of his texts. I didn't mean to impinge on his privacy, but you must understand the complexities of this particular situation. After all, it is my responsibility to maintain the security of this place. If anyone and I mean ANYONE, finds out about this place, it's my neck on the line. Which brings me to my next question. May I ask how you and your friend were able to find this place? It's not exactly on the grid—if you know what I mean."

"Just stumbled across it," I lied.

"You have to do better than that, Zack. Why don't we just be honest with each other? There's no point in keeping lies behind these walls," he said, waving his arms all around. "Fair enough?"

"All right," I said, reluctantly. Things couldn't get any worse telling the truth, could they? "When Nick was younger he inadvertently witnessed a 'drop off.' He saw those…those…people, if you can even call them that, escorted inside this very cave. We just wanted to scope the place out—honestly. We never really believed we would be able to find a way inside. But…"

"You did find a way in, didn't you?"

I nodded. "Yeah, but none of that matters anymore. I just want to find Nick and get the hell out of here. You have my word, I won't say anything."

Dr. Vox ran his filthy hands through his unkempt beard before reaching into his pocket. *A gun*, I thought, *HE'S REACHING FOR A GUN.* Eyes locked on his every movement, my heart nearly skipped a beat when he yanked his hand out holding something large and metallic. I breathed a sigh of relief after noticing that it wasn't a gun. It was a large, bronze Folger Adam key.

"Now, I'm going to open up this door and I need you to promise me that you won't do anything stupid. I'm not making any promises, but if you help me out with your friend, maybe…just maybe…I'll let the both of you go. If anyone else had been here," Dr. Vox shook his head with a blank stare, "you'd never see your family again. Are we clear?"

I nodded, horrified at that nightmarish revelation.

"As you can see this place isn't as *lively* as it used to be. There hasn't been an outbreak for quite some time now, and aside from my continued research, this place is essentially shutdown. If I do decide to let you and your friend go, which I haven't made up my mind about yet, just know there is a contingency plan set in place. This entire cave is rigged with explosives, ready to wipe out any evidence that this place ever existed. If anyone…and I mean anyone…ventures over to these parts, I'll have no choice but to ignite. The government agency I work for won't mind a few casualties to maintain this highly classified operation."

Glancing down at a severed limb, crawling with maggots, something wasn't adding up. How long was *"quite some time now,"* in Dr. Vox's world? Days… weeks…months…years? There was no way to know for sure. Then again, I knew virtually nothing about the infection so who was I to talk. Maybe the "infected" were just like the zombies from the movies, where the only way to kill one of them was through severe trauma to the monster's brain. If that were the case, maybe the still decomposing bodies were Dr. Vox's last batch of test subjects. Regardless, none of that mattered any longer. What did was getting out of the cave alive and doing everything in my power to prevent it from disappearing off the map.

"When you said you needed help with Nick. What did you mean by that?" I asked, returning to my main concern.

Dr. Vox then jabbed the Folger Adam key into the keyhole and turned it sharply to the left. "Your friend isn't doing too well. He will have to stay here as long as it takes for him to fully recover—something that may never happen, Zack. I don't mean to be overly direct and sound cold, but your friend is in critical condition. He will need round-the-clock care, something I cannot do alone."

"What if I just took him out of your hair and carried him to the nearest hospital? I promise, I won't say anything about this place. And when Nick wakes up, I'll make sure he does the same!'"

"It's not that easy, Zack. Aside from the particulars regarding his currently incapacitated state, of which there are many, it'd go against my Hippocratic Oath to allow him to leave in such a critical state." Dr. Vox suddenly swung the cell door open and gestured for me to enter. "Now, I don't want this to sound threatening, which it is, but I'll need you to accompany me. If you were to make a break for it, be warned, I'll have no choice but to obliterate this place. I don't think either of us wants that to happen, now do we?"

I shook my head. He had me by the…well, you know. And he knew it too. My only prayer at that moment was for him to reconsider and let us both go. "Okay," I said taking a step towards him, "anything you say."

"Excellent, Zack, but, first thing first, I'll need your phone. I cannot risk having it traced. You understand, don't you?"

I nodded, then realized after putting my hand in my pocket that it wasn't there. It must have fallen out of my hand when I tumbled into the sea of the death. It couldn't be far from where the…*pickaxe* was lying. Oh, how the pickaxe could solve everything. One perfectly executed swing and my nightmare would be over. He could blow this cave to high heaven and it wouldn't matter as long as Nick and I were able to escape. Of course, without knowing where he kept the trigger, it could be on his person for all I knew. It was a move far too risky to take.

"Hold on a second, I need to find it. I must have dropped it when I fell."

"Hurry," he replied impatiently.

Assuming it was in the same general vicinity of the pickaxe, I ran over towards it—the handle almost calling my name—and began searching for my phone. With the bright spotlight illuminating most of the cave, casting ghostly shadows here and there, I found my phone with relative ease. Crouching down to pick it up, my hand brushed against a jagged bone the size of a large screwdriver. Part of a lower arm or leg, it was hard to decipher which, the bone's sharp edge looked as if it could do substantial damage if stabbed in just the right place. It wasn't the pickaxe, but it was something.

Simultaneously grabbing the jagged bone and cell phone, I tentatively rose to my feet, and discreetly slid the bone underneath the inside of my shirtsleeve, carefully holding it in place with my middle and ring fingers. Then, feeling slightly better, defenseless no more, I turned around and approached Dr. Vox. "Here, you go," I said, tossing my phone over to him.

"Thank you," he replied politely, his decaying, black teeth in stark contrast to his pale, ivory skin. He then took the phone and immediately dismantled it, placing the battery in an opposite pocket than the rest of the phone. "Follow me," he said, waving his still bloodstained red hand.

Trailing several feet behind (the putrid stench permeating from Dr. Vox made it impossible to follow any closer), I nearly puked in my mouth after inhaling a strong waft of his vile scent. Consciously or not, after that repulsive shock to my system, I stopped breathing through my nose altogether. Sadly, that didn't solve the problem. With each nauseatingly, rancid breath inhaled, a rank aftertaste coated my mouth. My stomach twisting and turning, like a terrified seal in the presence of a starved polar bear, I began holding my breath for long stretches, only coming up for air when absolutely necessary. Before reaching the steel door, stationed directly under the spotlight, I took notice of the highly secured vault-like door. Staring at its complicated locking system, it suddenly dawned on me that the secret hatch door, located in the rear of the cave, had been left unlocked. That seemed strange. With all the secrets and damning evidence hidden inside Timmonds Rock, leaving it unlocked seemed highly risky. So why had it been? Had it purposely been left unlocked and was all part of Dr. Vox's master plan to eliminate both threats if the moment presented itself?

He must have known I would come looking for Nick, I thought, nervous tremors erupting all over my body. If so what was his exit strategy if I had gone straight to the police? Would he have fled the lab and waited until he was far enough away to blow the mountain into smithereens— incinerating anyone in the blast radius. As crazy as it was to think, coming alone might have been the smartest move I made all night.

Chapter Ten

The Lab

Stepping inside the lab, it became immediately apparent that the place had seen better days. As if a mini tornado swept through the 20 by 20 room, there were papers, dust, computer towers, medical supplies, monitors, security cameras, and glass strewn all over the floor. Nearly everything in the room was damaged in some type of fashion. In fact, the only item still standing was a grimy, dented steel table covered with stacks of weathered notebooks, slides, and a powerful microscope. On each side of the room stood tall steel doors, conveniently labeled with braille for the visually impaired, leading into the infirmary (straight ahead), the barracks (off to my left), and the holding cells/experimentation room (just to my right).

"I have your friend stationed in the infirmary. I apologize for the mess, I don't get many visitors and my work has been quite frustrating. I'm aware it's a bit childish, but in recent months I've become extremely volatile towards this place."

Hearing about his temper was worrisome. If he could do that to a room—what's there to say he wouldn't do it to a curious young man looking for his "lost" friend? Massaging the end of the jagged bone, fingers caressing the splintered end, I wasn't above using my makeshift shank in defense—a broad area in my opinion. If at any moment, Dr. Vox's actions were viewed as overtly aggressive, I'd have no choice but to react. After all, throwing the first punch sometimes works out for the best. Sometimes not—it got me into this entire mess if you really thing about it.

Keep him talking, I encouraged myself. *Remember to listen carefully to monitor his mental state. Working down in this abyss of death must have taken its toll on him. You don't want to end up looking worse than his lab, do you?*

"Didn't you mention that there hasn't been an outbreak for quite a while now?" I asked to get a sense of his mood.

"I did, but my work's not done yet. Won't be until a cure's discovered. Till then, I'm stuck in this place with nothing to do but search for a cure, or a means to treat, a seemingly untreatable virus. Over time, it can really *eat* away at a person's brain."

"If there hasn't been any new outbreaks, couldn't they just shut this place down and stick you in some fancy lab?"

Dr. Vox stopped and glared at me.

Uh-oh! I thought. *Now you pissed him off! Maybe keeping him talking isn't the smartest idea.*

To my relief, Dr. Vox wasn't angered. Instead, he let out a short-winded chuckle, the type of laughter Ms. Maddows often released when a student asked a question so stupid, so illogical, all she could do was laugh. "I wish...but without a viable cure or treatment...this place will never shut down. And because of that, someone has to be responsible for it. Turns out—like it or not—that person is me. Now, come on, let's hurry. I need to check your friend's vitals."

THE BOMB, THE BOMB, THE BOMB, I screamed to myself. *Find out more about the bomb. What kind of trigger mechanism does it have? And furthermore, where the hell does he keep it?*

"H-how devastating will the explosion be? I mean, what type of range are we talking about?"

Grabbing hold of the doorknob leading into the infirmary, Dr. Vox turned to me and stared through me with his soulless black eyes. "Quite significant," he said poignantly. "This place is rigged with enough explosives to incinerate everything within a half-mile radius. Within a mile-and-a-half radius trees will uproot and any animals in the area will die immediately from the blast force. If it comes to that, trust me, Zack, there will be nothing left of this place."

"What about you?" I asked, hoping to lure him into talking more about the trigger mechanism. "How could you possibly set it off and get away in time?"

"The trigger is portable. However, in the event I am unable to flee and destroy the evidence in time, I'll have to...well, I'm pretty sure you get the point..."

"Go down with the ship," I mumbled.

"Right, you are. Now, I must warn you, like the lab, the infirmary has seen better days. I cleaned up a small area for your friend, but that was about all. I have him hooked up to some of the monitors and devices I was able to salvage from my last outburst. For the time being, he has everything he'll need to fully recover. That is, as long as there are no complications. But let's not think about that right now."

Dr. Vox then swung the door open and gestured for me to enter. Passing him, a waft of his stench assaulted my senses—sending my stomach lurching and saliva pooling in my mouth. Not wanting to make a scene, I resisted the urge to vomit. Once inside the dimly lit room, its only source of light coming from a flickering florescent bulb hanging from the ceiling, it was easy to see that the infirmary was in comparable shape, if not more worse off than the lab. There were medical supplies, IV poles, broken glass, medical records, curtains, vital signs monitors, defibrillators, colostomy bags, catheters, computers, and various other machines damaged and scattered all across the dusty cement floor. On both sides of the room rested fifteen steel restraint tables, each spaced a solid ten feet from the one adjacent to it. Of all of the tables, the one located far off in the right corner of the room had a dark red curtain surrounding it.

"Your friend's on that table over there," he said, pointing towards the only one with a curtain draped around it. "Go see for yourself."

As I approached the table, the faulty lighting added a more dramatic and creepy effect to the room. Similar to a strobe light in a haunted house, the flickering light made everything seem as if it was happening in slow motion— and maybe it was—I was moving so cautiously through the infirmary. Glancing over my shoulder, I was relieved to see that Dr. Vox was at a safe distance, sluggishly trailing a few feet behind. In fact, it was actually preferable. With him, and his god wretched stench, trailing at least five feet behind, I was finally able to overcome the sensation to puke.

Cautiously maneuvering through the room, studying the sturdy metal tables as I passed, thoughts of being restrained to one of those tables sent chills bulleting through my body. From the looks of it, with the safety of the scientists in mind, the now dangling restraint straps were designed to keep movement at a minimum. There were thick restraint straps that went around each foot and knee, each wrist and elbow, the entire midsection, chest, and a padded one for the neck. The only thing missing on the table was space for a bedpan. However, judging by the abundance of colostomy bags and catheters scattered about the floor, there must not have been any "so called" bathroom breaks. It must have been a nightmare to live out your remaining days on one of those tables. I'm not an advocate of suicide, never have been, but in that type of situation a bottle of booze and pills sure beats out the alternative. It was unknown what types of heinous experiments were conducted on the "infected," and frankly, I didn't care to find out. My curiosity died the second Nick went missing. My only concern at that moment was getting him, and myself, out of that god-forsaken place in one piece. If it meant pulling up some chairs next to Nick's table, playing cards with the creepy and rank smelling doctor, so be it. I'd stay down in that hellhole as long as it took for the both of us to make it out alive.

Sliding my hand (the one armed with the shank) in front of me to conceal it from Dr. Vox, I allowed the bone to descend down into the palm of my hand. Tightening my grasp around the shank, I was prepared to use it if absolutely necessary. "Please be okay, Nick," I whispered to myself drawing closer and closer to the curtain. Heart racing at a dangerous pace, I glanced back and and locked eyes with Dr. Vox. Staring at me intently, it looked as if his icy, dark eyes penetrated my soul. Returning my gaze to the curtain, I noticed that there were small, circular droplets of blood splattered all over the floor surrounding the table. It was a disconcerting sight, blood always is; nevertheless, if Dr. Vox's story rang true, the blood spatters could have originated from Nick's head injury.

There's no turning back now, Zack. You have to do this, I thought reaching for the curtain. *Everything's going to be okay. He's just in a bad spot right now, but he'll get better. I know he will. We're going to get through this...*

Taking in a deep inhalation, my fingers tugged at the curtain, slowly pulling it aside. After only sliding the curtain over a foot or two, I suddenly stopped, frozen in fear. It took a moment for my brain to process what it was seeing. There, lying only a few feet from me was an almost unrecognizable fleshy mass, mutilated from head to toe. I say "almost" because I knew with a 100% certainty that it was Nick's ravaged corpse lying on the bloodied table. How it was possible to identify a faceless carcass? That was the easy part. With his blood-soaked clothes ripped to shreds and his body mauled as if he had been devoured by a pack of hungry wolves, all it took was one glance at his footwear to know it was him. There poking out of the soles of his blood-stained sneakers were those stupid metal thumbtacks.

As traumatizing as Nick's death was, there was no time to mourn his passing. Cast into a dire situation, I had to act fast just to save my own hide. I turned to my left just as Dr. Vox was in the process of swinging a long retractable baton at my head. My reflexes springing to life, my arms shot up in an attempt to thwart the attack. It partially worked. My head was still intact, but that didn't mean my body escaped unscathed. Crashing painfully into my raised arms, the momentum of the blow sent me wheeling backwards where my body bounced off the steel table and fell to the floor. Remarkably, my arms (in particular my left forearm), absorbed *most* of the impact. I say "most" because the baton still managed to strike my left ear, inducing a disorienting tuning fork-like ringing in my head.

In total survival mode, instincts and adrenaline completely taking over, I attempted to hurl my body underneath the massive steel table for protection. Dr. Vox wasn't having any part of that. Slithering underneath the table, Dr. Vox was more than ready with his instrument of destruction. He slammed the baton violently into my left calf, sending lightning bolts of pain radiating up and down my body. Screaming in agony, my legs shot under the table faster than a frightened turtle retreating inside its shell.

My leg and arm writhing in pain, I found myself tucked in the fetal position praying for a miracle. Staring up at the slab of steel above my head, I at least had one thing working for me. The metal examination table, which currently housed the corpse of my best friend, was moderately spacious. Lying directly beneath it, with the bottom shelf approximately two-and-a-half feet from the ground, there was roughly three feet of space all around me. Unless he got down on his hands and knees, the baton was at least neutralized for the time being. If he wanted to give it another go with the baton, he'd have to drag my kicking, punching, biting, and scratching body out to do so. Hurt or not, I had no intentions of making it easy on him.

Eyes glued to Dr. Vox's decrepit, old shoes, a long, yellowed toenail popping out from a sizable hole, it suddenly dawned on me that my shank was gone. Even if the jagged bone was pathetic at best, it was still a weapon. I guess when you're faced with a life-or-death situation, even the most primitive of weapons can still give you comfort of mind. It's kind of like the puncher's chance in boxing. Even if a fighter is clearly outclassed in every way, there's always that one miniscule chance to score a knockout. With my weapon nowhere in sight, all signs pointed to an abrupt, vicious knockout.

With my optimism waning—how the hell was I going to get out of this mess?—I couldn't help but to feel powerless. There was no way I'd survive the night. How could I? He had every conceivable advantage. He was bigger, stronger, and because of my leg, faster. The only thing going for me was my rapidly thumping pulse, meaning I was still alive, and even if the odds were stacked against me, there was a chance, however small, of making it through my nightmarish ordeal.

Understanding that outrunning him was impossible, my leg wouldn't allow for it, baiting him was my only option. If I could just get him down to my level, a well-executed kick to the neck, jaw, or groin could give me the upper hand long enough to find another weapon or steal the baton away from him. It was a long shot, but worth a try. Were there any other options? If there were, I couldn't think of any.

Still cradled in the fetal position, I rocked myself onto my back and trained my eyes on his feet. With my knees hoisted to my chest, I envisioned myself unleashing a barrage of deadly kicks into Dr. Vox's mangy face. If he even did so much as peak under the table, he was going to get it.

Eyes zeroed in on his feet, I made sure to follow his every movement. If he went left, I went left. If he went right, I went right. Regardless of his direction, one thing was constant. I was always poised to strike on a moment's notice. My head still ringing, as if I was submerged in water, I heard a faint, distorted voice off in the distance. Desperate to regain my hearing, I jabbed my finger into my left ear and began using it like a plunger.

While fingering my ear, I heard the same muffled voice again followed by a piercing metallic *clang*, coming from directly above my head. Though the words evaded me, it was easy to decipher the origins of the deafening sound. Dr. Vox was pounding on the steel table with his fists, the baton, or possibly a combination of the two. The tremors rattled the steel table, sending hellish chills tearing through my body. Would it really be possible to stop that monster with a few leg kicks? My confidence rapidly dwindling, I tried to filter out those negative thoughts as much as possible as Dr. Vox continued slamming on the top of the steel table with enough force to rattle the entire table.

Finally, after another minute or two of Dr. Vox carrying on like a lunatic, the ringing began to subside. And as if I was listening to the radio on its lowest volume, I was finally able to hear what he had been saying. Over and Over, in-between vicious blows to the table, Dr. Vox screamed for me to come out from underneath the table. He vowed that if I didn't listen to him, in lieu of a quick and relatively painless death, he promised he'd take his time with me. Considering both options were vastly unappealing, okay admittedly, one more undesirable than the other, I chose to stay put. If Dr. Vox was going to take his time with me. He was going to have to work for it.

"You ANGER me, Zack," he yelled. "I'm giving you the opportunity to die a quick, relatively pain-free death, and you still choose the highly unpleasant and regrettable alternative. If you continue to antagonize me, I'll have no choice but to give you the hell you deserve."

Dr. Vox then began pacing back and forth. "Out of curiosity, Zack," he continued, "have you ever been privy to witnessing a chimp mauling a human. What am I thinking? Of course you've never watched such a rare and wonderful occurrence. I'm sure you've heard stories about how gruesome their attacks can be. Chimps are wonderful pets when young—almost like little people. And like people, they change as they age. Some stay friendly. Some get real, real mean—especially after reaching puberty. I've heard countless tales of chimpanzees mauling people, tearing and biting off fingers...toes...limbs...noses...large chunks of flesh...and even genitalia. Yes, Zack, they target some of our most sensitive areas. You understand where I'm going with this, don't you?"

It was loud and clear what he was getting at. If Nick's mutilated corpse was any indication of what the crazy doctor was capable of, Dr. Vox fully intended on pushing my pain tolerance to the brink—and then some. If he managed to catch me, my worst imaginable fear, Nick's bloodied corpse was going to look like a paper-cut compared to what would be in store for me.

"I actually viewed a video of a chimp mauling," he added, tapping the bottom shelf with his baton. "It started off kind of humorous, almost like a gag. There was this balding, middle-aged man wearing a birthday hat, carrying a cake through a chimpanzee sanctuary. The silent footage, which was grainy and out of focus at times, added to the comical effect. Think Benny Hill, minus the music, if you even who that is. Well, to make a long story short, the cake goes flying, the party hat gets bloodied, and the man loses his face amongst other appendages. Unfortunately for Coco's sake, Coco was the chimpanzee in case you're wondering, workers at the sanctuary gunned him down before he could finish what he started."

Dr. Vox then walked clear to the other side of the restraint table. As if I was a clock, I swiveled, keeping my feet always poised to go on the offensive. "You know something, Zack? Coco and I are a lot alike. We have an innate need to cause bodily harm. But don't be mistaken, Zack. Where Coco failed to get the job done—I won't. You see, the man lived. Probably wished he hadn't, but he did. Now let's be real, Zack. We can do this the humane way or...the not so humane way..."

Okay, to be fair, out of the two undesirable choices, the quick painless death was by far the more appealing option. My body was sure to be ravaged, just as Nick's had, but at least it would take place postmortem. Resigned to keep quiet, I refrained from responding to him. Judging by his mannerisms, my vow of silence appeared to be getting under his skin. Using his baton, he struck the lower shelf of the restraint table again—this time more violently. His cold, calculated demeanor was long gone by that point, replaced by a sudden sense of urgency. He could have attacked me at any moment leading up to the discovery of Nick's corpse, yet he hadn't. It was as if he wanted me to see what was in store for me before he did me in. Simply killing me wasn't enough. It didn't satiate whatever sadistic and innate drive that was fueling his need to kill. Housing hordes of brain-dead test subjects, ones he could do as he pleased with, must have been a dream job for him.

After circling around the table like a shark—presumably waiting for the perfect opportunity to strike—

Dr. Vox suddenly stopped and faced the table. It wasn't clear as to why he hadn't made a move on me yet, but it was bound to happen sooner or later—that much was for sure. Maybe he just didn't want to place himself in a vulnerable position, where he could possibly lose the upper edge, even if only for a few seconds. Plus, like a polar bear hunting seals, why waste the time of swimming in frigid waters, when the defenseless seal is bound to come up for air sooner or later. It was reminiscent of an old war strategy where an attacking army surrounds a castle or barracks and forces the other army to make a choice—die on the battle field or die of starvation.

With his decrepit black shoes facing me, Dr. Vox slowly approached the table. Moments later, there was a dull tearing sound, followed by the undeniable sound of masticating. He was chewing on something. Chewing on someone!

"MHHMMMM...HMMMMMM! That really hit the spot," he announced, sounding chipper. "Your friend must be Italian—he has an oily quality to him, you know. You should try some."

A large mass of flesh then splattered against the floor, spraying tiny droplets of blood all over my hands and face. I gagged at the sight of Nick's flesh and the sudden realization of what had actually become of him. Dr. Vox not only brutally murdered him—he had consumed his flesh as well. My stomach convulsing, gagging at the thought, any hope for a miracle vanished. There was no doubt in my mind that if Nick was the appetizer, I was destined to be the main course.

"Where are your manners, boy? Don't you know it's rude to sit under the table during dinnertime? I'll make a deal with you, Zack. Join me for an exquisite feast—a last supper so to speak—and when it's your turn, I'll go easy on you. Do we have a deal?"

That was the last straw. I couldn't contain myself any longer. "YOU'RE SICK," I screamed. "If I get out of here, I'll make you pay for what you did to Nick."

"*If*...you survive. If...you escape. If...If...If. I'll tell you one thing, by the graces of God, if you manage to get out and hunt me down, then by all means, make me suffer, make me pay for what I did to your friend. But let's be real, Zack. You and I both know that isn't going to happen. You can ask Nick how well that worked out for him. So, since you're finally talking, which will it be...a slow harrowing death...or a relatively painless one? I have all types of drugs that can do the job quickly and effectively. So what'll it be, Zack?"

"GO TO HELL!"

"Have it your way. Slow and painful it is!"

It happened in an instant. The massive steel table suddenly lifted from above me and crashed to the floor. Shockwaves of terror, mixed with astonishment, shot through my body. Not only had Dr. Vox been able to lift one side of the heavy table up, an incredible feat for someone his size, but he was also able to flip it over as if it weighed nothing. Terrified, my eyes met his gaze as the sole light in the room continued flickering away. Staring intently into his soulless, dark eyes, I kicked my feet out with as much force as my jittery legs could muster. I had to succeed, if not, my fate was sealed. With my legs hurling forward, the room went black...then white...then black...then white...then...

My feet collided with Dr. Vox's bony knees, launching him backwards onto the cement floor. To my relief, I saw his instrument of pain catapult out of his hands, landing a solid ten to fifteen feet from where he fell. With my safety net uplifted, like a startled insect, I began scurrying away on all fours. Moving as fast as my injured arm and leg would allow, my eyes scanned the floor for anything that could possibly be used as a weapon. Glancing over my shoulder, taking notice of Dr. Vox slowly rising to his feet, provided me with all the motivation to search harder and crawl faster. Then out of the corner of my eye, I spotted my trusty shank.

"I'll make you pay for that!" Dr. Vox screamed, his words echoing throughout the infirmary.

Shuffling towards the bone, scraping my hands and knees on all the broken shards of glass in the process, I glanced back and saw that Dr. Vox was ready to pounce. The look on his face said it all. He was out for the sweet taste of my tender flesh. Panicked, I kicked it into high gear and lunged for the shank. In one quick motion, I scooped it up with my good hand (my left hand was virtually useless at that point) and staggered to my feet. With the shank gripped tightly in my hand, ready to unleash its jagged edge into Dr. Vox's delicate neck, I turned to face him for a showdown of epic proportions.

Unfortunately, if round three was the rubber match, with him winning round one and myself winning round two, the third round went to the sadistically, evil doctor. Cutting the distance between us like a charging 250-pound linebacker, Dr. Vox lowered his shoulder and plowed right through me. The collision instantly knocked the wind out of me and thrust me backwards without any conceivable way of bracing my fall. Although happening in real time, probably only a fraction of a second, it seemed like an eternity before my upper torso and the back of my head smashed violently into the concrete floor. For the second time that night, my diaphragm went catatonic on me. No air was going in and no air was coming out. Attempting to force air into my lungs while my head felt as if it was going to explode, my attention was diverted away from the real threat to my safety.

Dr. Vox took no pity on me. Completely helpless, Dr. Vox hurled himself on top of me and placed his blood-stained hands around my neck. Swiveling my hips back and forth in an effort to repel him off me, my oxygen-deprived muscles proved no match for his much larger frame. Leaning forward, Dr. Vox tightened his grasp and began applying intense pressure. His motives were relatively clear-cut, he was either going to kill me right then and there or render me unconscious so he could proceed with his plans of providing me with a slow, painful death.

Retaliate! My brain screamed. *His eyes—don't forget his cold, soulless eyes!*

Desperate for air, and willing to do whatever was necessary to weaken his attack, my fingers found the fleshy insides of his eye sockets. Letting out a thunderous howl, Dr. Vox immediately released his python-like grasp from around my neck. My convulsing diaphragm suddenly burst back to life, flooding it with gust after gust of stagnant air. Trying to buy myself more time to recuperate, I dug my thumbs deeper and deeper into his skull, pressing them against his hard, rubbery eyes. Maybe if one or both of his eyes exploded under the tremendous pressure, rendering him blind, freedom would be within my grasp—literally.

Dr. Vox saw otherwise. He wasn't going to allow a little eye-gouging to ruin his plans. He easily slapped my hands away, and in what I refer to as a "pure act of rage," grabbed my left hand, and ferociously bore down into it with his jagged, decaying teeth. I screamed in pain as I yanked my hand way from him, a costly reaction that cost me a quarter-sized chunk of my flesh. Blood began dripping all over my face, most of which found its way into my eyes and mouth. Dr. Vox began chewing the wad of flesh as if it was a piece of red taffy.

Ready for more, he must have really enjoyed my taste, Dr. Vox sprang back into action. Sitting more upright to avoid another painful eye gouging session, Dr. Vox's hands lunged out and quickly grabbed a hold of my tender, inflamed neck. Squeezing with all his might, Dr. Vox showed no pity for me. If something wasn't done, and fast,

I was going to lose consciousness. With darkness beginning to creep in, a vision of an abdominal exercise popped in my head. Bicycle crunches. A rigorous floor ab exercise performed by alternating between bringing your left knee all the way up to meet your right elbow, and vice versa. I had never been a huge advocate for that particular ab exercise. Too much cardio involved in my opinion. But at Lonnie's encouragement, I got into the habit of doing them at the conclusion of every training session—or at least the sessions where I worked out with him. It wasn't a perfect solution, not in the least. However, I surmised that if my knee smashed into just the right place with enough force, his spinal column per say, substantial damage could be inflicted. So that's exactly what I did.

Stretching out my good leg, like a missile firing off, I launched it directly into the middle of his back with as much power as my adrenaline-revved body could garner. He immediately arched his back, grunted in pain, and released one hand from around my neck. Reaching for the middle of his back with his other hand to smother out the singeing pain, Dr. Vox left himself open for another strike.

The second blow did the trick. Already off balance, Dr. Vox lurched forward, forced to use his hands to brace his fall. Swarming through my enflamed throat, sweltering hot air never felt so good. The darkness that had been engulfing me suddenly vanished, birthing me back into my nightmare.

Not one to give up so easily, Dr. Vox leaned back onto my squirming body, mounted himself on my lower stomach, and grabbed a handful of my hair. Then staring at me with hate in his eyes, he began bashing my head into the concrete floor. By the fourth blow, my brain sufficiently jarred, my body went limp. I wasn't knocked out completely—thank God for that—but close to it. I'm guessing it's some type of defense mechanism, you know, sort of like an opossum playing dead when faced with immediate danger. Go limp, and maybe if you're lucky enough, the attacker will get bored and leave you alone. It's either that or your brain just gets so rattled you temporarily lose control over your body.

Effectively taking most of the fight out of me, before I could even lift a finger, Dr. Vox had already slid down, shifted his weight atop my waist, and gently returned his bloodstained hands to my raw, engorged neck. His strategy was simple. From that position, he could decapitate two birds with one vicious bite. He would be able to continue choking me out while reducing the overall effectiveness of my retaliatory strikes. I could still knee him in the back, I wasn't completely helpless, but the amount of force behind the blows had been sufficiently neutralized. What Dr. Vox didn't anticipate was that I'd change my strategy as well. Instead of one kick at a time, I decided to do two while simultaneously sweeping the ground in search of a weapon. Like the trail of a slug, my hand, covered with tiny lacerations, left streaks of red all over the dusty floor.

On the verge of exhaustion, muscles weakening in their oxygen-depraved state, there was no way I could keep it up for much longer. Fading fast, my heart and lungs feeling as if they were engulfed in flames and ready to burst, eyes feeling as if they were bulging out of their sockets, and blood vessels popping all over my face, a thick, black fog swept in. Then, just as I was beginning to succumb to the darkness, my hand swept across something smooth and jagged. I attempted to pick it up with harrowing results. My blood soaked fingers just kept sliding right off it. I was devastated. I was on the verge of losing consciousness and my last conceivable shot at salvation was literally slipping through my fingers.

THINK, ZACK, THINK! My will to survive shrieked.

Then it hit me. What's the best way to pick a penny up off the floor if your nails are too short? Slide it up against something and flip it up. Works every time. With what was undoubtedly a large slab of glass lying off to my side, all I had to do was slide it closer to me and use my body as leverage. Hoping to buy myself some time, I struck below the belt—literally. I plunged my other hand between his legs, grabbed a handful of his manhood, and began twisting it in a counter-clockwise direction. Howling at the top of his lungs, droplets of his putrid saliva and sweat raining down on my face, Dr. Vox immediately released his powerful grasp from around my neck and lunged for my hand. Clarity rushing back into my head, I slid the object, which was in fact a large shard of glass, over to me and flipped it on its side. The size of a slice of pizza, resembling it too with all my blood staining it a deep red, the shard was the perfect size. Ignoring the piercing burn as the sharp glass dug deeply into my hand, I tightened my grip. The pain was secondary to my will to live.

With fresh blood oozing out of my burning hand, I was ready to unleash my "secret weapon." Peeling my hand away from his genitals, Dr. Vox's fiery glare made it abundantly clear that he was going to make me pay for my "dirty" tactic. He was going to make me pay for that cruel tactic, possibly return the favor in due time—just not with his hands. Concealing the razor-sharp shank off to my side, I patiently waited for the perfect opportunity to strike. That moment didn't take long to present itself. Dr. Vox backhanded me across the face before pouncing back on my neck, squeezing and pushing down on it so forcefully, my larynx felt as if it was being crushed from the immense pressure. With his hands, and attention, completely absorbed on ending my existence, I swung and jabbed the long shard of glass in his face, sending him lurching backwards. It was the perfect shot. Impaled in his right eye socket, the shard of glass dripped a steady flow of red down his face. His neck may have been a more deadly target, obviously, but with his shoulders and arms shielding most of it, his eye was a workable and extremely painful alternative.

Screaming in pure agony, Dr. Vox's body quivered and convulsed as I wiggled free. Gasping what felt like liquid fire through my swollen and enflamed esophagus, a cocktail of mucus and blood began involuntarily spurting out of my mouth. Shuffling backwards, a pinkish, foamy goo flowed freely from my mouth. With a line of the pink, foamy goo hanging from my chin, I staggered to my feet. The drilling pain in my ravaged throat, increasing with every swallow and gasp for air, dulled everything else out. That actually worked in my favor, especially considering the rest of my brutal injuries. Trying to regain my equilibrium, my head still cloudy and lost in a hazy fog, I watched in pure horror as Dr. Vox raised himself to a seated position. Then, if that wasn't bad enough, he began pulling at the shard of glass. Dr. Vox wasn't finished with me quite yet. Splayed eye or not, he was going to see it through until the end.

Under different circumstances, one that didn't involve him trying to murder me, I may have actually felt pity for his traumatic injury. It's only human to feel that way. Instead, pure rage took over. That man...no monster...had experimented on countless people, murdered my best friend, and mangled my body. He didn't deserve pity. He deserved death. And I was going to deliver it to him. With the same mercilessness Dr. Vox showed me, I returned the favor. I sprinted...well, limped...over to him and stomped on his face with the heel of my shoe, lodging the shard of glass deeper into his skull. Blood sprayed out of his destroyed eye socket as he keeled over. I'd love to say my foot made contact with his face a few more times, you know for good measure, but I had more pressing matters to attend to—mainly, getting my butt out of the cave as quickly as possible. I'm aware that in the movies it's the biggest mistake a character can make. You know, assuming the antagonist or, in this case, monster is dead or incapacitated, only for the antagonist to rise again—even more determined to tear you to shreds. And faced with such a dilemma, I can say one thing in my defense: the man, the beast, the devil incarnate, terrified me. So much so, I wanted to get as far away from him as possible. There was, of course, a secondary excuse—mainly the bomb, which could incinerate us both. Without knowing of the trigger mechanism's whereabouts (would a full on assault incite Dr. Vox to pull the trigger in desperation?), it was in my best interest to my gluteus maximus kicked into high gear.

Without even an ounce of guilt watching him writhe in agony, I prayed the shard of glass lobotomized him. He was due for a change in personality anyways. Exiting the lab, I took a slow, agonizing breath, relieved that my nightmare was finally over...

"YOU'LL NEVER GET OUT OF THIS CAVE ALIVE," Dr. Vox screamed, reigniting my fear.

In a fraction of a second, I went from feeling ecstatic to fearing for the worst. I was astonished at his pain tolerance, and immediately regretted my cowardliness when it came to finishing him off. Colossal mistake. One that may have just cost me my life. Glancing back over at the sea of death, estimating just how long it would take me to pass through in my current condition, one thing was certain: outrunning him wasn't going to happen. He and I both knew that. There was always the pickaxe, but that involved engaging in another brutal exchange, one my body just wasn't up for.

That left only one viable option. Finding a place to hide, and fast. Shuffling towards the cell door, my eyes bounced around all corners of the cave, desperately searching for a place to seek refuge. Aside from the cooler—talk about painting yourself into a corner—there was nothing but skeletal remains and wide open space. There was always the possibility of burrowing underneath the skeletal remains, had seen it done effectively in the movies; however, that seemed too time consuming and utterly revolting. There had to be a better option. Glancing back at the cooler, knowing it was an enormous mistake to even consider it a feasible option, I limped over to it to get a better look. Closing in on the cooler, feeling droplets of blood dripping from my fingertips, it suddenly dawned on me that I had left quite the trail. *Follow the red blood-splattered road.* Burying my hands into my pockets to absorb as much blood as possible, I quickly backtracked and snuffed out the trail of blood by sweeping mounds of dirt over it with my feet. It wasn't a perfect solution, but a viable one. I then made my way back over to the cooler, praying for a miracle. If by the grace of God, Dr. Vox made a crazed dash for the secret hatch, maybe, just maybe, it would allot me enough time to barricade myself somewhere else in the lab. Wishful thinking I realize, but what other choice did I have?

Flicking on the light switch with my shoulder—thank God the switch was on the outside—I quickly yanked open the massive steel door and peeked inside. The dimly lit cooler was moderately spacious, filled to capacity with countless boxes and crates. Finding a place to hide was going to be easy. The only unknown was whether or not Dr. Vox would go straight for the secret hatch door or make a pit stop in the cooler.

Hearing a door slam open, presumably the one leading into the lab area, I was forced to make a rapid and potentially life altering decision. Hide and pray, make one more stand, or will my aching body to compete in a literal death race. There had to be another option. Then, while staring at the cooler door's bloody handle, knowing I'd never be able to completely cover my tracks, the perfect solution came to me. Well, almost perfect. I had never actually tried the stunt before, had wanted to on many occasions, just never got the chance. In cartoons, it always seemed to work. Without giving my plan another thought, I shook my bloody hand inside, and all around the cooler, grabbed the handle, and opened it up all the way, stopping a mere foot away from the cave wall. I then slid behind the cooler door, my feet completely concealed by the rubber draft guard. Corked in-between the jagged rocks and the cool steel door, I held my breath and attempted to remain as motionless as possible.

Please, God, let him be the coyote! I prayed.

"Where are you, Zack?" Dr. Vox growled after storming out of the lab. "Play time's over, young man. I have a feast to return to. You seem smart enough, Zack. You should know that raw meat tends to spoil rather quickly. Even faster if flies get to it. The offer's still on the table. Come out from where you're hiding and I'll euthanize you instead of the painful alternative. Regrettably, I won't enjoy it as much, but I'm a man of my word. You see, Zack, meat tastes much better when there's still life—and fear—coursing through it. So what do you say?"

I said nothing. I closed my eyes and allowed a faint, shallow breath to part my lips. My lungs, presumably suffering from an episode of PTSD, released the shallow breath the instant it felt oxygen-depraved. Just way too much trauma for one night. My heart racing, stomach in a twisting vice, brain pulsating as if there was a demolition crew jack-hammering the back of my skull, I prayed Dr. Vox would venture inside. I'm fully aware that in the cartoons, the crafty character stands in front of the door and swings it open at the last second before sending its arch nemesis bolting into a room with no floor (usually crashing hundreds of feet down), but you work with what you have. Mine was just of the slower and more calculating variety.

"Are you in there, Zack," he said, his footsteps coming to a halt in front of the cooler's entrance. "If so, I should probably thank you. I actually prefer my *sushi* a little on the chilled side."

PLEASE GO IN, PLEASE GO IN, PLEASE...PLEASE...PLEASE! I chanted to myself.

Blood dripping from my hands, subsequently affecting my grasp on the cooler door's handle, I suddenly realized a catastrophic error in my planning. What if there's no lock? I had never even thought of that nightmarish possibility when putting my impromptu plan together. Not fully thinking out your plans usually leads to failure. In my case, failure would ultimately lead to death—a painful one at that. Peeking through a miniscule sliver between the door and its frame, I watched as Dr. Vox followed my trail of blood into the cooler. He appeared tentative in his approach, his eyes zeroed in on the tiny blood splatters that led into the dimly lit room. The shard was still poking out of his head, dripping a steady flow of red down his face.

"Are you in there, boy? In case you are, just know, there's no way out. And, just so we're clear, you will pay for what you did to my eye. I'm not above going *Josef Mengele* on you. I think your eyes are due for a lighter shade of blue, don't you think?"

The moment Dr. Vox fully vanished from my line of vision, with my face pressed against the chilled metal door, I began feeling around the handle for a locking feature. If there wasn't one to be found, I'd have no choice but to abort the mission. Even if I succeeded in slamming the door on Dr. Vox, there was no way my fatigued and ailing body would be able to contain him inside. A few minutes maybe—not much more than that.

HALLELUJAH, the word chimed in my head after fingering a small opening (the perfect size for a lock) with my finger. That was great news, and should have lifted some of the weight off my shoulders, yet it didn't. There was one other major problem. Like most people, I don't ordinarily carry around a lock with me in the event a psychotic doctor needs to be imprisoned inside a cooler. With no way of locking him inside the cooler, I was back to square one…

Wait a minute, I thought to myself. *What if I use…*

Then, to my horror, before I could even finish my thought, my hand slipped off the handle, sending the door lurching forward. I had blown my cover. Dr. Vox let out a howl of recognition and began gunning for the door. Forced to react, I lunged forward pushing the thick steel door with all my might. Eyes closed, adrenaline charging up my depleted energy reserves, nothing was going to stop me. Not my bum leg, not my busted-up forearm, not my exhausted body, and especially not my arch-nemesis, Dr. Vox. Within seconds, the door crashed shut and I heard the sweat sounds of Dr. Vox screaming in defeat. As it turns out, he wasn't screaming because he had been bested. Not at all.

Glancing slightly to my left were four engorged fingers jutting out from the steel doorframe. In all the commotion of attempting to flee from the cooler, Dr. Vox's hand paid the costly price. Wedged between the massive steel door and doorframe, his crushed hand, bones surely pulverized, convulsed as if it had a heartbeat of its own. Taking no pity on him and his shattered hand, I pulled the door back just a tad, and began smashing it shut in rapid and painful succession. I wasn't going to make the same mistake twice. Ruthless or not, nothing was going to stop me. After mauling his ruined hand for about thirty-seconds straight, as if I had won a prize, four little souvenirs fell to the ground. I stared at the four bloodstained fingers and actually had a hard time comprehending how not long ago those destroyed fingers were wrapped firmly around my neck. I basked in the glory of inflicting an insurmountable amount of pain upon my friend's murderer. And, judging from his intense guttural moans, the pain must have been almost unbearable.

Not out of harm's way just yet, I still had one final task to complete. I flicked off the light switch, casting Dr. Vox into pure darkness, and frantically reached into my pocket to retrieve my *salvation*. Lonnie had been right after all. Glute-Boots were lifesavers. Well, in this instance, a part from the Glute-Boots—the karabiner hook that I had swapped with my keychain. With the karabiner hook in hand, I jingled all my keys off it, allowing them to fall to the ground.

Taking in a slow painful breath, I sprung open the karabiner gate and was about to fasten it in place when Dr. Vox suddenly stopped screaming. Still finagling with the karabiner and the lock hole, I turned my head slightly and listened in on Dr. Vox. It was difficult to hear anything through the thick steel door, but what I was able to hear sounded as if he was shuffling around inside the cooler. With no time to spare, Dr. Vox was predictable in the sense that he had no quit in him, I crouched to get a better view of the lock hole. Although a tight fit, the karabiner appeared as if it could penetrate the hole with ease. Of course, like someone's "first time," that's easier said than done; especially, with my bloodied, sweat-filled hands trembling uncontrollably from a combination of fatigue, adrenaline, and anxiety coursing through my system.

After several failed attempts to "thread the needle," so to speak, I heard thunderous footsteps approaching the door. It almost sounded like a herd of buffalo were stampeding towards me. *WHOOMP!* The door vibrated, impaling a cold chill through my spine. Then another *WHOOMP*...and another...and another. It was as if he was hurling himself blindly at the door. Fortunately for my sake, the door failed to budge an inch. Then to my horror, he unexpectedly changed his strategy. It sounded as if he was patting down the door, feeling around for something, perhaps a door handle. Too focused on what Dr. Vox was up to, I missed the latch lock again. Time was running out. If he located the door handle before the karabiner locked into position, I was finished. He may not have been capable of

Consumed

choking me out any longer, his severed fingers attested for that, but if nothing else, he was resourceful. He'd find another way to prep me for his dinner table.

Prying open the hook gate for fourth or fifth time, my bloodied and slick hands making this seemingly easy task extremely challenging, the door handle began trembling as if it was seizing. Realizing that Dr. Vox had located the handle, terror ripped through me. Distraught, heart racing a million beats per second, I closed my eyes and went with blind faith. If it was meant to be, then it would...

My eyes shot open after feeling the karabiner slide into place and snap shut. Releasing the hook, relief shot through me as I watched it dangle like a hoop earring. Still staring at the hook, I was in shock. God must have really been on my side for that one. And not a moment too soon. Not even a second later, the door handle began jiggling up and down, Dr. Vox's last-ditch effort finishing a close second. Had he not wasted his time trying to bash the door open, who knows what the outcome would have been?

Physically exhausted, and in need of immediate medical attention, I limped over to the lab. I wanted out of that cave of death in the worst way; however, my injuries needed to be tended to immediately. Besides, if what Dr. Vox had been telling me about the bomb was true, there was no way I'd make it out of the blast radius anyway. My only hope in those regards was that the trigger mechanism was anywhere but inside the cooler.

T.S. Charles

Chapter Eleven

Aftermath

After entering the lab area, I made it halfway across the room before dropping to my knees. Physically and emotionally drained, tears paved white paths down my blood-splattered face. I wiped away the tears, smearing fresh blood across both cheeks in the process. Glancing over at the door leading into the infirmary, I began crying even harder. I felt personally responsible for Nick's untimely demise. Had I been there for him, he'd still be alive. I failed him in the worst imaginable way. My actions were unforgiveable. I didn't deserve first aid. No, I deserved to bleed out. With tiny pools of blood forming on the dusty floor and salty, coppery tasting tears running into my parched mouth, I wasn't doing Nick any justice by sitting there feeling sorry for myself. People needed to know the truth surrounding Timmonds Rock, and there was only one person who could deliver it to them.

Glancing over in the far corner of the room, I spotted Dr. Vox's stacks of notebooks. In honor of Nick, I stumbled to my feet and staggered over to the table. I grabbed the pile of notebooks, stamping them with large, bloody prints and headed straight for the barracks. Every step I

- 182 -

took felt like someone was jabbing a serrated knife directly into my left calf. Dangling limply at my side, my swollen left forearm ached, but was manageable when left alone. Once inside the barracks, engulfed in total darkness, I began feeling around for a light switch.

"Jackpot," I cried after finding it.

The barracks certainly had all the goods, and then some. Filled with about five triple bunks, cubbies, a dining and kitchen area, huge file cabinets, several closets, and a bathroom at the rear of the room, it had everything a soldier would need while stationed inside the secret military base. Quickly scanning the room for a first aid kit, my search came up empty. It didn't mean there wasn't one lying around somewhere. It just meant the search needed to be expanded. I checked out the closets first. The first one was busting at the seams with linens, while the second one contained heavy-duty white hazmat suits hanging from a steel rod. But no signs of a first aid kit. I further expanded my search to the kitchen area, meticulously inspecting every shelf and drawer. Again, no first aid kit. I did, however, find some type of cream labeled, Zyprolenia Cream 0.25%. Medically speaking, I had no clue what it was for, but the name seemed interesting so it found itself buried in one of my side pockets. That left just the bathroom to explore.

Approaching the bathroom, an intense stench (almost as foul as the one emanating from Dr. Vox, filled the stagnant air. I plugged my nostrils shut and kept on moving. Once inside the bathroom, I flicked on the light and nearly puked at the sight that lay before my eyes. It was terrible. Like a chocolate ice cream cone left outside in the sun too long, every clogged toilet had feces pouring out over its side. Just nasty. As it turns out, Dr. Vox wasn't lying about the atrocious plumbing issues in the facility. To make matters worse, there was even an area off in the far corner of the room designated as the new dumping ground—literally.

I couldn't believe what my eyes were seeing. I was aware that Dr. Vox's hygiene was poor and inexcusable, but his bathroom antics went well beyond appropriate behavior, even for a psychotic, cannibalistic doctor. On a whole, from a purely grossed out beyond belief perspective, I'd say the barracks bathroom was by far the sickest image I had ever seen—Nick's mutilated body falling a close second.

Out of nowhere, laughter spewed out of my mouth. I couldn't stop envisioning Dr. Vox straddling the toilet bowl trying to take a dump without falling into his own unsightly creation. After my laughter sufficed, I came to a realization that no matter how evil somebody is, everyone defecates. In a way, it humanized him, which in turn, completely bummed me out. Underneath his merciless and ruthless exterior was a person who had to listen to *Nature's Call*, just like everyone else. Except, unlike most hygienic adults, when it came to such a *call*, I think he skipped the whole wiping part. I'm aware I'll never know that definitively; however, judging by the absence of toilet paper in his brown mess, I'd say it's a pretty fair assessment.

Unable to look at Dr. Vox's masterpiece any longer, I turned my attention to the walls, hoping to find the coveted first aid kit. "Thank God," I muttered after spotting one near the mound of hardened foulness in the far corner of the room. With my hand cupped around my nose and mouth, the smell of fresh blood dulling out most of the wretched stench, I shuffled over to it, stepped carefully over a few *stragglers* scattered about the floor, and yanked the entire kit off of the wall. Rushing back to the sink area, I tore the lid off faster than an eager kid opening up a gift on Christmas. It was sad and pathetic, indeed, but I was actually thrilled to find a single alcohol swab and several rolls of yellowed gauze. It was a start at least.

Committed to stopping the profuse bleeding in my hands, of utmost importance, I began rinsing them under cold water. Ignoring the singeing pain, I gently rubbed them together to get as much dried blood and dirt out as possible. A whitish hue returning to my hands, I was finally able to see the true extent of the damage. In addition to a plethora of tiny cuts, there were two deep lacerations on my right hand and a sizable chunk of flesh missing from the other. Spanning the palm of my hand and all four fingers, the cut ran so deep bone and rubbery tendons were visible. After running my hands under the cold water for a few minutes, with dire hopes of slowing the bleeding, I knew I had to disinfect the wounds as much as possible.

Knowing that it had to be done, the cave was one massive petri dish filled with unimaginable contaminants, I tore open the alcohol swab and quickly rubbed it over my wounds. I'm aware that the active ingredient in an alcohol swab is *alcohol*—that's a no brainer—but I swear that particular swab must have been doused with hydrochloric acid. With my hands feeling as if they were melting away, I wasted no time in wrapping the yellowed gauze rolls snuggly around them. It was a grueling yet necessary task. Once completed, guttural groans slipped out as I squeezed my hands shut in an effort to apply direct pressure to my wounds. With my hands looking ready for boxing gloves to be thrown on them, I began examining the rest of my injuries.

Laced in colors of purple and deep red, my neck appeared as if a minion of toothless *succubi* went to town on it. Stretched across the nape of my tender and swollen neck, it was almost possible to make out Dr. Vox's large handprints. Speckled all over my face, mostly around my eyes, were droves of tiny red dots, commonly referred to as broken blood vessels. They were without a doubt disturbing, but paled in comparison to my next discovery. Staring intently into the foggy, grimy mirror, there were fiery red eyes glaring back at me. Apparently, when it felt as if my eyes were bulging out of my head—they really were.

"Wow, red really brings out the blue in my eyes, I joked to myself in a pathetic attempt to divert my attention away from my grotesque appearance. "I guess Dr. Vox got his wish of making my eyes bluer, after all."

I must have been straining so intensely when Dr. Vox strangled me, my eyes hemorrhaged, turning the whites a deep red color. I immediately glanced away from that disturbing sight and studied the deep gash above my eye. The bleeding had long ceased, leaving in its path streams of caked blood all over the side of my ragged and bloated face. I didn't even bother cleaning it up. What would be the point? Contagions or not, I'd worry about that later—after all, the dried cocktail of dirt and blood was doing an excellent job of acting as a sort of sealant. As for the lump on the back of my head, nearly the size of a golf ball at that point, it was out of my line of vision; thus went ignored, as did my scraped knees. My ear, on the other hand, didn't go unnoticed. Swelled three sizes larger than normal, I could almost feel the blood and fluids swishing around my ear whenever I poked it.

Sick of staring at my battered face, blood-filled eyes, and cauliflower ear, grateful just to be alive, I grabbed the journals and limped out of the bathroom. Gimping through the barracks, I suddenly stopped midway and walked over to one of the bunkers. With my hands still held in tight fists, journals tucked under one of my arms, I yanked an old charcoal gray blanket from a bed and slung it over my shoulder. A waft of dust swirled upwards, sending a disturbing reminder of the human matter potentially ingested earlier in the night. Making my way over to the exit, I was just about to leave when the slightly ajar refrigerator door caught my eye. The chances were slim, but what if there were medications, in particular antibiotics or painkillers, stored in the stainless steel fridge. It was worth a shot.

I hesitated only for a brief moment before hurling it open with my foot. At first glance the fridge wasn't all that impressive. There were traces of rotted fruit, soured milk, containers filled with an indescribable black goo that may have once been edible, and off in the far corner of the fridge was a dark brown medicine bottle. My first inclination was that it was a bottle of hydrogen peroxide—a disinfecting lifesaver. If it was, I wasn't above dousing my entire body with what was left in the bottle. Opening up my left hand, the one with the gaping hole, I reached for it. As I did, a faint red stain, resembling a bloody yin-yang symbol, was already forming on the outer layer of the aged gauze. It's never a good sign to see blood seeping through fresh…well, nearly fresh…bandages.

"Chloroform!" I muttered after grabbing the dark brown bottle. "What the heck did they use this for?"

Maybe, just maybe, before Dr. Vox completely lost his mind, the "infected" were treated much more humanely than I had previously thought. Regardless of the reason, holding the bottle in my hand, a sudden urge to pop the lid off and take a quick whiff kicked in. I don't know why there was that completely reckless urge, but there it was front and center, forcing me to twist the cap off. I almost needed to know. It's kind of like when a friend comes up to you and asks you to smell something. Knowing how foul it must be to garner such attention, deep down you really don't want to smell it, yet you find yourself taking a quick sniff, regretting the decision every time. With the cap off, more than ready to take a short harmless inhalation, something unexpected happened. Although a rarity in the teen years, common sense prevailed.

Twisting the cap back on, I shook my head thinking, *this is the type of inane thing you do when you're friends are around. Not when you're all by yourself.*

Still curious about the scent, I placed the bottle of chloroform in my other side pocket for later use. Then without even giving it a second thought, I opened up the freezer. I really didn't believe there would be any medications up there (I mean, how often are meds kept in the freezer?), but I figured it was worth a shot. The moment the frosted light flicked on, casting an almost mystical glow, I stumbled back after noticing an assortment of freezer burnt limbs and appendages. The sight was gruesome—the realization much more harrowing. Food, specimens, or a combination of the two—I slammed the door shut with little interest of learning the truth.

Deeply disturbed, I stormed into the lab. Glancing towards the door leading out to the cave area—my salvation—my dejected heart wouldn't allow me to leave without paying my final respects to Nick. It's the reason I grabbed the old wool blanket in the first place. He didn't deserve to be left like that. Nobody did. Well, I take that back, Dr. Vox and his cruel minions would have deserve it.

Back in the infirmary, I followed the trail of blood, some mine, some Dr. Vox's, all the way back to where my nightmare had begun. Tentatively approaching the table, my head pivoted at such an angle to avoid looking at Nick's mutilated corpse, it was still impossible to come to terms with what had happened to him. He was only sixteen-years-old—not even old enough to legally buy beer, cigarettes, or an X-rated movie. He may have been stubborn and reckless to the core; especially, when he put himself in such a precarious situation, but that didn't mean he deserved the fate that was bestowed upon him. Dr. Vox took his life from him, leaving an unrecognizable bloody mass in its wake.

My plan was simple. Ease Nick's body to the ground and cover it with the wool blanket. Things didn't go accordingly, forcing me to improvise. Instead of unbuckling all of the restraints (my war-torn hands weren't up for the job), I took the blanket and carefully slung it over the side of the table, covering everything except the red mess beneath my feet.

With the light still flickering on and off, like a photo shoot gone wrong, I made my way over to the side of the overturned table and sat down. I purposely positioned myself against the leg of the table nearest his gutted face. There was a faint coppery scent in the air, somewhat masked by the musky stench from the wool blanket. Resting my head again the cold steel, which provided slight relief to my bulbous welt, I opened up one of Dr. Vox's marble notebooks and began reading aloud to Nick. If Nick's soul was anywhere in the vicinity, I knew above everything else, learning of the lab's secrets would at least close out one chapter in his short life.

April 17, 2009

I am no closer to finding a cure or viable treatment for the virus. I am beginning to lose all hope that a cure is even possible. Test subject 000892 showed no improvements with my newest strain of antiviral. Three years of work down the drain. I fear that if I do not produce results in any type of facet, my services will no longer be deemed necessary. I need more time.

The passage went on and on for several pages going into a detailed explanation of the antiviral medication Dr. Vox had developed. Some of it was interesting, most of it was not, just a bunch of medical jargon, way above my intellectual capacity. I eventually stopped reading after Dr. Vox went into grave details of the chemical composition of his newly developed medication. Skimming through the journals, I noticed that they were all in chronological order, dating back to the onset of the first outbreak. Ms.

Maddows would kill me for doing this, any English teacher would, but she wasn't there to stop me, so I pressed forward starting from the end. Opening up the most recent journal, I began reading from the last dated entry.

March 20, 2013

> *I need to feed soon. My time is near-*
> *ly running out. If my calculations*
> *are correct, there should still be a few*
> *days left, but I do not think I can*
> *wait that long. It has already been*
> *nearly 15 days since my last feast. I*
> *am aware that the hunger keeps hit-*
> *ting me sooner and sooner, but I*
> *have to hold out as long as possible.*
> *My survival depends on it.*

What kind of feast are we talking about? I wondered flipping through the journal searching for the March 5, 2013 entry log. I located it with ease.

March 5, 2013

> *Success! I ate well tonight. I need to*
> *be vigilant about my ways, though.*
> *If I am ever caught, it is all over. The*
> *cure—my life—everything!!! I will*
> *resume my work on a satiated stom-*
> *ach tomorrow. I have plenty to keep*
> *my mind occupied for the next 20 or*
> *so days...*

His journal didn't outright specify it, but I was begin-ning to get the feeling that he was referring to cannibalism. That part was easy to figure out; especially, with his most recent meal a mere foot away from my head. However, what didn't make any sense was why he needed to eat within a certain timeframe. To me it sounded more like a necessity than anything else. Almost like he didn't have a choice in the matter. I needed to find out what was going on.

I flipped through several more sections only taking the time to read the good parts aloud to Nick. By the time I finished the most recent journal, two things had become abundantly clear: Dr. Vox was eating people every 15-20 days and the underlying reason why was buried somewhere in one of his journals. Ignoring the aching pain, blood loss, and painful memories, I plowed forward, determined to unlock Dr. Vox's darkest secret.

January 1, 2010

The joys of New Years Eve! My methods may seem extreme; however, in the grand scheme of things, they are more than necessary. With test subjects a rarity to come across now-a-days, my little infection spree in Louisville, Kentucky, should pay dividends. Of the twelve people I infected with the virus if "just" three manage to make it to my lab intact, I will be satisfied with those results. I am confident that my new strand, although not a cure per say, will prolong the inevitable transformation...

It took me nearly twenty minutes to sort through his journals to figure out what that transformation was. Apparently, according to Dr. Vox's research, if infected with the virus he commonly referred to as the "EATS virus" (Extreme Anthropophagite Temperament Syndrome virus) the mortality rate measured at a perfect 100%. The rapidly spreading virus, which initially presented with flu-like symptoms (on average four to five days after being infected), gradually progressed as the person's health deteriorated, much more rapidly if the person's immune system was already compromised. In addition to presenting with a constant fever of above 100 degrees Fahrenheit, the infected person would rapidly lose weight, skin would appear ashen, facial orifices would begin weeping a dark, gooey pus, and if not cared for immediately the person would become dehydrated before the end of the first week. According to some of his own personal tests he conducted, if a subject was administered fluids to maintain hydration, the eventual transformation took on average about *three* weeks. Never longer than *25* days, though. While in contrast, if a subject was neglected fluids, he or she would go through the process in about half that time.

Speaking of the transformation, in the final stages of the virus the person would begin to exhibit symptoms of dementia before ultimately slipping into a coma. Once in that comatose state, there was no turning back. The person would rise to see another day, just not as the person he or she had once been. No longer feverish, malaise, or cognizant of their surroundings, the infected person was reborn as cannibalistic monster—a seemingly indestructible force—possessing no fear, remorse, or the ability to feel pain. All of which made for a lethal combination. Something I was all too familiar with.

I was learning so much, yet so little. Staring at my blood-soaked bandages, my right hand troubling me with every drop of blood that dripped to the floor, I wanted to leave, but felt compelled to continue reading. It was as if something was telling, no forcing me, to continue looking through Dr. Vox's journals. Maybe it was Nick or my parents looking out for me from above...you know...pushing me to locate that elusive secret. A secret for my eyes only, perhaps. Regardless, my eyes led the way.

January 11, 2010

> *Louisville provided me with eight beautiful specimens. Oh, the things I did with them. They were a pleasant group, six vagrants, a prostitute, and a schoolteacher. How she got thrown into the mix, I'm not sure. Who knows, maybe she's not as clean as one would be led to believe. Regardless, I will be preparing my newest "subjects" with the latest strand of antiviral. As always, I will have a control group. Since my contaminated needle did not infect the attractive young schoolteacher, and it is impossible to determine her date of infection, she will be used in other ways...*

I read on and learned just what he had in store for her. Brutal...just Goddamn...brutal. What he did to her was unthinkable and flat out ruthless. In an effort to study (which by that point I referred to as zombies—what else could the monsters be described as?) the long-term effects of regular feedings, Dr. Vox cold-bloodedly chopped her into pieces and fed her to an "infected" test subject he had stowed away in an observational holding cell. Dr. Vox was more than pleased with the results. Although he didn't understand the virus, he made what he referred to as "a major breakthrough." His "discovery" boiled down to the fact that if one of the transformed subjects fed off human meat for a prolonged period, *its* body reacted in a fascinating way. As if human meat acted like a steroid to the beasts, the more meat consumed the stronger and faster *it* would get. Whereas, his control group revealed that if one of the transformed subjects wasn't fed human meat, it would rapidly lose those qualities and would begin to decompose from the inside out. Hence, the human remains scattered about the cave and the insatiable appetite the *monsters* exhibited.

February 24, 2010

I believe that General Ackerman and his unit may be onto me and my extreme methods. I need to construct an emergency exit in the rear of the cave...

Everything was beginning to make sense. A secret hatch door had never been in the blueprints. It was Dr. Vox's exit strategy in the event he found himself on the wrong side of the cell door.

March 22, 2010

The hatch door is finally complete. It was a shame I had to terminate my remaining subjects to clear the lab of the military presence. But there will be more. There always are. And, when things get slow, I just have to improvise. I'll let things die out for a few months before I venture out again to recruit more subjects...

I wanted to stop reading out of fear of what could be ultimately discovered, but just couldn't. From everything I had read, it was all boiling down to one reality that didn't settle well with me. Like his subjects, "he" was eating for a reason.

September 12, 2010

General Ackerman and his troops thought they bested me by throwing me in with my subjects. Little did they know I had a way out. Prior to being thrown to the "wolves," General Ackerman informed me that a witness had come forward reporting a rather suspicious tale. The witness stated that someone, fitting my exact description, dragged an unconscious man into an alley, at which point the "alleged" assailant flipped the man onto his stomach and injected a needle into his rectum. He took the witness by his word and conducted his own investigation, destroying my lab in the process. It didn't take him long to find the evidence he was looking for—a stash of my contaminated needles. Fortunately, for the sake of my research, he wasn't able to locate my journals. It may take some time for the dust to settle, but my work's not done. Not making it out of the cave unscathed has made sure of that...

I read on in horror, only to discover that Dr. Vox had suffered a bite while making a desperate break for the exit. I wanted to vomit at that exact moment. Studying the deep red stain on my bandaged left hand, directly above the savage bite mark, tears began welling up in my eyes. The red blot no longer resembled a yin-yang symbol to me. No, regardless of its circular, swirling pattern, all I could see was…death.

Tears streaming down my face, I fully understood the implications. The "EATS virus" was coursing through my veins, courtesy of Dr. Vox. But something didn't make any sense. How, if Dr. Vox suffered the infectious bite on, or around, September 12, 2010, was he still alive? His research clearly specified that if infected, you would inevitably transform into a cannibalistic beast within a span of 15-25 days. No longer worried about my health—I was a walking time bomb, after all—I ventured on.

September 24, 2010

I have kept my body hydrated to the max, drugged myself beyond image with all my strands of antiviral, and still I am struggling with fatigue and all the other ailments associated with the virus. I need to see if my theory will work. It has to work…

September 30, 2010

It took me close to a week, but I am finally in a position to test out my "Carrión" theory. I am in the basement of an abandoned house on the verge of making history, or putting the good people of Stone Creek in harm's way. I am leaving my journals here in the event that things do not go according to plan. My re-

search, regardless of my unethical and inhumane ways, may one day help us understand more about this alien virus. I cannot wait any longer. My lucid thoughts are few and far between now. The "Memorex" has proved useless in terms of combating the increased symptoms of dementia. I will either wake up tomorrow and not know whom I am, not wake up at all, or if my theory proves accurate—reborn as something this world has never seen...

The latter proved to be the case. I spent the next fifteen minutes reading all about Dr. Vox's transformation from man to zombie-hybrid—a killing machine with conscious thought and awareness. He went into grave details about his feedings, of which took place on average every 16-19 days, with Nick being the only victim not mentioned in his journal. Although not a cure, Dr. Vox's feedings slowed the progression of the virus, thus providing him with more time to conduct his research. He theorized that as long as he continued eating, he could delay the inevitable transformation indefinitely. Dr. Vox was unsure why the virus reacted in such a fashion, other than the simple fact that it did. He also had plans of taking his experiments to all new levels, including cloning human embryos infected with the virus with hopes that the 2nd generation virus would reveal possible clues on how to combat the seemingly indestructible virus. His journals also referenced a desire to reconnect with an old associate of his, Dr. Allen Fish (a leading virologist previously stationed in Dr. Vox's dungeon), to further assist him with his brutal experiments. His journals never revealed whether or not he pursued that disturbing collaboration.

August 26, 2011

A year has almost passed since my first feast and I have never felt better. My body seems to be functioning at an accelerated level and sleep is no longer necessary. I am stronger, faster, more alert, and my visual and auditory senses have been heightened. I can now detect the undeniable scent of human pheromones; and as if I was one of "Pavlov's dogs," I salivate at the scent. I believe that with regular feedings, my timetable may have increased, but I am too wary to test the waters without any scientific proof. Until I am able to put that experiment to test with new subjects, I will continue medicating myself every 15-20 days. Unfortunately, test subjects are much more difficult to come by. And the ones I am able to recruit, usually end up on my feeding table. I will prevail though, as I have no choice. As a doctor, scientist, and man, it is my responsibility to find that elusive cure in the event the virus ever resurfaces...

There was much more to read through, too much in fact, so I decided it was best to leave. Besides, I couldn't take much more anyway. Placing the journals next to Nick's body, away from the pools of blood, I placed my hand gently on the top of his blanketed head.

"You should have these, Nick. They have everything you were ever looking for, and much, much more. It's time for me to leave this nightmare behind and contemplate my future. Huh…funny…contemplate my future," I shook my head in disgust, "more like, contemplate my death. Looks like we'll be having a reunion real soon, Nick. I just want to let you know that I loved you, and that all this," I waved my arms around the room, "is my fault. If I had just skipped the…goddamnit why hadn't I skipped the party…well, none of that is important now. We can talk all about that when we meet up again on the other side. Take care, Nick…"

Before making my way out of the infirmary, out of the corner of my eye, I spotted Nick's white—well, mostly white—backpack lying in a pool of coagulated blood resting in-between the top and bottom shelves of the steel table. I immediately opened it up and searched through its contents. Neatly organized, as always, were his house keys, his cell phone, a white flashlight and camera, and even a sandwich made out of "white bread." Aside from his phone and the flashlight, everything else was useless to me. Removing the weird cream and the chloroform from my pockets, I tossed them into the backpack before slinging it over my shoulder, smearing blood on the entire left side of my back in the process. I probably should have kept the journals, they were evidence after all, but considering the path ahead of me, they were better off with Nick. If someone was able to stumble across Nick's corpse, the journals would do an excellent job of explaining exactly what happened to him.

Before heading off into the cave area, I stopped back inside the lab, determined to find the bomb's trigger mechanism. Even if I wouldn't be around to see it, the lab's exploits should come to light one day. After rummaging through all of Dr. Vox's desks, I finally stumbled across a stainless steel suitcase, the size of a small lunchbox, in one of his desk's drawers. Examining it, I saw that it required two different keys and a combination to open it up. Without any way of opening it, the entire suitcase found itself stuffed away in Nick's backpack.

Making my way back into the cave area, I made sure to move as discreetly as possible. Dr. Vox may have been securely contained inside the dark cooler, but that didn't mean it was a good idea to stir him. Never wake a sleeping, cannibalistic beast was my new motto. I took four or five steps before tragedy struck in the form of accidently kicking a small rock into cooler door. It took only a matter of a millisecond for Dr. Vox to explode.

"ZAAACCCCCKKKKK!" he screamed through the thick cooler door. "LET ME OUT OF HERE. YOU CAN'T DO THIS TO ME. IT'S MURDER IF YOU LEAVE ME HERE TO DIE. YOU HEAR ME? MURDER!!!"

I wanted no part of exchanging words with Dr. Vox. There were more pressing matters to worry about—mainly, my current infliction. I tried to block his words out as much as possible as I ventured over to the cell door. Dr. Vox continued shouting at the top of his lungs for me to let him out, and when I failed to respond, he began taking his frustration out on the cooler door.

Slamming his body, or crates, or whatever against the door, Dr. Vox was relentless. With every strike, the door rattled, dust stirred, and small chips of rock crumbled away from all around the cooler's doorframe. That was all the motivation I needed to get my "glutes" moving.

Chapter Twelve

Fresh Air

After successfully climbing through the secret hatch door, a slow, painful process, I rolled over onto my back and stared up at the heavens. I drew in a long, deep breath and exhaled. The cool spring air may have soothed my swollen throat, but did little to ease my fragile mental-state. Even entombed inside the cooler, Dr. Vox managed to ruin the moment for me. I should have been ecstatic, yet there was absolutely nothing to be excited about. I managed to escape, but for how long? It didn't matter how much distance was between the lab and me, because my "deadly" condition imprisoned me, permanently destroying any possible sense of freedom. Like an active volcano, I could feel the depression boiling up inside, readying itself to erupt.

Taking in a few more deep breaths, my throat feeling as if flaming embers were searing it with every inhalation, rest wasn't an option. I had to keep moving. As much as the depression was eating away at me faster than the virus, I couldn't allow it to get the best of me. Not yet at least. It would have its time soon enough. That much was certain.

Rising to my feet, I slammed the hatch door shut, threw Nick's bloodstained bag over my shoulder, and began hiking through the treacherous woods. My leg ached with every step, a deep stabbing pain that only seemed to be getting worse.

Through the slow hike through the woods, I thought long and hard about my immediate future. The next 15-25 days to be exact. Should I voluntarily turn myself in, potentially becoming Dr. Vox's *cellie*? Possibly. Should I take matters into my own hands? Another possibility. Or finally, should I allow the virus to run its course and endanger the general populous? That one didn't sit too well with me. When really thinking about it, none of the options seemed appealing. Regardless, a decision would eventually have to be made concerning my immediate future.

Warm tears trickled down my face while lost in depressive thoughts about my family and friends. My mind was entirely consumed with visions of my parents' gruesome attack, Nick's half-devoured corpse, and the concerned expression tattooed across Tiffany's face when I left the party. She looked so concerned, so troubled, so damn beautiful. I was falling for her, and hard. When she said yes, my mind raced with vivid thoughts of how our relationship would blossom and flourish over time. I envisioned all the adventures we'd happily embark on together. The rest of high school...the college years...maybe even marriage—that is, if I played my cards right. Clenching my fists, a painful reminder of my new reality, my thoughts quickly turned depressive. There'd be no future for us. No happy-ending. No more kisses that tasted of strawberries. No more anything. Just a mirage of what could have been. Utterly depressed by that point, I felt an awful sensation in the pit of my stomach. It was as if the butterflies had gotten into an all out drunken brawl.

Stomach twisted in barbed-wire knots, I finally made it out of the woods. Certain my bike was totaled in bicycle terms, you know, the cost of repairing a busted tire out-weighs the actual worth of the bike, I didn't even bother looking for it. In need of a means of transportation, I searched the surrounding woods for Nick's bike. Hidden behind yet another spruce tree, it didn't take long for me to locate Nick's bike.

Remembering the promise I had made to Tiffany, as much as I couldn't bear to hear her voice—still too painful to think about—I pulled Nick's phone out of his backpack and turned it on. While punching her number into the phone it dawned on me that Dr. Vox still had my cell phone. Although not entirely comfortable with the idea of Dr. Vox having a means of communication, I felt confident that there was no way he'd get reception inside the cave, much less trapped inside the confines of his steel tomb.

"Hello!" Tiffany whispered suspiciously into the phone. "Who is this?"

For a moment, I was confused. *How can she not know it's me?* I thought. Then it hit me like a runaway Dr. Vox. I was calling her from a foreign number. "Hey, Tiff, it's Zack. I'm using Nick's phone. I really need to see you," I said, regretting my words. I did want to see her, just not in my current condition. She didn't deserve to be dragged into my nightmare. No one did. "Some...some...something's happened..." I couldn't even finish my sentence. My emotions got the best of me and left me sobbing like that little boy who lost his parents all those years ago.

"What happened, Zack? Is everything all right? Please speak to me, Zack. You're scaring me!"

Wiping the tears away with the back of one of my heavily bandaged hands, in an effort to regain my compo-sure, I began taking slow, painful gasps of air. It took me another minute before I was finally able to speak. "L-l-look...I-I...c-can't really talk...r-right now..." I paused to take several more agonizing breaths. "C-c-can...w-we meet up?"

"Of course, Zack! Do you want to come over here?"

"Y-yes." I mumbled into the phone, a line of brown snot (the dust and bone particles were still making their way out) latching onto Nick's phone.

"Okay, just text me when your outside. Please hurry, though. You're freaking me out."

"I will," I replied, cutting the snot cord.

After hanging up, my eyes went at it again. I wasn't sure if it was hearing her voice, or the culmination of everything that had transpired over the course of the night; regardless, I was at the mercy of my emotions. Powerless to stop the unexpected onslaught, I took a seat next to Nick's bike and waited out the storm.

Several minutes later, the clouds of emotions finally parting, I began firing off text after text to Tiffany. In those text messages, I asked Tiffany to gather together medical supplies including: ace-bandages, Band-Aids, gauze pads, rubbing alcohol, scissors, tape, more ace-bandages, and as much antibacterial cream as she could find. Out of curiosity, I also asked her to look up what the Zyprolenia Cream 0.25% was typically used for and if she would be able to put a change of clothes together for me. As would be expected, Tiffany demanded that I tell her everything. It was hard, but I managed to avoid telling her anything significant. The less she knew, especially over the phone, the better.

With a long ride ahead of me, I tossed Nick's phone into my pocket and jumped onto his bike. Excruciatingly painful, yet necessary (the walk to Tiffany's house would take far too long), I gripped the handlebars with my raw, tender hands and squeezed. Feeling the searing pain jolt through my body, doubt began to creep in. How was I going to ride the entire way to her house in my current condition? There was only one way to find out—give it a whirl.

Gripping the handlebars even tighter, an effective, yet painful way to apply direct pressure to my open wounds, I gritted my teeth, and slowly began peddling down the street, heavily favoring my left side.

Switching between riding and walking when the pain became too unbearable, or when faced with monstrous hills, I cut through the streets of Stone Creek, moving so slowly it was like watching a tortoise climb stairs. After traveling a fourth of the way to Tiffany's house, I stopped after hearing Nick's phone ringing. Jumping off the bike, my hands in need of a break anyway, I pulled the phone out and saw that it was Tiffany.

"What's up?"

"Let me guess, tanning bed?" she asked sarcastically.

"What are you talking about?"

"Look, Zack, just because I agreed to go out with you doesn't mean I'm going to sleep with you right away. It's not even on the table right now."

"I'm not following you, Tiffany. What are you talking about?"

"Maybe you're sexually active and cool with it, but I'm not. Personally, I think sleeping around in high school is gross, but I guess that's just me, right Zack?"

I had absolutely no idea where she was going with the conversation. Never once had I pressured her into anything, much less sex. Things were getting crazy, and this conversation needed to be nipped in the bud. ""Tiffany, please just tell me where all of this is coming from? I'm in a great deal of pain, so can we please just cut to the chase."

Tiffany fell silent for a moment. "Fine, if that's how you want it, Zack. I think that you're embarrassed about your past, and because of it, came up with an elaborate ploy to bring up a touchy subject with me. You know, get me talking about it so you don't have to. Are you following me, Zack?"

"I have no idea what you're talking about?"

"Does the Zy-pro-lemia, or lenia, or whatever heck it is, ring a bell?"

"What about it? Did you find out what it's used for?"

"Crabs, Zack! It's used for the treatment of genital lice—as if you didn't already know."

Sickened by that unexpected development, I took the cream out of Nick's backpack and tossed it into a large forsythia plant. "Are you kidding me? That's what it's used for…" *And I touched it with my bare hands*, I cringed at the thought. "Honestly, I had no idea."

"Then why did you have me look it up for you?"

"I don't know! I just thought it might be important. Trust me, Tiff. Everything will make sense once we meet up."

"All right, Zack, I believe you. Please just get rid of that crap before you get here, okay?"

That wasn't a problem, especially since it was already resting in the innards of the budding forsythia plant. With my hands rested, and anxious to see Tiffany, I jumped back onto Nick's bike, and continued on my way. After what seemed like an eternity, my journey ended in front of Tiffany's house. It was 1:53 A.M. Exhausted and emotionally drained, I texted Tiffany to let her know of my arrival, and then found a nice resting spot next to the side door. Purposely or not, I found myself entirely concealed in the shadows of night. Maybe, just maybe, if I stayed in that particular spot, she wouldn't see the true extent of my injuries. Destined to never see her again—too risky considering my "infectious" condition—leaving the image of my brutalized face engrained in her memory didn't sit too well with me. She should remember the Zack Treadwell prior to his exit from the party, not the disturbing version of him filled with gruesome battle scars. Call me insecure, call me whatever you want, but having red and blue eyes is typically not a turn-on. Running on fumes, I drifted off to sleep, my head resting against the chilled, yellow stucco wall.

The coldness of the gravelly surface, reminiscent of the steel restraint table, actually provided slight relief to my sizable welt.

"Oh my god, Zack!" Tiffany cried. "You look terrible. What happened to you?"

Unaware that I had fallen asleep in the first place, I nearly jumped out of my skin at the sound of her voice. Like a drunkard, I staggered to my feet and stared at Tiffany with an intoxicated glare. Although 100% sober, I got my first taste of what a raging hangover must feel like. With my vision coming in and out of focus, slightly nauseous, and my head throbbing, standing was becoming more and more laborious. Stumbling backwards, I was forced to use the house for support.

"ZACK!" she cried, covering her mouth with her hands. "What happened out there? Please talk to me!" I could see and hear that she was speaking, but nothing was registering through the thick fog. Her words seemed to pass through me, almost as if she was communicating in a foreign language. Trapped in that particular trance-like state, the ability to reply evaded me. Half-sleeping, half-alert, it was as if I was watching our interaction—well, her interaction and my catatonic trance-like state—from afar.

"Zack, why aren't you answering me? You're scaring me. I'm calling 9-1-1!" she bellowed, pulling her phone out of her pocket.

Hearing her mention 9-1-1 jolted my awareness. She didn't know this about me (how could she?), but going to the hospital was out of question. Still undecided in reference to my immediate future, going to the hospital was a certain death sentence. All it would take was one simple blood test, a few phone calls, and *violà*, off to Timmonds Rock, or the incinerator, I go.

"N-noooo," I mumbled. "Don't!"

"Zack, you look like hell. You're covered in blood and…"

"I'm fine," I said, finding my way out of the fog. "I'm banged up...but I'll manage. Did you...bring the...stuff?"

Tears welling in her eyes, Tiffany held the bag up for me to see.

"Thanks," I replied, then reached for the bag. "I'll tell you everything...but first...I need to clean myself up.

Still holding firmly onto the bag—no signs of letting it go—Tiffany shook her head animatedly. "Are you kidding me, Zack? You're in no condition to fix yourself up. I mean look at your hands. Do you honestly believe you'd do a better job than me?"

"No, I don't. But it's not...safe for you. I'd feel better if I did it myself. Not all of this...is my blood..." *As if my blood is so pure now*, I thought harshly.

Tiffany's expression immediately changed. Tears streaming, she had a bewildered look in her eyes. "What happened out there, Zack?"

"Nothing good..."

Unable to look at me, Tiffany turned away and faced the door. "Follow me! I'm not taking 'no' for an answer. You hear me? Either you follow me or I'm calling 9-1-1."

I nodded, then followed her inside. Presumably afraid to wake her parents, Tiffany left the lights off as we descended the stairs, heading towards the bathroom nearest the gym. Along the way, she whispered to me that the downstairs bathroom was rarely, if ever, used at night. My anxiety grew when we entered the bathroom. In a matter of seconds, there was going to be no more hiding the true extent of my injuries. I closed my eyes in anticipation, a last-ditch effort to conceal one of my more grotesque and problematic features. I'm sure she noticed something was off with my eyes, but because of the dark, she probably didn't see just how bad they really were.

With the flick of a finger, bright light filled the room. Tiffany immediately gasped in horror, and she had yet to see the main event. I slowly opened my eyes, the reddish hue parting like curtains in a theater. Her hands jerked up and covered her mouth—fresh tears streaming down her mortified face. Out of sympathy or compassion, couldn't tell you which, Tiffany *attempted* to place a hand on my shoulder. *Attempted* is the operative word. Seeing her hand steadily approaching my contaminated body, I freaked out and lunged backwards, crashing the small of my back into the porcelain sink.

"My...God...Zack! What happened? Please tell me?"

Seeing her tears was all it took. I joined her in a duet of muffled cries and labored breathing. Unable to face her, I jerked my head to the side and covered it as much as possible with my arm. I kept trying to talk, only for my words to evade me yet again.

Tiffany finally broke the silence. "Z-Z-Zack...y-your neck...a-and eyes!"

Wiping away fresh tears with my shoulders, I took several deep, burning inhalations before replying, "I'll be okay...I just need...to get myself...cleaned up. We can talk...afterwards."

Tiffany nodded, then placed the bag on the floor and began rummaging through the supplies. "Let me help you, Zack."

I shook my head. "No, Tiffany, I need to do this...on my own. Okay?"

I then proceeded to peel the blood-soaked bandages off my hands. It was an arduous and painful task, especially in the areas where the blood had hardened, forming an adhesive bond between the bandage and my lacerated skin. Similar to pulling off a scab before its ready, fresh blood began to well up from the deeper of the gouges. After ripping off (I say ripping even though the process was slow moving and gentle only because that's exactly what it felt like) the last of the bandages, I carefully placed the highly "infectious" rags into the garbage can. Hoping to avoid contaminating her floor with my highly toxic blood, I jerked them over her sink just in time to watch crimson red droplets make artwork of her shiny white sink. The contrast was beautiful. The pure white magnified the little red splatters of death.

"This is ridiculous, Zack. You can't do this on your own. Look at your hands for Christ's sake. One looks like an old cutting board and the other looks like something tore a chunk out of it. What happened out there?"

I shook my head unable to come up with a retort. She was right. I couldn't do it on my own. But asking her, of all people, was out of the question. I'd rather bleed out in her sink than risk her catching the "EATS virus." I could deal with my own death, if it came to that, not hers.

Tiffany didn't bother to wait for a response. She simply turned around and darted out of the room.

"Tiffany," I whispered after her. "Where are you going? Come back! Tiff..."

She wasn't coming back. That much was for sure. But what was she up to? Was she going for her parents? Her brother? Needle and thread? I had no clue. All I knew was that my butt wasn't going anywhere. Even if I wanted to chase after her, it wasn't going to happen with my *venomous* fluids leaking all over the place. From my limited understanding of blood borne pathogens, I was aware that some were capable of living outside the body for minutes, hours, even days, just waiting to latch onto an unsuspecting host and do what they do best—ravage a person's immune system. Staring at my mauled hands, blood dripping worse than a leaky faucet, I was grounded.

Glancing around the room, I spotted the bag Tiffany had prepared for me off in the far corner of the bathroom. If I could just get to that bag, maybe, just maybe, there'd be enough time to fix myself up and make a quick dart for the exit. It was worth a shot. With my hands hovering over the sink, I lunged for the bag with my foot. After a few unsuccessful tries, my foot finally caught the bag's handle, and I was able to carefully slide it over to me.

In total desperation mode, motivated by the thought of Lonnie and Allison making a surprise visit (courtesy of Tiffany) into the bathroom, I turned the faucet on and began rinsing my hands under the cold water. Stopping the bleeding serving as my primary objective, even if only for a few moments, would allow me the opportunity to harpoon my hand into the bag and grab one of the thick rolls of gauze. After that, with an even quicker wrap-job, I could be out of the bathroom in 90 seconds tops. Wishful thinking, without a doubt, but if I worked efficiently and ignored the searing pain anything was possible.

"Okay, it's now or never," I mumbled to myself.

Rinsing off the remaining blood from my swollen left hand, of which a greenish pus was beginning to ooze from the site of the deep bite wound, I readied myself for the snag. About to plunge my hand into the plastic bag, I heard the terrifying sound of footsteps vastly approaching. *Abort! Abort! Abort!* I hollered in my head. There was no point in bloodying up the bag and my change of clothes if the mission was going to fail anyway. Eyes glued to the door, I nervously waited for it to open.

Seconds later, the door swung open and a faint laugh parted my dried, chapped lips. There was no Lonnie, no Allison, no Rick ready to force me against my will to seek immediate medical attention. Nope, none of them were in attendance for what would undoubtable be my *low-key* going away party. No DJ. No ice sculptures. No paparazzi. No catering service. No foam party. No nothing. Just a quiet send-off with the youngest of the Kent gang clad in oversized purple gloves—so big, they had to be folded over at the elbow just to fit her. It was a tremendous relief.

"I know, I know. These were the only gloves I could find. My mom has a tendency to disregard sizes when she shops for things like this. She once bought a belt for my dad that was a size 46—only off by a good 14 inches."

"You had me scared there for a minute," I admitted. "I thought you had left to call for backup."

Tiffany glared at me pensively. "You know full well I should be waking them up. It's crazy that I'm not. Have you seen yourself, Zack? You look like you were left for dead. Did someone try to strangle you?"

I nodded. There was no point in denying it. The evidence was tattooed in a colorful array of reds and purples all around my enflamed neck. It still hurt to breath, even worse to swallow.

"You have to give me something, Zack. Did you find your friend?"

Again, I nodded. "I did..." I paused clenching my teeth in anger, trying to push back the visions, the memories, the unavoidable tears. "...Oh, did I ever."

"You're scaring me, Zack!"

"Look, Tiffany, I think it's in our best interest to clean me up first. I promise, I'll tell you everything. I just really need to get out of these clothes. All the blood is making me sick..."

"Of course, Zack," Tiffany gestured towards the toilet, "sit and let me take over. I volunteered at a summer camp a few years ago. Bumps and bruises are nothing new to me."

"You got it Nurse Kent," I joked, hoping to lighten the mood, for her sake more than my own.

Reaching into her bag, Tiffany pulled out several rolls of gauze, sterile gauze pads, antibacterial ointment, medical tape, *rubbing alcohol*, and a brown bottle that resembled the bottle of chloroform I had swiped. My eyes fixated on the bottle of rubbing alcohol. A flashback of the acid-like alcohol swab melted through me. What was I thinking when I added that to the list? Did I hate myself that much? If I had intended on diluting it enough to drink—that would have made much more sense than pouring the liquid fire on my wounds. I turned away unable to look at it any longer.

Grabbing the bottle of rubbing alcohol, Tiffany waved it at me. *Is she trying to torture me, waving it in my face like that?* I thought, my skin cowering in anticipation.

"Zack, I know you asked me to grab this for you, but honestly, I'm not sure if I have it in me to use it on you. Not without anesthesia that is. With how deep your cuts are, it'd probably feel like I was pouring boiling oil over them. But—"

Oh, the infamous *but*. Just when things are looking up, and a sense of relief sets in, there's always a "but." I know you want to go to your parents' funeral, "but" we don't feel that's in your best interest, Zack. I understand that you want to live with your grandmother, I truly can sympathize, "but" she's old and frail and is in no condition to care for a small child. Zack, I know we can inspect the cave tomorrow, come all prepared and all that crap, "but" it's not going to happen. I'm going tonight—whether you like it or not. And last, yet certainly not least, you manage to survive a hellish ordeal, the odds stacked heavily against you, "but" now you have to deal with a little thing called the "EATS virus." All my life, a "but" preceded tragedy. Why should now be any different?

"—I think this will work much better and sting a whole heck of a lot less," Tiffany added, holding up a bottle of hydrogen peroxide.

"Whatever you say, Nurse Kent," I said, relief sweeping through me. "I'm at your mercy."

"Will you stop calling me that, Zack? You know a real nurse should be looking at you—not me."

"I know, Tiffany. You're right. I should be at the hospital right now. *BUT* there's a reason I can't go to one. I promise everything will make sense in due time."

Tiffany shrugged her shoulders dryly and got to work. Soon enough my hands resembled Tiffany's pool from earlier in the night, bubbling and fizzling all over like the suds from her foam party. The hydrogen peroxide still torched my hands a bit, just not on the same level of intensity as the lone alcohol swab. After thoroughly disinfecting my hands, Tiffany lathered a thick coat of antibacterial ointment on both hands before carefully bandaging them. She then repeated that same process with my knees and on the deep gash above my eye. After finishing my wound care, sweat glistening on her forehead and upper lip, Tiffany carefully wrapped ace bandages around my calf and forearm and helped me change out of my blood-soaked clothes. With fresh boxers, socks, sweatpants, and a promotional long-sleeved Glute-Boots shirt on, I thought we were done. Was I ever wrong!

"Okay, so I guess the stage is—"

"We're not done yet," she interrupted. "There's one more thing we need to do. Hold on, I'll be right back."

Tiffany left and reappeared minutes later holding a stack of ice packs. "You need to apply ice to reduce some of the swelling, Zack. It's going to suck, but if you don't, things are only going to get worse."

The infamous "but" reared its ugly head again.

Tiffany then spent the next several minutes binding the ice packs to my swollen calf and forearm, both hands, the back of my head, a smaller one for my engorged ear, and two for my neck—wrapped snuggly around like a cervical collar. It took a few minutes for the cold to kick it, and when it did, I detested Tiffany's astuteness. Bearing in mind Tiffany that was still in the dark about my condition, she was right about one thing—things were only going to get worse—much, much worse. The swelling, the pain, the excruciating discomfort bound to settle in over the course of the next few days, mattered little. I didn't plan to stick around long enough to see how badly things could get.

Throwing all of my infectious clothes and contaminated materials in a bag for proper disposal, Tiffany glanced up at me, and smirked.

"What's so funny?"

"Oh, nothing, Zack," she replied, now almost laughing. "We've only been dating for a few hours now and look at us. You look like you were just in a death match and I'm picking up the pieces. I can't wait to see what's in store for us."

Her explanation stirred up the brawling butterflies once again. This time it was an all out weapons match. The simple fact remained, there was nothing in store for us, just a short and painful goodbye. Of which, needed to get underway.

"Nick's dead!"

"What do you mean he's dead? That can't be. Please tell me you're just messing with me?"

"I'm not."

"How?"

I shook my head slowly, staring at her with a distressed glare. "He was murdered!"

"Murdered?" she cried. "What do you mean murdered?"

"I mean he was savagely—"

"Shhhhhh," she whispered suddenly, cutting me off. "I think someone's coming down the stairs."

As if it was on cue, a light abruptly flicked on in the hallway, sending paralyzing fear coursing through my body. Tiffany looked as equally scared as me, panic setting in her widening eyes. Had someone heard us? I thought we were being relatively quiet, but then again, sound tends to travel in houses, even ones as big as the Kents' mansion. With the footsteps quickly approaching, I shrugged my shoulders and mouthed the words, "What should we do?"

"Just be quiet," she whispered almost inaudibly into my ear.

I took her advice, as if there was an alternative. Moments later, to my sheer horror, the footsteps abruptly stopped right in front of the door. If things couldn't get any worse, whoever was standing outside of the door, gently knocked on it three times, sending a cold chill pin-balling up and down my spine. I immediately locked eyes with Tiffany, hoping she would come to the rescue. After thirty seconds of pure silence, her shell-shocked face still contorted with her jaw almost of its hinge, I knew it was up to me to save the day.

Thinking on my feet, or more appropriately on my glutes, I flushed the toilet with my elbow, and in my best Tiffany impersonation said, "Hello," with a slight rasp in my voice. The rasp actually came naturally with my enflamed and shredded esophagus.

Tiffany's jaw snapped back into place. Pulling at her hair in frustration, she mouthed the words, "Are you crazy?"

"Is that you, Tiffany?" Lonnie asked through the door. "Is everything okay? You don't sound like yourself."

Tiffany then shot an evil glare my way before sliding a finger across her throat—a clear signal that I was a dead man. She had no idea how right she was. Then, after clearing her throat, she replied, "Sorry, Dad, I'm not feeling too well right now. My stomach's killing me. I think I ate too much at the party."

Impressive rebound. However, that only solved one problem. Why was Lonnie downstairs in the first place? A late night workout, perhaps? If so, how long did he plan on hitting the weights?

"I'm sorry to hear that, sweetie," Lonnie replied, sounding concerned. "Is there anything I can do for you? You know what, why don't I just run upstairs and grab your mother. She's always been good with those types of things."

Dear God, NO! I thought, immediately panicking.

If Lonnie was apprehensive about walking in on his sick, little girl, Allison would not be. Of course, I didn't really have any basis for this theory, but she was a woman, and women typically migrate to bathrooms together. Why should this be any different—especially, with the deathly ill picture Tiffany was painting?

"No, Dad, I'll be fine," Tiffany moaned. "It just has to run its course. Once it does, I'm sure I'll be okay. I have my phone with me so if it gets real bad, I'll call. Okay?"

"Speaking of phones, I just came down here looking for mine. I can't find it anywhere. Is it in there by any chance?"

"Hold on a sec," Tiffany grunted, her eyes bouncing around the room, searching for Lonnie's phone. Caught up in the moment—my battered self, Tiffany on her hands and knees desperately hunting down her father's phone—I nearly burst out into laughter. *If only Mr. Kent could really see what was going on behind closed doors*, I thought gleefully to myself. Noticing the emerging smirk on my face, Tiffany smiled as well, presumably thinking the same thing as me.

"I don't see it in here, Dad. Why don't you check in the gym, isn't that where you always leave it?"

"You're right about that. I'll go check it out, sweetie," he announced before trouncing down the hallway.

"That was close," Tiffany whispered into my good ear. "Let's wait untill he leaves and go outside. We'll have more privacy there."

I nodded in agreement. Several minutes passed before we heard the door to the gym swing open, followed by Lonnie's heavy footsteps thumping down the hall. When he reached the door, he knocked on it gently again, and said, "I found it, Tiff. Give me a call if you need anything. I'm spent. That party really wiped me out. Hope you feel better, sweetheart."

In pure silence, we listened as Lonnie made his way back to the master bedroom. I had never actually seen the master bedroom, but from what I heard, like everything else in the house, it was massive. The word on the street—straight from Mike's highly exaggerative mouth—was that you could fit a Boeing 747 in it and still have enough room to make the "magic" happen. After waiting a few more minutes for Lonnie to get settled in, we made our move. Throwing all of the ice packs in a bag for outside use—damn her, and her first aid ways—Tiffany slung the bag over her shoulder, and took the lead. With all of the lights still off, I followed closely behind. As graceful as a highly trained ninja, Tiffany conquered the stairs without producing even the slightest peep. She could do no wrong. As for me, I offset her complete silence by making a loud ruckus. Even attempting to mimic her every move, my feet stepping in the exact same places as hers, I still made enough noise to wake the entire household. It was like I was tap dancing on bubble wrap.

Unable to voice her frustration, Tiffany kept shooting looks in my direction, as if to say: *Are you trying to get us caught?* Fortunately, because of Tiffany's nimbleness, everything equaled out in the end and it sounded as if only one person was clumping up the stairs—perhaps, an over-tired person with digestive issues.

"Okay, Zack it's important that you stay close. My parents have the entire backyard rigged with motion detectors. If any of them go off our cover will be blown. My dad is a light sleeper and is hyper-vigilant about protecting his family. Just last week he was outside hunting prowlers in his boxers with a shotgun slung over his shoulders. If he sees any of the lights go off, he won't hesitate to investigate. So do everything I do—and don't screw up. I'll go first. After I reach the first 'safe zone' I'll wave you over. Got it!"

I nodded, terrified to mess up. I then watched as Tiffany crouched down and began duck-walking behind a row of tall bushes that ran parallel to the fence. Just before making it to the corner of the fence, Tiffany performed a smooth summersault across a spot where a small section of bush was missing, triumphantly jumping to her feet once passed it. Turning around to face me, Tiffany waved for me to go. Although not as elegant as her—the summersault killed my aching body—I also made it without incident.

"One down, two to go," she whispered before taking off again.

Crouched behind a large rectangular shaped box bush, I watched in horror as Tiffany eased herself onto her belly and began shuffling military-style, her chin mere inches off the ground, behind a long line of sprouting flowers. After making it about twenty-five feet, passing the pool house on her left-hand side, Tiffany sat up from behind a large rose bush and gave me the thumbs up. Taking inventory of my injuries, I wasn't sure if my body could manage. How was I going to crawl military-style with my hands, arm, knees, and leg banged up as they were? It didn't seem possible. Then again, if I could escape from the clutches of Dr. Vox, was there really anything out of the realm of possibility? I thought not, then pressed forward.

Easing myself to the ground, pain radiated up and down my left side as I began the grueling task of shuffling military-style towards the rose bush. With my eyes closed, teeth clenched like a vice, sweat oozing out of my pores, I slithered forward like a snake after a substantial meal, traveling a few feet a time. In contrast to the minute it took Tiffany to reach the safe zone, it took me ten. Out of breath, my body on fire, once there, Tiffany hoisted me to a seated position. My mind was so rattled it didn't even register in my head that she had touched me with her bare hands—a tremendous no, no—that need not be repeated.

"Okay, Zack, just one more. But I must warn you ahead of time—you're not going to like it. In fact, you're probably going to want to kill me afterwards."

Without uttering another word, Tiffany slid through a small opening in the rose bush, and once through, adjusted her position and began rolling in the direction of the pool house. Once completely behind it, she stopped herself, took a moment to regain her equilibrium, and jumped to her feet. With her hands extended out in front of her, she began gesturing for me to come to her as if I was a dog. *Come here, boy! Come to momma*, I imagined her saying. *You can do it...I know you can.* Listening like the good doggie, I threw myself onto my stomach and began "inch-worming" my way through the small opening, scratching the back of my head and neck in the process. After popping through the rosebush like a well-trained dog, I could almost imagine what Tiffany would say next: *That's a good boy, Zachary. Now roll over...*

I did, and as soon as my wounded forearm hit the ground, that stupid voice I had imagined ceased to exist. Actually, everything, aside from the inferno of pain, ceased to exist. With the blank chalkboard of my brain on fire, I had to force myself to dig deeper just to keep moving. Like an overweight crocodile with a bad heart and arthritic knees, my roll was slow moving, torturous, and pathetic at best. I'd get moving, stop mid-roll, rock back and forth for a moment to gain momentum, and after harnessing enough force to flip over, I'd crash painfully to the ground. Tiffany was right—I did want to kill her. After finally making it over to her, fifteen torturous rolls later, my body felt as if it was on the verge of exploding.

"Are you okay," Tiffany asked, leaning over me.

Staring blankly at her, my breathing labored, I shook my head. "Not at all! I should be...fine in a minute or..."

Just then, out of nowhere, one of the sensor lights went off, triggering the rest to turn on. The backyard lit up like a football stadium during a night game. Panicked, I jolted up, dizzy and all, and shuffled over to the back of the pool house. Beating me there, Tiffany held her finger up to her lip, and shook her head, whispering, "Don't move…make any sounds…or even breathe!"

I did an excellent job of the first two. The breathing one was a completely different story. After the violent exchange with Dr. Vox, holding my breath for any amount of time was a recipe for another PTSD episode.

"GOD DAMN RACOONS," Lonnie shouted off in the distance. "They're eating all the crap off the ground."

"Just let them be, Lonnie," Allison grunted. "Besides, it'll be less to clean up tomorrow.

Tiffany and I both shared a deep sigh of relief. "You don't know how lucky we are, Zack. Let's just hope those raccoons stay over there and don't venture over here. Those things have nasty bites."

"Speaking of bites," I said, staring at my freshly grass-stained bandages. "I should probably go ahead and tell you everything that happened."

Tiffany edged closer to me and placed an ungloved hand on my leg. It didn't go unnoticed this time. I immediately jerked my leg away from her and glared at her wide-eyed. "Not without your gloves, Tiffany. It's not safe—"

"Can I ask why you're so toxic all of a sudden?"

I took a slow breath in and exhaled. The pain still lingered in my throat, reminding me of just how close to death I had been. It also reminded me of my looming fate. "Tiffany," I said, somewhat hesitantly, "have you ever heard of the 'EATS virus?'"

"The what?"

Not holding anything back—what would be the point—I laid everything there was to know about the virus and conspiracy on the table. I told her about my parents, Nick's discovery of the secret military lab, and my gravely encounter with the evil Dr. Vox. Without going into extremely graphic details, I also told her about Nick's brutal murder. She appeared horrified by my tale, but did not interrupt. Instead, she sat there quietly listening as I explained all about my battle with Dr. Vox and his secret journals. The same journals that spelled out my fate.

Before going into intimate details about my new and "deadly" condition, Tiffany broke her silence. "We have to go to the police, Zack," she cried. "If that monster is still inside the cave, he needs to pay for what he did to you and your friend, Nick."

I waved my bandaged hand at her—the one with the huge bite mark. "It's not that simple, Tiffany."

"What do you mean it's not that simple? It is that simple. You call the police, show them where you found the secret hatch, and wait for them to do their job."

"I can't go to the police."

"That doesn't make any sense, Zack. Are you afraid of getting in trouble for trespassing on a military base?"

"No."

"Then what are you hiding from me?"

I hesitated, then cued her in on my *toxic* little secret. "Dr. Vox was infected with the 'EATS virus,' Tiffany. Which means—"

Eyes welling with tears, her eyes fixated on my heavily bandaged hands, Tiffany finished my sentence: "—you're infected too."

The tears erupted out of her eyes. Watching her head and shoulders bopping up and down like an infant in a jumper, I couldn't help but to join in. The worst part was that I couldn't even console her. It was far too dangerous.

"It's okay, Tiffany."

Eyes bloodshot, snot dangling from her nose, Tiffany shot a look at me. "How is everything okay, Zack? If everything you told me about the virus is true—you're as good as…dead!"

"I know that, Tiff. And I've already come to terms with that," I blatantly lied. "But for now, I have more important things to worry about."

"What could possibly be more important than your life?"

"You for instance. I have to make sure nothing happens to you or anyone else for that matter. It's one of the reasons I've been so hyper-vigilant about any physical contact. The virus may be my curse, my nightmare, my death sentence, but that doesn't mean it has to be yours too."

"Can't you just go to the hospital and make sure you're really infected?"

"It's too risky. I've seen what happens to the 'infected,' and I don't want to end up like one of them. Besides, I just have to wait for the fever set in to know for sure. Once it does, it'll be proof enough for me."

Tiffany broke down crying again, her head now tucked in between her legs. "There has to be another way," she said, raising her head.

"There is no other way," I replied, forcing thoughts of Dr. Vox's *miracle elixir* out of my head. "When it's time, I want to go out on my terms—no one else's. Understand?"

"What now, Zack?"

I paused, knowing exactly what needed to happen next. Tiffany and I would need to go our separate ways. Wiping away a fresh tear with my sleeve, I shrugged my shoulders meekly. "I think you know the answer to that question."

Tiffany shook her head in defiance. "It doesn't have to end this way. We can still—"

"No, Tiffany, we can't! I have to leave and never look back. It's too risky for you to be around me. And, frankly, it's too damn depression for me to hear your voice. I'm only here tonight because you deserved to hear it from me directly. And because, I—"

"Stop it, Zack! We're not saying goodbye just yet—and that's final."

I glared at her, wondering what she had in mind.

"If tonight is our last night together, I want to spend it with you. We can sleep under the stars and pretend that everything's fine. Maybe it's selfish of me, but I'd prefer my last memory of you to be special. The virus may be stealing you away from me, but that doesn't mean we can't enjoy what little time we have left."

She made a valid argument. If it was going to be the last time we ever saw or spoke to each other, it should be memorable. We should be able to reflect back on our last night together and see a glimmer of happiness instead of pain. Of all the things we would miss out on—I tried to block those thoughts out as much as possible—we would still have the kiss we shared and the night we spent together under the stars.

"Okay, I concede, but what about your parents? Won't they kill us if they find us out here?"

Tiffany threw her arms up in the air. "Who cares? I'll take my chances. You're worth any punishment my parents can dole out. Here let me put the ice packs back on. It's about that time."

Without even having to remind her, Tiffany threw her purple gloves back on applied the ice packs. When she was finished, she took her gloves off and informed me that she would be right back. I then watched as she got into position and rolled towards the rose bush before darting through the small opening like a fleeing rabbit. Exhausted, I rested my eyes while waiting for her to return. I fell asleep almost instantly. I'm not sure how much time elapsed, but the next thing I knew Tiffany had returned holding a stack of pillows and blankets piled up so high, they nearly covered her pretty face. I also noticed that she had a backpack slung around her shoulder and had changed into pajamas. On instinct, I jumped to my feet, my now warmed icepacks flopping to the ground like dead fish, and offered to help.

"They're just blankets and pillows, Zack. I think I can manage."

I backed off and let Tiffany do her thing. After putting the finishing touches up on our sleeping area, something finally dawned on me. "Wait a minute! How did you not set off the motion detectors carrying all that stuff? There's no way you took that same route as before."

"Oh, that. It was easy," she replied humbly, "I just turned them off."

Tiffany and I shared a glance before erupting in laughter. I could, and rightly should have been mad at her, but with so little time on our side, it seemed a waste of time. Besides, it was incredibly funny—the irony torching my ailing body.

"In case you were hungry," Tiffany said, opening up the backpack, "I brought out some leftovers—including a piece of cake. I felt bad that you didn't get a chance to have any."

The gesture was truly appreciated. Beyond imagine. Except, I wasn't sure if, or how much my raw esophagus could manage. "Tiffany," I began. "That was very thoughtful, but..." I paused as Tiffany's expression changed. Not wanting to hurt her feelings, I backtracked. "—I don't think I can wait for desert. That cake looks delicious. Do you mind if I start with that?"

"I don't mind at all just as long as you share it with me."

Splitting the piece of cake in two, giving herself the much larger piece after I declined, we devoured the cake within minutes. I made sure to masticate slowly, chasing each bite down with a large gulp of cold water. It still burned on the way down, nearly unbearable at times, but if nothing else the cake put some food in my depleted body and overrode the dreadful aftertaste that had been lingering in my mouth since my clumsy spill into the dusty graveyard. After finishing the cake, I picked at some of the other leftovers, more so to provide the illusion to Tiffany that she was taking care of me.

"Here, take some of these," Tiffany said, handing me over several Ibuprofen pills. "It may help with the pain."

I swallowed them down, one by one, and then eased myself onto my back. Snapping the purple gloves back on, I knew what was in store for me—another icing session. Pulling out a fresh batch of ice packs from her backpack (the type you have to smack around for a few minutes to activate), struggling to crack them open, Tiffany threw them to the ground and began stomping on them. To my astonishment, out of the eight ice packs, she only busted one of them, staining the rear of the pool house with that weird, jellylike blue goo. After activating the last cold compress, Tiffany scooped them up, minus the deflated one, and went to work.

"All done," Tiffany said, pulling off the gloves. "Just twenty more minutes, Zack. Trust me. You'll thank me in the morning."

"Isn't it morning already?"

"Very funny, Zack. You have to do it, though. Cause if you don't, you'll swell up worse than a dictionary left in the rain."

I quit my gabbing. I could talk my head off and it wasn't going to change anything. Nurse Kent was dead set on icing my injuries, so that's exactly what she was going to do. Splitting time between staring up at the heavens and into Tiffany's deep blue eyes, I decided to try to impress her with my primitive knowledge of astronomy. "Hey, Tiff, that's Orion right there…and the Big Dipper's over there," I said, pointing off to the left. "Do you see it?"

Tiffany burst into laughter.

"Spit it out," I demanded. "What's so funny?"

"Really, Zack, that's the Big Dipper?"

I nodded, confidence waning.

"Well, I may be wrong, but I could have sworn the constellation you were pointing to was Ursa Minor, a.k.a. Little Bear, a.k.a. Little Dipper. Which, to be honest, is pretty impressive since most people have difficulty spotting it. Ursa Major, a.k.a. Great Bear, a.k.a. Big Dipper, is over there…much more prominent and easy to spot."

My face blushed. "Okay, Tiffany, you caught me red-handed—literally and figuratively. I really don't have any astronomical skills. I was just trying to impress you."

Tiffany rolled over to her side and faced me. "You don't have to try to impress me, Zack. I like you the way you are—astronomically challenged or not."

I turned, met her gaze, and saw a strength in her not previously noticed. Tiffany knew what was on our plate, yet she was attempting to do something unimaginable, and at the same time, completely selfless. Tiffany was trying to make our last night together memorable, and in the process, force out any negative thoughts about my dismal future. She wanted to squeeze every last drop out of our relationship before it had a chance to dry out. I loved that about her. In fact, I just loved her, period. She was the type of person you could marry and never, not even for a fraction of a second, feel as if you missed out on anything. In today's society where playing the field is the norm, most people frown upon a person's first real relationship going the distance. Their motto always being: how do you know that you caught the best fish in the sea if you never snagged anything else on your line? Unfortunately, we would never get to prove them wrong. Our relationship was on life support, and, by morning rise, the figurative plug was scheduled to be pulled.

"Where are you, Zack?" Tiffany asked, sitting up. "What's on your mind?"

My lips bowed upwards. "I was just thinking about stuff. Nothing important. Since you're the astronomy buff, why don't teach me a few things."

"Okay, but I must warn you, this girl knows her stuff. I took an advanced astronomy class in grammar school."

"Impressive! Now let's see if you can put your money where your mouth is."

"Over there is…" Tiffany began shooting off constellation after constellation, even providing me with a brief history of each. After a while, Tiffany slowly edged closer and closer to me. Her closeness made me extremely uncomfortable, but since she wasn't physically touching me, I decided not to say anything. Even if she was, it probably would have mattered little, considering how well she had bandaged me up.

We spent the remainder of the night gazing into the stars, making small talk, flirting, and feeling the moderate closeness of each other's bodies. It was clear that neither of us wanted to fall asleep. We must have wanted the night to last as long as possible, it being our last, and all. Although we made a valiant effort to stay awake, at some point during the early morning hours, we both drifted off into sleep.

Chapter Thirteen

A New Day

The next day, well literally the same day but later, I awoke to the sounds of birds chirping and Tiffany's warm hand nudging me on the shoulder.

"Wake up, Zack," she whispered. "You need to get up. My parents usually wake-up around six to exercise."

Even though my head felt groggy and my body ached, I forced myself to cut through the thick, black fog and sat up. As painful as it was to lift myself to a seated position, small explosions erupting from all different parts of my body, I found myself in a surprisingly pleasant mood. Tiffany played a major role in that. With her hair scrounged and all knotted up, her makeup smeared all around her puffy, sleep-deprived eyes, and a whitish mucus in the corners of her mouth, Tiffany still managed to look stunning.

For a brief moment, watching Tiffany kick her cleaning efforts into high gear, there were no thoughts of Nick, Dr. Vox, or the virus that was rapidly multiplying inside of my body. To be honest, I almost felt normal, as if everything was going to be okay. Then, just as a sense of normalcy returned back into my life, my eyes drifted downwards. One glimpse at my heavily bandaged hands was all it took. It served as the catalyst that set off a volcanic eruption in my brain, sending depressing thoughts floating like ashen soot to the forefront of my consciousness. Void of any hope, I crawled over to the pool house and used it to hoist myself to a standing position. Once upright, I ran a mental checklist of extreme pain vs. soreness while Tiffany continued with the cleaning.

Falling into the category of extreme pain were my head, both hands, neck, throat, and forearm—basically everything. The only thing that actually felt slightly better was my calf. The swelling had gone down significantly—thanks to Nurse Kent's painful icing sessions—and was only mildly uncomfortable to stand on. Walking was a different story, but was by far much more manageable than the previous night.

"How are you feeling?"

"I'll manage."

"I hate to rush you…especially in the condition you're in…but—"

"I know…your parents."

Tiffany smiled crookedly. She began shaking her head as fresh tears paved a path down her flustered face. "I can't believe it's come to this, Zack. I can't keep the act up any longer. I tried so hard to be strong for you last night. But it's eating me up inside."

I could relate to the "eating me up" part. Except in my case, it was the "EATS virus," which in due time would undoubtedly wreak havoc on my immune system. Of course, reminding Tiffany of that little tidbit of information was completely unnecessary. "I know we don't have a lot of time. But before I go there's one thing you should know…" I paused, turning my grotesque gaze away from hers, "Tiffany…I…I…I love you."

"I love you too," Tiffany cried, pulling me into an embrace. "I'm going to miss you so much, Zack. I'm going to hold out hope that by some miracle, some will of God, you're not infected. Before you go, you have to promise me something, Zack."

"Sure, whatever you need."

"Please promise me that you'll let me know before you…you know…go through with it."

"I will," I replied, catching a glimpse of her inviting lips. "You don't know how much I want to kiss you right now. To taste your lips one last—"

Before I could do anything to stop her, Tiffany planted a kiss on my cheek, the corners of our lips briefly locking. She felt and tasted too good to pull away—yet it had to happen, and fast—her life was in jeopardy. Jerking my head away from hers, I cried, "Are you crazy, Tiffany? Did you not hear what I said about the virus and the risks associated?"

"Don't worry, Zack. I'll be fine. Besides we barely touched lips."

"Yeah, but I don't know how contagious this virus is. For all we know it can be as contagious as hepatitis. You have to wipe your mouth off with something—anything."

Tiffany shook her head, then reached into her backpack and pulled out a small bottle of hand sanitizer. After squirting a small amount of the clear substance in her hand, she scrubbed the side of her lip that touched mine. Once fully sanitized, she wiped her mouth off with her sleeve and stared at me searching for approval.

"Please tell me that didn't burn!" I cried, completely paranoid for her safety and well-being. I was aware that she took excellent care of her lips, evidenced by the sweet taste of strawberries so early in the morning—still it didn't hurt to be certain.

"Not at all, Zack. Why would it burn, anyway? It's just hand sanitizer."

"Most sanitizers contain alcohol, so my thinking was that if you had any open wounds on your lips it'd probably burn. Makes sense, right?"

"I guess so."

"Oh, and don't forget to wash all the sheets in hot—"

"—water!" she finished my sentence. "Zack, I think you're being a little obsessive right now. Nothing's going to happen to me. I know you don't believe this, but I have faith that we'll see each other again. That monster may have bitten you, but that doesn't necessarily mean you're infected. For all we know, he could just be a complete whack-job, and all that time spent in isolation fried his brain. Maybe he's even convinced himself that it's all true and he's been eating people to feed into that psychotic delusion."

I smiled, hoping and praying that she was right, although doubtful that she was. "I'll know soon enough, Tiffany. If nothing does happen…you will see me again. Either way, I promise to contact you one last time…," I shrugged my shoulders weakly, "…before everything goes down. Please, no calls or texts. I need to put everything from my past behind me to focus on what needs to be done. Understand?"

Tiffany nodded, new tears welling up in her eyes. Her bottom lip quivering, she gave me one last hug, and whispered that she loved me. I said it back to her, turned around, and exited from her backyard, and from her life for good. There would no turning back. The line, carved deeper into the earth than the lacerations on my hand, was there to stay. Our paths were not destined to cross again. Wanting to forget everything, I jumped on Nick's bike and began my journey back to my foster parents' house.

The ride back was not as amnesic as I would have hoped. The pain and grueling hills helped a little, just not enough to eliminate the depressing thoughts altogether. No matter how hard I tried to focus on anything else, thoughts of Nick, Tiffany, and my own mortality weighed heavily on my mind.

Arriving at my foster parents' house shortly later, anxiety reared its timid head while trying to figure out how I was going to sneak past Bill and Susan. Like everything else with the Baniaks, their morning routine was vastly unpredictable. Sometimes they'd wake-up super early in the morning, and do God knows what, and at other times, they'd oversleep and act like complete psychos running all around trying to get ready for work. It was hit or miss with them. Walking Nick's bike up the driveway, it was a good sign that all of the lights were off. They were probably still sleeping, or meditating, or engaging in an activity best not mentioned. Regardless, the only thing that mattered was gaining entrance into the house and reaching my room undetected. Just as with Lonnie and Allison, I couldn't risk the Baniaks seeing me in my current condition.

Parking Nick's bike behind the garage, I quietly approached the house from the rear. When only an arm's length away from the door, my heart suddenly slammed itself into my pancreas after realizing my keys were still inside Timmonds Rock. I cursed myself for being so stupid. I couldn't believe it, well, actually that's a lie, in all the chaos, my keys were the least of my concerns. But still, it was a highly irresponsible oversight on my part.

Without keys or any feasible way inside the house until Bill and Susan left for work, waiting them out was my only option. In no condition to walk the streets, my hindquarters kept Nick's bike company behind the old, raggedy garage. It was 6:23 A.M., meaning the house wouldn't be vacated for at least two more hours. Even on those chaotic mornings when they hit the snooze button one too many times, Bill and Susan were always out of the house by 8:30 A.M.

Still groggy from the night before, I rested my head against the garage and tried to sleep. I say tried because sleep evaded me. The problem wasn't fatigue—I was more than exhausted. No, what was making sleep so evasive was my throbbing headache. It almost felt as if an immense force was crushing my skull, and at the same time pinning my brain against it, making it virtually impossible to focus on anything but the excruciating pain. Think deep sea diving with some lunatic pounding on your skull with a meat tenderizer. Although not a medical professional, a severe concussion was my initial diagnosis. Freaked out, I began visualizing my brain swelling with blood and fluids, pressing dangerously against my skull. I had heard stories of people dying under such conditions because they didn't seek out immediate medical attention. For my sake, I prayed that didn't come into fruition. It was a scary possibility.

Under different circumstances, I would have already been at the hospital begging for someone—anyone—to examine my head. I'd let them run me through whatever gamut of tests they needed to in order to ensure a healthy recovery. I wouldn't even complain either. I'd sit down with my mouth shut, follow whatever instructions were provided, and let them crack my skull open if they had to. But I wasn't under a different set of circumstances, and a visit to the hospital was out of the question. Then, while entirely engrossed in thoughts of death and the unbearable throbbing sensation in my head, it suddenly dawned on me. Who cares? If my head injury proved fatal with me dying from a severe brain edema wouldn't that just save me the trouble doing it myself? Plus, if suicide is a sin in the eyes of God, that'd be a colossal burden lifted off my aching shoulders. A win, win, so to speak. I don't have to potentially transform into a cannibalistic monster, putting countless people at risk, and I certainly wouldn't have to force myself to do something that goes against the very fabric of my being. I mean, for most species the driving instinct is survival, not the morbid alternative.

As the thought of my brain exploding inside my head became more and more appealing, I began wishing it upon myself. The pain was already so agonizing it didn't seem as if it could get much worse. Anticipating my demise, I closed my eyes and waited for my life to slip away. After an hour of waiting, the only thing that was actually closer to death was a family of birds (one attentive mother and two baby chicks), chirping the morning away from a nearby tree. Ordinarily, the sounds of nature are enjoyable, especially cheerful birds singing the morning away, but in that particular instance, those hungry, little bastards were driving me insane. Their relentless high-pitched chirps made my head feel like someone was taking a jackhammer to it. I didn't know how much more I could, or would be willing, to take.

In the end, I covered both ears with my huge cotton ball hands and no blood was shed. After another hour, finally on the verge of passing out, the sound of the backdoor swinging open jolted me out of my half-somber. Seconds later, the engine to Bill and Susan's lime-green hybrid coughed to life, and they peeled out of the driveway. It was 8:52 A.M. They were running late.

Approaching the backdoor, I prayed that they had left it open. They did that sometimes, either out of forgetfulness or faith in the community they loved. Regardless of which, it instilled hope of an easy entrance. Turning the doorknob, I mumbled to myself, "Please open, please open, please…"

"Dammit," I shouted after discovering that the door was locked. "Of all the days to be responsible," I growled, "they picked today. What the fu…"

Wait a minute, I thought. *Didn't they mention something about a spare key hidden somewhere on the property?* I checked my memory bank and came up empty. If they had, nothing was registering. Of course, that's not surprising since I often tuned them out whenever they talked. But that was beside the point. I had a scavenger hunt to attend to.

On my hands and knees I searched all the obvious places: underneath the doormat, in the mailbox, on top of the doorframe, the light fixtures, under all of the garden decorations, and even in the mulch surrounding the front stairs, all to no avail. Coming up empty, I resorted to plan B—finding an alternative entrance into the house. I quickly checked all the windows, and as expected, they were all securely locked. With little options remaining, I found a softball-sized rock and picked the cruddiest window to bash in, which just happened to be a grimy basement window covered in cobwebs. I hated to resort to such extreme measures, but finding a way inside took precedence. About to hurl the rock through the window, the sound of a neighbor's car starting up stopped me dead in my tracks. Realizing that breaking into a house in broad daylight was tremendously risky (and deadly in my case if apprehended by the police), I dropped the rock and resorted to plan C— texting Bill to inquire into the status of the elusive spare key. I made sure to mention that Nick was with me and we were using his phone because mine had run out of juice.

He took the bait.

Bill: *It's under the propane tank in the grill out back. Hope you had fun last night. Susan and I are dying to hear about the party. Catch up with you later.*

Thank, God, I thought.

I immediately ran over to the old grill, located the key, and once inside the house, darted all the way up to my room. I wasn't there to reminisce, rest, or anything along those lines. No, I was there strictly for business. Like a bank job, my goal was to get everything I needed and be out of the house within minutes. Once in my room, after pulling a large duffel bag out of my closet, I filled it to capacity with clothes, a pillow, a blanket, anything related to "The Project," money, toothpaste and a toothbrush, deodorant, antibacterial ointment, hydrogen peroxide, a bottle of Tylenol (minus the six pills I forced down my swollen gullet), gauze rolls, tape, a flashlight, batteries, and a picture of Tiffany. After sealing Nick's bloodstained backpack airtight in a large black garbage bag, it found itself in the bag as well. No point in carrying around any extra baggage if not absolutely necessary. One carry-on bag was all that was necessary for the trip I had planned.

All packed up and ready to hit the road, I made a quick pit stop in the kitchen. Eating may have been the last thing on my mind at that point; however, that didn't mean I wouldn't eventually succumb to the urges. Besides, with the path ahead, knowing just how much energy was going to be exerted, regular refueling sessions were going to be a necessity. I grabbed a couple loafs of bread, cereal bars, a few bottles of water, and pita chips—basically everything my body had survived on while living with the Baniaks.

Before heading out the door, I threw a sharp cutting knife in my bag for good measure. Still undecided in reference to what my exit strategy was going to be, the knife surely could come in handy. By that point, my bag felt so heavy, it seemed as if cinderblocks had been neatly packed inside instead of clothes and some other basic supplies. The weight really worked against me. Instead of riding off into the sunset, which had been my initial plan, I had to walk using Nick's bike to bear the brunt of the load.

Making my way through the streets of Stone Creek, the heavy duffel bag slung over the crossbar, it took me a total of three hours to cross the border into Dangsten Mills. Known for its nonunion operated coalmines, of which its employees earn right around the minimum wage mark, Dangsten Mills was a complete dump. After passing through a small rundown section of the impoverished town, with nothing but wilderness and abandoned buildings on both sides of the main throughway, it seemed like the perfect area to settle down and rest. My plan was simple.

Find a nice, comfortable place to fall asleep for hours, maybe days, maybe forever...

Traveling through the treacherous terrain, I navigated Nick's bike through an array of obstacles: fallen trees, jagged rocks, small streams, and dense shrubs that seemed to grab and claw at me every chance they got. After trekking nearly two miles in, I found what appeared to be a nice resting spot. Face and neck tore up from the unforgiving branches, I cared little that it was on a slight incline and that there was a musky, dank smell in the air. I needed a break—deserved one actually. Utterly exhausted, I yanked a blanket and pillow out of my bag, eased myself onto the ground, and the next thing I knew it was nighttime. It was amazing. I had actually slept through the entire day. I probably would have slept even longer had it not been for the distressing dream that stirred me out of my slumber.

There I was completely submerged in a greenish-brown murky water, desperately trying to swim to the surface. My lungs burning, arms and legs seemingly working against me, no matter how hard I tried, my body kept sinking further and further into the abyss of darkness. Time was running out. Then, while flailing my arms around, with the little light still remaining through the dark-green fog, I noticed trails of blood pouring out of a lacerated wrist, streaking the water red. The dream seemed so real I woke up gasping for air while holding my wrist.

Although never one to take dreams too seriously, that particular one really affected me. As if my dream was an outlet for my subconscious, it illustrated to me precisely how I should accomplish my toughest challenge. It told me to locate a deep body of water, find a good jump point, slit my wrist for good measure, and dive in. Possibly overkill, I chalked the wrist cutting part up as more of an insurance policy than anything else. You know, in case my will to live, to breathe, to seek out the surface, overrides my unnatural need to perish. Although fatal in its own rights—

many have succeeded—the essential purpose of slitting my wrist was to diminish my overall resistance. After all, if I'm all groggy and lightheaded before I even dive into the frigid waters, the chances of swimming to safety were slim to none. Judging by my triumph over Dr. Vox, I could see why my subconscious wouldn't take any chances. It terms of pain and discomfort, it wasn't the most desirable way to go out, but my dream, or subconscious, had spoken, and it was time to listen up.

With a solid method set in place, there was just one more thing that needed to fall into place. It was imperative to find out if I truly was infected. That would take time, though, roughly four to five days according to Dr. Vox's records. Then, once the fever sets in, which in my opinion was all but certain, it'd be go time. In the mean time, there were things that needed to be done. In addition to locating the perfect body of water and jump site, as much as possible, I still had to live life and recuperate from my injuries. If not, there was no way to know for sure if my mind and body would be strong enough to move forward with what needed to be done—a literal suicide mission.

Pulling Nick's phone out of my pocket and turning it on (I had previously powered it off before going to sleep), I saw that there were countless missed calls, emails, voicemails, and text messages. In no mood to read or listen to any of the text messages or voicemails—it was just too much to take in—I texted bill one last time.

Zack: *Bill, you and Susan have been great! You're both amazing people/parents/role models. This decision had absolutely nothing to do with either of you. Nick and...*

Zack: *I decided to go off on our own to soul search or something like that. We may never come back. Tell his parents for him. This will be our last message. I've al-...*

Zack: *ready destroyed my phone so don't even bother attempting to call it. Send his love to his parents for him. It may not seem like it, but I hold a special place in...*

Zack: *my heart for you both. Please take care of your-selves and know that this was for the best. —Zack*

I then shut Nick's phone off and contemplated my next move. Staring at the phone, a dreadful thought crossed my mind. *Can the police trace Nick's phone?* I wasn't entirely sure. In the movies and on television they certainly could. Then an even more horrifying realization popped into my head. *If so, could mine be traced as well?* I didn't even want to consider that nightmarish possibility. In the end, I decided it was probably best not to have Nick's phone in my possession—or anywhere near me for that matter. I also eased my concerns about my own phone by recalling how Dr. Vox had essentially cut its life force out by remov-ing the battery. It had to have a pulse to be traced, right? Again, I wasn't entirely sure.

Still in need of a means of communication, there was that "whole" promise thing with Tiffany, I grabbed the phone, disconnected the battery, sealed it airtight in a few plastic bags, and stuck it inside a small tree hollow. I felt confident that the phone would be okay, even in the event of a torrential downpour. I, on the other hand, would not be all right. Heavy rain would be disastrous for me and my limited supplies. So disastrous I'd probably have to seek refuge in one of the many abandoned buildings. Not desir-able considering the potential of running into hungry rats or worse—vagrants—yet still viable if the weather forced me down that particular path.

The following day, after a treacherous hike through the woods, I located the perfect jump spot. Running alongside Crater Lake, the largest and deepest body of water around, I found a steep cliff ideal for my purposes. At an elevation of roughly 90 feet, the plummet itself was going to be bru-tal. Probably not fatal, but certainly debilitating enough to rattle my senses. Inspecting the water below, I calculated that it was approximately 25 feet deep. It was not an exact measurement, but it was a fairly accurate assessment based off my makeshift depth-detecting device. Constructed from a long strand of rope nabbed from one of the abandoned buildings, all I had to do was tie a rock to its end and lower into the murky water until it hit the lake bed. Then after marking off the spot and pulling it out of the water, all that was left to do was measure it off with my footsteps. Like I said, not an exact measurement, but pretty darn close.

As expected, the fever set in a few days later. It was a little early—too early. However, Dr. Vox's notes clearly specified that if the infected person did not stay well hydrated, the progression of the virus would rapidly accelerate. That bill certainly fit me well as I had barely eaten or drank anything prior to the onset of the fever. In fact, aside from locating a suitable jump site, I barely did much of anything, other than sleeping that is. It's kind of hard to motivate yourself to stay active and find enjoyable things to do when (A), you're staring death in the face, and (B), you need to conserve your energy as much as possible because of your limited resources.

With no reason to conserve food any longer, I waited until night set it before indulging in what would become my "last meal." As last meals go, it was unquestionably sad and pathetic. I'm sure whole grain bread and pita chip crumbs probably doesn't rank high on anyone's list on death row. And honestly, it didn't rank high on mine either. A nice home-cooked meal, courtesy of the Kents or Tindersons, would have been much higher up on my list. Devouring every last crumb and drinking what remained of my water supply, I felt refueled and ready to follow through with my greatest sacrifice.

Fulfilling my promise to Tiffany, I retrieved Nick's phone and sent her one last text message. I told her about the fever, how deep my love for her was, and that it was time. I kept it brief and to the point. I'm aware she probably would have preferred actually talking to me, but hearing her voice had the potential to complicate things. Already an impossible task, one that went against my instinctual drive for self-preservation, any unwanted distractions could spell disaster. If, for instance, my suicide was put off for a day, what's there to say I wouldn't put it off for another, and then another, and so on. And the next thing I know, or more appropriately don't know, my mind gradually slips away and I'm left wandering around the woods, a prisoner of my fried brain. Then, because of my negligence, I undergo the final transformation and, if not stopped in time, the potential for another outbreak. Horrified by the lethal implications associated with that particular fate, impersonal or not, Tiffany would have to understand why passing up on the opportunity to speak to her one last time was imperative.

Turning the phone back off, I carefully removed the battery before hurling all of the pieces into Crater Lake's frigid waters. There was no turning back now. I had no phone, no food, and after ghost riding Nick's bike into the lake, no means of transportation. I was giving away all of my worldly possessions—bestowing them to the same lake I'd donate my body to. If the ancient Egyptians were right when it came to their concept of an afterlife, jumping in with my duffel bag slung tightly to my back (a makeshift weighted belt so to speak), I'd be pretty well off on the other side. I'd have a change of clothes, linens, a pillow, a phone, a few bucks to my name, some personal hygiene items, and most importantly, a bike to get around.

With the heavy duffel bag slung over my shoulder, I began the ascent to the top of the peak—my designated jump site. Once there, I leered over the side and nearly slipped in the process. The near fall rattled my nerves and sent my heart bouncing up and down my torso like a pinball caught between two active bumpers. It was ironic that

I go so worked up about almost falling to my death when that was the precise reason I was there in the first place. But it was my suicide, and it needed to go down as planned. No mess-ups or *slip-ups*—literally—just a sacrifice for the good of humankind.

Sitting down with my legs dangling over the ledge, I plopped the duffel bag beside me and opened it up. I retrieved the knife, stabbed it into a growth of moss, and zipped the bag back up. I then slung the duffel bag back over my shoulder, made sure it was snug enough not to fall off when I plunged into the water below, grabbed my cutting tool, and stood up. In a matter of minutes, there would be no more Zack Treadwell—just a body fitting his description slowly decomposing at the bottom of Crater Lake. Staring at the sea of black ink 90 feet below, I had never been so scared in my life. My emotions were waging a war inside my tensed body. Alternating between wanting to cry, laugh, and scream at the top of my lungs, I was on the verge of hyperventilating and my stomach felt as if it was being churned with a morning star. My hands, arms, and legs all trembling, sweat beading all over my face, heart still bouncing all around, following through with my suicide was going to be near impossible. I didn't want to die. Not yet—not ever. It just wasn't fair.

My mind began racing with thoughts of the unknown. How painful would it be? Where do you go when you die? Would my extreme measures be enough? All terrifying questions I didn't want to find out the answers to. Then, after stepping closer to the ledge, knife trembling in hand, there was an unexpected rustling sound coming from somewhere nearby. Had someone found me? Unable to ascertain the true origins of the sound, and fully understanding the consequences of an intervention, I used it as the much needed motivation to propel myself over the ledge—literally and figuratively.

Visualizing the blade slicing through my tender wrist, I drew a deep breath, ready to end it all…

Chapter Fourteen

Death

Suddenly, a loud voice screamed, "What are you doing? NO...PLEASE...just put the knife down! You don't have to do this..."

His words went ignored. Instead, my focus shifted downward, glancing at the sharp knife at peace with the decision I had made. There was no turning back now. I had come too far to abort the mission. Whether I had it in me or not, *it* was going to get done. It had to get done.

Hesitation a luxury I didn't have, the knife was put to good use. With one swift and violent cut, warm blood began spurting out. I didn't scream, overreact, or regret my actions. I stood there motionless for a few seconds watching the blood squirt out like a mystical blood fountain. The Mayans would have been proud. Lightheaded and dripping with warm blood, I drew in a long, deep breath and dove headfirst into darkness.

It was an amazing, euphoric feeling. It almost felt as if I was floating. The moment I had dreaded for so long was now becoming a very pleasurable one. I had never felt such a rush—such a rage of pure ecstasy. I just closed my eyes with hopes of enjoying the moment for as long as it would last. Deep down, I relished the idea that this was the end of the line for Zack Treadwell.

Moments later, I crashed headfirst, and hard, into the abyss of darkness. I was hoping all the pain and regret would be gone, but it wasn't. Everything was still intact. Nothing changed. I was still wide-awake, fully aware of what was going on.

Truth be told, I wasn't submerged in the cold, murky waters of Crater Lake, the weight of the large duffel bag immersing me deeper and deeper into the enveloping wet blackness. Nor was blood pouring out of a deep laceration to my radial artery. The reality of the situation was that I was sitting on a dirty cement floor in an abandoned building. I was covered in coppery scented blood, but none of it belonged to me. I stood up from the floor and approached a large metal table, reminiscent of the one on which Nick had died.

"HELLO!" I yelled.

"HELLO…HELLO…HELLO!" I yelled even louder.

"ARE YOU STILL WITH ME?" I hissed while vigorously shaking the unresponsive man confined to a restraint table.

There was no response, and after checking his vitals, one thing was obvious: the man was dead. Unfortunately for him, I was far from finished.

"Well, there's no point in wasting a good meal," I joked cruelly to myself.

Chewing on his tender thigh muscle, I couldn't get over the fact of how exquisite it tasted. I thought it'd be repulsive, especially raw, but it wasn't. Not at all. It was heated to the perfect temperature, ninety-eight degrees, with freshness that couldn't be topped—not even by sushi. The warm blood, serving as a sort of creamy gravy, aided the chunks of flesh traveling down my gullet. I opted to stay away from the internal organs, mainly focusing on the flesh and muscles. I relished the knowledge that in future meals, my horizons could be expanded by incorporating delicacies such as brains, livers, intestines, or even an eyeball or two. The possibilities were endless. I was elated that Dr. Fish was in relatively good shape considering his age (mid-fifties) because nothing's worse than eating meats filled with rubbery fat deposits. Unable to stow any of the meat away like Dr. Vox had done so in his freezer, I had to make the most of my kill. I kept eating and eating until my stomach felt like it was going to burst.

Finishing up shortly later, fatigued and still funning a fever, I rested hoping Dr. Vox's "miracle elixir" would alleviate some of the symptoms of the virus. Two hours later, I woke up revitalized and ready to conceal the evidence. The fever, fatigue, nausea, and achiness, all gone, I had no problems digging the ditch that would ultimately become Dr. Fish's final resting spot. Filthy and covered in a cocktail of blood, human matter, and dirt, I grabbed a reasonably clean outfit from my bag, got changed, and then tossed the evidence-laden materials beside Dr. Fish's remains. I then proceeded to fill the grave back up, concealing its freshly dug appearance by topping it off with a combination of rocks, dried leaves, and a large "bonfire-sized" pile of branches. Satisfied with my handiwork, I made my way back to the site of my first feast. There was blood all over the place and no amount of effort was going to change that. So I did the next best thing. Instead of cleaning it up, I grabbed handfuls of dirt and slathered a thick coat of it all over the floor. With the floor squared away, I wiped down the metal table, grabbed my stuff (including a lone sheet of paper speckled with blood droplets), and exited the building. Thinking back, it was kind of crazy how I had gone from standing on the edge of the cliff to becoming Dr. Vox's pseudo apprentice.

***

Hearing the rustling sound for the second time, over-come by curiosity, I turned around to see what had been making all of the ruckus. Discovering that it was a squirrel foraging for food, and not a cop or some member of a search team, I had an epiphany. There was *one* way to slow down the progression of the virus indefinitely. Con-sume the flesh of the living. It was a hard decision to make—bordering on impossible. Yet, as hard as I tried to force out the intrusive thoughts, they kept coming one after the other. They wanted justice and, more importantly, vengeance. After all, the virus and subsequent cover-up had cost me my parents, my childhood, my best friend, and was about to cost me my life.

Stepping down from the edge of the cliff, I made my way back to the throughway. I wasn't sure where my deci-sion would ultimately take me, but I had an idea of who deserved to be my first victim. A cohort of Dr. Vox, Dr. Allen Fish was by no means an innocent man. He, along with his evil counterpart, was an integral participant in the gruesome experiments and heinous measures used in an effort to alleviate the threat of the virus. All I needed to know was that he had spent some time in the secret lab to cast a guilty verdict down on him—thus, sealing his fate. Locating his whereabouts was priority number one.

Scoping out the poverty-stricken Dangsten Mills—what was left of it, that is—I eventually located the local library (equally as rundown) and stopped in to conduct some much-needed research. As it turned out, locating Dr. Fish's precise location was not as challenging as I had as-sumed it would be. I just Googled his name and saw that he worked for the Center for Disease Control and Preven-tion, in Hagerstown, Maryland. It even had a headshot of him smiling with his thick, bushy mustache and balding head. I printed out his photo, looked up bus routes heading in that particular direction, and made my way over to Dangsten Mills Transit Authority. I was fortunate to have just enough cash to purchase a ticket to Denbrou, Maryland, the closest town to my final destination.

Once in Denbrou, I hiked the rest of the way to Hagerstown. With the symptoms of the virus setting in—increased fever, malaise, obliterated appetite, and constant nausea—the forty-mile trek took nearly two days. Out of money and extremely paranoid over the idea that a code 10-57 (missing person) had been put out on me, I avoided people at all costs. I slept in abandoned buildings or in wooded areas whenever possible, always staying out of sight. With my appetite non-existent, I literally lived off water—and tons of it. I still felt the most intense hunger pains imaginable, but foods suitable for human consumption did little to satiate this hunger. In fact, they only made things worse. I learned this lesson the hard way. After scrounging together nearly a dollar in change, most of which was found in nasty gutters, I purchased a fresh bagel and took two bites before the nausea kicked in, sending bodily fluids shooting out both ends. A nasty mistake that resulted in an extra-long bathroom break and a change of clothing.

Water, on the other hand, a necessity to keep myself hydrated, didn't affect my stomach at all. It did little to appease my hunger, but it served its own important purpose. If nothing else, it was a tool to slow down the progression of the virus. I was aware that it may have been a little late—Dr. Vox's secret journals clearly specified that hydration was the most important thing right after becoming newly infected—yet it was worth a shot, even if it was just an afterthought. With that in mind, I drank water whenever it was available. I no longer cared about germs. I drank out of filthy bathroom sinks, streams not fit for human consumption, and, as a last resort, from brown puddles when no other sources of water were available. I figured any bacteria or organisms ingested wouldn't stand a chance in my body. I imagined the little "buggers" entering my body with hopes of wreaking havoc on my immune system only to be stopped dead in their tracks like flattened road kill at the hands of the "Mack Truck" of viruses.

Shortly after entering Hagerstown, I spent a night in an old, abandoned psychiatric hospital I stumbled across on my voyage through the town. Scoping out the building, I found a dilapidated restraint table in the east corridor of the hospital. The table swayed from side to side, and appeared on the verge of collapsing (not ideal for its intended purpose), but the thick, faded leather straps (similar to the ones used in Dr. Vox's infirmary) sealed the deal for me. A touch of irony if you ask my opinion. If everything worked according to plan, Dr. Fish would finally get to see what it was like to be on the other side of the table. I didn't worry too much about the table collapsing, an initial concern of mine, after spending a few minutes jumping up and down on it to gauge its structural integrity. I almost fell a few times, but the table passed my test with flying colors—mostly shades of deep red. And with my knife held to his neck, limiting Dr. Fish's mobility seemed an easy enough task.

With the perfect feast site located, all I had to do was pick up my "takeout" meal. That was going to be the hard part—or so I thought. After finally locating the Center for Disease Control and Prevention late in the afternoon, void of any real plan at that point, I hid within the prickly arms of a large pine bush not too far from the main entrance, and studied each person that entered and exited the building. If I was fortunate enough to spot him and establish which car belonged to him, developing a strategy to sabotage him wouldn't take much effort at all. Essentially, all I would have to do is catch him off guard and hold him hostage with my "trusted" knife. Highly dangerous with unimaginable complications—but worth a shot, I thought. It's not like I had a choice in the matter. It was either go all in with my risky sabotage plan or go all in with my self-imposed execution. For my sake, it had to work.

Then, as if my brain was functioning on autopilot, the second he came into my viewpoint, exiting briskly from the building, I abandoned my "extremely high-risk" plan and improvised. "Dr. Fish," I shouted, popping out of the pine bush waving my filthy bandaged hands in the air. "Hold on a second. I need to talk to you about something."

He stopped and glared at me suspiciously. "Do I know you?" he asked, eying me up and down from a distance of about twenty feet. It been nearly a week since my encounter with Dr. Vox, and although most of the throbbing pain was gone, my body was still in shambles. Eyes still bleeding red, faded yellow and purple strands strewn across my neck, and my bandaged hands now resembling toasted marshmallows, it's a miracle he didn't make a break for it after catching a glimpse of me.

"No, you don't," I said, jogging over to him, "but you're going to want to listen to what I have to say. Can we talk somewhere in private?"

He shook his head. "I'm sorry, but that's not possible. Now, will you please tell me what this is all about? I'm expected somewhere."

I uttered the two lone words destined to change his tune, "Timmonds Rock!"

He glared at me, eyes fiery, nostrils flaring, and grunted, "Follow me!"

He escorted me over to his car and gestured for me to get in. I took a seat beside him in his black Cadillac Escalade. It was a beautiful car—by far one of the nicest I had ever had the luxury of sitting in. Turning to me, Dr. Fish asked, "Would you care to elaborate?"

"I will," I replied confidently, "but drive first. I think it's best if we find someplace private to talk."

"Just tell me what you want already. Is this about money? Do you really think you can get away with black-mailing—"

"It's not about money. Now drive!"

The inflection in my voice must have spoken volumes to him—told him I meant business—because seconds later, Dr. Fish's Escalade peeled out of the parking lot. In total silence, Dr. Fish drove a good ten miles before parking his car off on the side of the road. Surveying the area, seeing nothing but trees and a long strip of roadway, I felt the area was remote enough.

"Is this private enough for you?"

"It'll do."

"If you're not here about money, then what do you want?"

"First, I'd like a little help with changing my bandages. I think it's only fair that you help me, considering your old pal, Dr. Vox, did this to me."

Dr. Fish appeared shocked. "DR. VOX?" he said, looking confused. "That can't be...he's been dead for years."

"Nope," I replied calmly, undoing my bandages. "He looks dead, and probably is by now, but I assure you as of last Friday night he was alive and kicking—literally."

"Is this some kind of joke?"

I pointed at my neck and eyes. "Does this look like a joke? He did this to me. He tried to kill me, but I...never mind. I'll get to all of that in due..." I stopped and coughed a few times, "...time. Now, will you please help me with my bandages? I heard it's in your Hippocratic Oath to help people in need. As you can see, I need the help!" I held my ravaged hands up for him to see.

Stained red, dirt and dried blood crusted in the groves of my hands, with the deeper of my wounds still seeping a disconcerting greenish puss, there severity of my injuries were impossible to ignore. With limited supplies and fully intending to go through with my suicide, ensuring that my wounds were properly cared for didn't seem too important to me at the time. Now, that I had a reason to live, it was something that would need to be attended to—preferably by a doctor who knew a thing or two about *infections*.

"My God," he groaned, waving his hand in front of his nose, "I can smell the infection from here. Is that a...bite?"

"Look, we'll get into all of that later. What I need you to do is grab some gloves, a first aid kit if you have one, and treat them before they get any worse. Can you do that for me?"

Dr. Fish nodded. "Hold on a second...my first aid kit's in the trunk."

Dr. Fish then casually got up from his seat and walked over to the rear of his car. After popping the trunk open, he grabbed the first aid kid, returning several moments later carrying the huge toolbox-sized first aid kit. Had it been the night of my "near-death" encounter with Dr. Vox, I would have salivated at the site of the massive kit stocked with endless medical supplies. With utmost care, Dr. Fish cleaned out my heavily infected wounds, applied a substantial amount of antibacterial cream to them, and covered them snuggly with fresh dressings. Afterwards, he treated the deep, crusted gash above my eyebrow, slapped some antibacterial cream and Band-Aids on it, and examined my eyes.

"Your eyes look terrible, but I wouldn't worry about them too much. The blood will eventually dissipate—though it may take a few months. In the mean time, if I were you I'd purchase myself some sunglasses."

"I'll keep that in mind," I replied, catching sight of Dr. Fish's sunglasses, resting atop his bald head.

Cleaning up the small mess he had made while treating my wounds, Dr. Fish threw all of my old bandages into a biohazard bag, snapped off his gloves, throwing them inside as well, and tied it off. Then with his first aid kit in one hand and the biohazard bag in the other, he looked at me and said, "Let me put this stuff away and then we'll talk."

The instant Dr. Fish disappeared from my line of vision, I sprang into action. I pulled out Dr. Vox's bottle of chloroform, quickly looked for something to pour it on, then laughed after spotting the perfect material for the job. Dr. Fish returned just as the bottle found its way back into my side pocket.

"Okay, time to speak up. Tell me about your alleged 'run-in' with the late Dr. Vox," he said with a hint of sarcasm in his voice. "I have no doubt that you're privy to some highly confidential information, but it'll take a great deal of convincing to get me to believe that you had a violent encounter with the late Dr. Voxolomin. I know for a fact..." he paused and looked at me sideways, "what are you doing?"

"I don't know," I responded with the back of one of my bandaged hands inches away from my nose. "Are you sure these bandages are fresh. They smell kind of funky to me. Do they smell weird to you..."

***

Returning to Dr. Fish's Cadillac Escalade, which was parked right behind the building, I popped the trunk, threw my bag in, and retrieved the biohazard bag. After opening the biohazard bag up, I slid off the purple disposable gloves used to keep my bandages clean, and threw them inside. Although risky to travel around with potentially incriminating evidence—the gloves still had traces of Dr. Fish's blood on them—I decided to take the bag with me. It'd be easy enough to incinerate the bag—preferably a few states over.

After throwing the rest of my stuff in the trunk, excluding the blood-speckled sheet of paper, Dr. Fish's shades, and a wad of cash taken out of Dr. Fish's wallet, I jumped in the car and turned the interior lights on. I carefully examined the paper and was pleased to see that it was perfectly legible and easy to read.

> *Sergeant Major Dale Ackerman. Ethnicity/Gender: Caucasian male. Age: 40-45. Height: 5'11''-6'1.'' Distinguishing Features: shaved head, gray eyes, and missing the lower half of his left ear (shrapnel injury). Whereabouts: currently stationed at the Pentagon—living in the area. Hometown: Steward, Minnesota.*

> *Sergeant Major of the Army Emerson Herstow. Ethnicity/Gender: Caucasian male. Age: 50-55. Height: 5'8''-5'10.'' Distinguishing Features: short salt & pepper hair (crew cut style), brown eyes, and glasses. Whereabouts: not sure where he's stationed. Hometown: unknown.*

> *Dr. David Olin. Ethnicity/Gender: Asian-American male. Age 35-40. Height: 5'6"-5'8". Distinguishing Features: black hair, thin goatee, brown eyes, large birthmark on the back of his neck. Whereabouts: currently practicing medicine in New Orleans, Louisiana.*

> *Dr. Rebecca Harper...*

I was pleased with Dr. Fish. He did as he was asked. Although somewhat resistant at first, one threat to his family's well-being was all it took to get his writing hand moving. Of course, flashing a picture of his wife and kids after reading off his home address didn't hurt my cause—thank God for driver's licenses. In all, Dr. Fish provided me with eight names—a good start—but only the beginning. There would be more—many, many more.

Folding and placing the "ever important" list in my pocket, I fired up the ignition, and entered a destination into the GPS—New Orleans, Louisiana. I probably should have felt remorseful for my actions, a man had just been cannibalized by me, but I didn't. Not at all. Remorse is a human trait—something I no longer was. In fact, I felt the reverse. Society's rules governing what's right and wrong no longer applied to me. People put down lions that get a taste for human flesh, but that doesn't mean they actually expect lions to adhere to the laws of mankind. There's no judge, jury, trial, or anything along those lines—just what is referred to as a justified slaughter. If caught, I could see the same thing happening to me.

I don't like to brag; however, I'd say I'm on the top of the food chain. Call me a zombie hybrid, a monster, whatever you want—just understand that I'm far from done. My mission has only just begun. This is my new life now. I won't quit until I'm dead...cured...or all the guilty are eaten one satisfying bite at a time...

~*~*~